THE MANSON CURSE

Journalist John Harkness, on holiday in Cornwall, chanced upon an old friend who had mysteriously dropped out of London literary society several years earlier. Richard Manson, author of a smash-hit novel, now lives in remote Poltressor House, with his beautiful wife Eve, his young son James, and his eccentric older sister. Pressed to stay, John learns of the Manson Curse which dooms all the oldest-born sons of the family to an early death. Richard is obsessed by the curse and terrified for his son's safety. Soon the brooding atmosphere surrounding Poltressor grows steadily more threatening, until madness and violence erupt ... and events move to a terrifying climax.

THE MANSON CURSE

Dell Shannon

ATLANTIC LARGE PRINT

Chivers Press, Bath, England.
Curley Publishing, Inc.,
South Yarmouth, Mass., USA.

Library of Congress Cataloging-in-Publication Data

Shannon, Dell, 1921–
    The Manson curse / Dell Shannon.
        p.   cm.—(Atlantic large print)
    ISBN 0–7927–0814–8 (Curley : lg. print)
    1. Large type books.   I. Title.
[PS3562.I515M36   1992]
813′.54—dc20   91–18114
                                                                   CIP

British Library Cataloguing in Publication Data available

This Large Print edition is published by Chivers Press, England, and
Curley Publishing, Inc, U.S.A. 1992

Published in the British Commonwealth by arrangement with Victor
Gollancz Ltd and in the U.S.A. with William Morrow and Company, Inc.

U.K. Hardback ISBN 0 7451 8253 4
U.K. Softback ISBN 0 7451 8265 8
U.S.A. Softback ISBN 0 7927 0814 8

THE MANSON CURSE

CHAPTER ONE

It was damned strange, how I found myself involved in the affair.

I came back to England in January, six years after my last stint there. Since then I'd been a lot of places for two years and at home—New York or Chicago—the rest of the time. When Barclay went on sick leave, someone was needed to replace him in the London office, and I was offered the job; it was a step up to editorship, if only temporary. Whether Barclay came back or not, it wasn't likely that I'd get the London office on a permanent basis, nor did I particularly want it. An editorship, yes, but preferably somewhere at home. I'm a sedentary individual—read it sybaritic—and I like my creature comforts.

But I was pleased enough to spend six or eight months in England. I had a number of old acquaintances there, both British and American. I took over Barclay's bachelor flat in Bloomsbury and settled in quite comfortably.

There wasn't much going on just then in the way of news. Most of the previous year's anti-Americanism had been given decent burial, the Russians were remarkably quiet, and for once there were no visiting film stars.

1

Outside the office I pottered around, renewing my acquaintance with London and a few other old friends, and I started a series of articles, 'The Face of England,' primarily for home consumption.

In the middle of February I decided it was time to see something of England outside London so I took off in Barclay's old Morris to spend a week collecting a few different backgrounds for my columns.

I'd been in England for three years, on and off, that other time, but in an odd way much of the country seemed new and fresh to me this time around, because I came to it in a different frame of mind, maybe as a different man. My last six months in England, six years before, had been spoiled by my resentment of an enforced absence from home, and most of my spare time had been devoted to writing long cheerful letters to Betty. It's not easy to write that kind of letter to someone who is dying, someone you love, and it had taken a good deal of my time and energy. Well, that was over now.

*　　　*　　　*

I went west from London; I'd never seen the West Country. Most of it was fine, even in the rain; the weather cleared by the time I reached Devon, and the next day I drove across Dartmoor in watery sunlight. I stopped for lunch in Liskeard, over the Cornish border, and cut south for the coast.

Devon (with the exception of Dartmoor) is the picture on a chocolate box, but Cornwall—I remember somebody once wrote that in Devon one may meet pixies, but in Cornwall bogles. It was a wild coast; I liked it until the fog came in. The fog was not like river fog; it was thin and white, and I had to slow almost to walking pace on a strange road. I felt that I'd been creeping along three hundred feet above a dimly heard, menacing surf for hours, though my watch told me it was just past four, when I came to a scattering of small cottages that constituted a village, and on the other side of it was a larger building with a sign. Relieved at these evidences of civilization, I drew up. There would be, of course, no chance of whiskey; but I might be offered decent tea.

There are Londoners who collect pubs; I fancied this would be a star in my collection. To begin with, it was called The Drowned Man and its sign was gruesomely realistic. There was one long, low room with the bar at the back, a few chairs and scarred tables, two kettles beside an enormous hearth; the only ornamentation was a row of collection boxes ranged neatly along the mantel, which was at least nine feet high.

When I came in, all talk stopped dead and five pairs of eyes turned to me. These belonged to four customers at one table and the publican, who leaned on the bar.

There was neither surprise, hostility, nor friendliness in the eyes; only veiled curiosity and suspicion of the outlander.

'Good afternoon,' I said.

The publican grunted; the other four fixed their eyes on their glasses and were silent. 'I don't suppose,' I pursued, 'You can give me a whiskey?'

'Sorry, sir, none left. Beer.'

I'm not a beer drinker. 'Er—no. Tea?'

'Tea,' said the publican meditatively. He was a middle-aged man with a great barrel of a chest. He had a pale, broad, secretive face with slate-gray eyes; he was shining-bald, but his bare arms were covered with coarse black curly hair. 'Tea. I daresay—if you'd not be wanting anything with it.'

'Tea will do fine, thanks.'

Without a word the publican turned into the rear premises by a door behind the bar. I leaned on the counter and surveyed the room while I got out a cigarette. The others were all watching me—three older men, one young: they might be fishermen. Suddenly, in accord, they all looked away and began their talk again. They were like the men who laid out Stonehenge: timeless—the old distrust of the stranger, whether he be from ten miles distant or a thousand. Now they had dismissed me, summed me up: one of the

Americans, not important.

'Just you wait and see, that's all, Jem. Just wait.'

'What I say. It'll come, it will, and some strange way to it, too. You wasn't borned when young James was drowned.' The oldest man of all contented himself with a grunt of agreement also directed at the youth.

'You're a lot of bloody fools,' said that one, contempt and uncertainty in his tone. 'Things like that don't happen nowadays—if they did any time.'

'Young James was no fool about water,' said the oldest. 'Little bit of a boat he kept just for goin' about, likin' to be at the sea. I remember my da tellin' it. And it weren't a rough day, calm as a pond. But over she go and he drownded.'

'It was more than fifty year ago,' said the youth sullenly. 'We're not talkin' of young James.'

'Manson be Manson,' said the first man, 'and eldest son be eldest son, you can't get from it—that's what it do say.'

The landlord reappeared silently and set a cracked saucer with a violet-patterned cup on the bar. The tea was strong and scalding hot. I stirred it reflectively. Manson was after all a common enough name; but I had a sudden vague memory of Manson being from the West Country, though it was not a Cornish name. Manson: I hadn't thought of him in years, until just the other day.

'Old parson got a book with all that in. You'd ought to ax him to see it, Jem. In a book, all wrote out. And a picture.'

The youth laughed sharply. I sipped my tea, lit another cigarette, and wondered about Manson. I could understand Fowler's curiosity. When was it I had seen Fowler?—at the Press Club, ten days ago or two weeks...

'Manson? No, I've never heard of or from him since the day I left England.'

'I had the idea you knew him pretty well,' Fowler had said.

'At one time I did, fairly. Strange type—nervous. And if you say, "Well, he's a writer ..."' I'd said with a grin. Fowler did not laugh. His long equine countenance was gloomier than usual.

'Yes, well, I'd rather like to get in touch with him. More out of curiosity than anything else. Fellow seems to have dropped out of existence. No one's seen or heard from him in God knows how long. No one I know, anyway.'

'Perhaps he's dead,' I'd said idly.

'Not unless his ghost is endorsing checks. He's still collecting occasional royalties on *Troth*.'

'I should imagine so,' I said, a little enviously. 'Let's see, it's what—six years, seven...'

6

'Nearer eight. I can't make out what's happened to the man. I haven't laid eyes on him in three years, or heard from him either. His only address is his bank. It's a bit late,' said Fowler, 'to cash in on *Troth* now, but it could be done. What sort of fool doesn't follow up a best seller? My God, any sort of trash—and he doesn't write trash, you know.'

'No.' *Troth* had not been trash. 'Really. That *is* rather odd. As I say, I lost touch with him when I left England. Isn't he writing at all?'

'Not so far as I know. I've written him care of the bank, of course—not a line in answer. Pity, you know. We both made money with *Troth*—I'd like another Manson. Though God knows why, when they take it away as fast as I make it.' Fowler is executive editor of an old and respected publishing house. 'He was always a queer fish, of course—for all I know he's in China, or turned hermit, or breeding hens in the country.'

It was rather strange about Manson. That kind of thing happens so gradually you don't mark it; men you knew in another life, a different time, men you called friends, somehow fading away to acquaintances, and then altogether. As it was with Manson, so it was with Cunningham, Adams, Wakefield, a dozen others I had once known. But you assumed they were placed somewhere, at work in a routine even if you didn't know it.

7

The meeting with Fowler had brought Manson back to mind, and I speculated idly about him a little before dismissing it with a shrug. Now, I heard the name on the slow, rough tongues of Cornish fishermen, and at the same time remembered, with startling clarity, Manson sitting at a table in a dirty little Soho café, looking down his nose at the foreign proprietor and waxing nostalgic about the West of England. Had he said Cornwall? The West might mean anything, logically, from Cornwall to Cumberland.

It was odd that after all this time my mental vision of Manson should be so sharp: the slight wiry figure, the fair hair and clipped mustache, the well-bred, chilly, English features and the pale eyes.

'A shame,' said the oldest man. 'A pity it do be, the only one. But it'll happen.'

The publican, who had been leaning on the bar staring into space, unexpectedly entered the conversation. 'That's her blame, the London female. All sort o' sly tricks they know to keep from it, can't bother theyselves with a fambly. A bad day he married that one. He shoulda thought for it. I daresay she won't shed tears when it do happen.'

'No comfort to him, sure. That city way she have.' All the voices but the young man's were slow, ruminative, monotoned. The five of them took no more notice of me than if I'd been a piece of the furniture, and my own

8

voice startled me with its urban inflection.

'I beg your pardon—I couldn't help overhearing—you mentioned a Mr. Manson, I wonder if it's a man I know.' Of course it couldn't be. The intruding remark startled them, too. They all turned on me with one look, the chained watch-dog rearing up to examine the pauser at the gate. 'A Mr. Richard Manson,' I said, half sorry I had spoken.

After a silence the landlord said noncommittally, 'Ar? Mr. Richard Manson do live up Poltressor House.'

'Oh.' It was still a common enough name. 'Slight fellow, small, very dark, quick way of talking?'

They said nothing at all, looking at me. The young man made an impatient gesture; he was young enough that he would have been in the service, out and away from the narrow local insularities.

'That's Mr. Manson, sure. You be a friend of his?'

'Yes,' I said, and then wondered. Had I been, was I? Manson had always been a standoffish guy. 'He lives near here? Where am I, by the way? I don't know Cornwall.'

'This be Pentressor,' and the youth decided to append, 'sir. Poltressor House be a long mile there,' and he nodded up the road.

'Well,' I said. I had the irrational feeling that I was being manipulated by destiny for some unknown end. I hadn't been hunting Manson (as Fowler had hunted? Perhaps) but here he was. Undoubtedly the right Manson. Had I any desire to see the man again? Few things bore me so much as postmortems on the past. What would Manson and I have to talk about except what each of us had done and not done since we'd last met? I could just tell Fowler the address and let it go.

Even as I thought that, I felt it inevitable that I would call at Manson's house now, and inevitable that the reason would be a residue of faint curiosity, as I remembered what Fowler had said. The Manson I had known was no recluse. Why only the accommodation address? Why the unanswered letters? Why no more writing after *Troth*? Well, I am a journalist; they say we all have more curiosity than the average man.

'You can't miss it—sir. Up the road, the first house on your right. There's a gate and a wall.' The young man was in the conspiracy with destiny to bring me together with Manson.

'I see, thanks.' Because I knew I must, now, seek out Manson I didn't want to: a bore, a waste of time. Quite definitely, I did not want to see him again.

'Thank you. Odd to run across him after all this while.' They were looking at me expectantly. No use; I was committed, if only by the pure chance of it.

10

I paid for the tea and came out into a cold salt breeze. The fog was blown in trailing wisps, white and insubstantial. As I started the car and drew away from The Drowned Man I reflected that at least Manson might put me up for the night, a more comfortable lodging than any I was likely to find elsewhere here.

CHAPTER TWO

Poltressor House (the little rhyme chased round my mind like a puppy after its tail, 'By Pol, Tre and Pen you may know the Cornish men') might have been built by a recluse. It stood on a headland jutting out to sea, almost at the edge of a respectably tall cliff. There was a five-foot stone wall all around it, with ornamental iron gates; it was a square Georgian house, an inland intruder on the coast. The gates were shut and I sat for a moment wondering if, after all, I would not just go on my way. In the end I got out and tried them; they were not locked. I drove in by a curving broad way. No attempt at a lawn; a rock garden; a few pots. It was bare, but nothing grew well on the coast, no green, civilized garden stuff. There was an old-fashioned bellpull.

I waited on the step. Just before the door

opened I was thinking. I could still turn and go—now, quickly, before anyone answers.

The woman who opened the door was pleasant-faced, middle-aged, in a neat uniform. When had I last seen a uniformed maid? 'Good afternoon, is Mr. Manson at home?'

'Yes, sir, if you'd come in? What name, sir?'

'Harkness—tell him .Captain Harkness.'

She went down the hall. Whatever Manson was doing or not doing there was evidently no lack of money; the carpeting was thick, the visible furniture solid and good—some old, and lovingly cared for. Inside, the house was light and fresh-seeming, with ivory woodwork, ivory-painted walls, a glimpse of flower-patterned draperies in what would be the sitting room to my left.

'Oh?' It was a breathy gasp of surprise. I glanced up. Bogles, not pixies? This was surely a pixie. A tiny, gray, very elderly woman: she stood on the stair landing and gazed at me in consternation before running down to face me. A fierce gray terrier of an old lady: gray, old-fashioned dress with dark-gray beading at the shoulders, silver-gray pince-nez over pale gray eyes (yes; Manson's eyes), gray-white hair in an untidy bun, drab gray stockings, gray glacé slippers, and a knitting bag with gray wool protruding.

'Who are you? What are you doing here?

You must go away at once—at once! Who let you in? Elsie? Elsie, come here immediately!' Like a lapdog with duty done, the warning bark given, she backed away from me. 'Elsie!'

I felt absurdly tall and awkward. 'I'm so sorry if I startled you—my name is Harkness, I came to see Mr. Manson.'

'You can't see him. He doesn't want to see you. You must go away at once.' She ended on a gasp and her eyes looked beyond me. I turned.

'Of course Richard wants to see Mr. Harkness, Miss Manson, we mustn't seem so inhospitable.'

'Eve...'

Yes, Eve, I thought: indubitably, who else could it be? Infinite woman. She stood framed in the door of the sitting room, a tall slender woman, erect yet graceful. In this remote country place she was City, everything right and smooth about her. Dark brown hair in sleek curls, a deep widow's peak and smooth crown above a low smooth brow; pale matte-complexioned oval face with sleek-plucked brows, a mature painted mouth, lengthened dark eyes; soft blue frock so simple that it said Money, sleek silk slender legs and high heels. The voice was creamy and smooth, and she gave me a slow smile. 'You must forgive Miss Manson, she's nervous.'

'Of course, I'm sorry to have...'

13

'I'm sure Richard's in. Won't you come into the sitting room—it is Mr. Harkness? I am Mrs. Manson. Do sit down.' The little old lady had disappeared. 'You understand how it is—I hope you're not offended. Miss Manson's old and a bit strange.'

'Yes,' I said meaninglessly.

'I believe I've heard Richard mention your name.'

Another smile. It was not quite English, somehow; was it deliberately provocative? I thought, a bored urbanite in the wilds with a recluse for a husband? She offered me a cigarette, leaning forward. Un-English?—but not foreign. Celtic, yes: the high cheekbones, the eyes put in with a smutty finger. It was not deliberate, I decided; only natural charm cultured to smoothness, and wouldn't Manson, little, nervous Manson, be just the one to possess such a woman? Too bad of him to keep her away in the country. 'He'll be so pleased to see you,' she said, leaning forward again to my politely held match.

Somewhere a door opened and the grave sanity of Bach marched down the corridor. And then I noticed that despite the calmness of her voice, the poised serenity, her long white hands were shaking. A quick light tread came nearer, and she said, 'Please don't mention it, Mr. Harkness, but Richard has been ... hasn't been too well. He's sometimes ... a bit nervous. I know you'll overlook it.'

14

Was that the explanation, then? Manson's become a little ill, not enough to tuck away in a home but unfit for freedom in London? I could not altogether believe it. Manson as I remembered him had always been nervous.

Manson came in. He was absurdly unchanged, the Manson of three, five, ten years ago: a type that does not age, wiry, boyish. Only his voice had risen and taken on petulance.

'Eve—Eve? They said someone—a stranger, someone pretending to know me—what did he want?' He saw me then and checked.

I rose and offered my hand. 'Hello, Manson. Nice to see you again.'

Manson stared at me in silence for a moment. Then in a completely altered, normal tone he said, 'Why, Harkness—Johnny Harkness. And good to see *you*, old boy—what are you doing in Cornwall?'

I thought of Dorian Gray more than once as I looked at Manson, listened to Manson, dined at Manson's board, accepted a bed for the night. We were the same age, but he might have been twenty-six instead of ten years older. There was nothing wrong with Manson, certainly.

'You like the house? Rather a lonely spot, but it suits us—privacy at least.' Yes, he had always been something of a solitary, I supposed. 'It used to be quite an extensive

15

property, Poltressor—been in the family almost since Elizabethan days. In those times it was valuable—shipping, you know, and smuggling as well. A good deal of it's been sold off—my land runs up the coast a quarter-mile or so, just a strip of the cliffs, you see—the inland part's been sold. I expect some people would find it lonely—I don't mind,' and a careless smile for his wife. I wondered if she lied when she smiled back and agreed.

'You don't come up to London much, then? I was talking to Fowler the other day and he mentioned that he hadn't seen you in some time.'

'Oh—Fowler,' said Manson. 'Yes, of course. He was always at me to write another novel. Well, when I don't have to work at it ... ' and he shrugged. A trifle arrogant? Manson was not, apparently, the true professional, restless when he was not writing: he had no inner drive to write. Yet *Troth* was a good novel, in its own way. Of course, he'd made a small fortune from his one novel; the film rights alone would keep him comfortably for the rest of his life.

'No, we seldom visit London.' What a waste, this woman here. 'More coffee, Mr. Harkness? Richard, the milk, please. Richard?'

'Oh—yes, certainly. We're not Cornish, of course—the original ancestor acquired the

16

place in payment of a debt, I believe—late sixteen-something. I was brought up here except for school. No, we don't find it lonely.'

That was the third time he had said so. Nothing wrong with Manson but his usual, remembered nervousness. He was fidgeting with the cutlery, the glasses, the salt cellar. 'Elsie—where is the woman? Elsie!'

'You needn't shout, Richard'—quiet, modulated tone—'let me ring.'

'Elsie—there you are. Did you tell Evans to lock the gates?'

'Yes, sir.'

'Both gates. I found the rear one open this morning. That must not happen again.'

'No, sir. Evans is just gone out to lock up, sir.'

'Very well.' Manson passed his cup to his wife for more coffee; he said, 'There are sometimes tramps—you have to be careful in the country.'

The little gray woman had joined us at the table, speaking scarcely a word. Now and again I found her eyes on me, suspicious. Before the coffee was served she excused herself in a tight trembling voice and vanished. Manson took little notice of her, calling her Aunt Belle, vaguely polite; only an odd little nonentity, the poor relation, and it could be inferred what Mrs. Manson thought of her by the way she used the more formal

17

address.

We adjourned to the sitting room, and through the flow of talk—mostly Manson's—I began to feel something a little unnatural about the atmosphere. It was not just that Manson was obviously starved for conversation: in this place there must be few men of his age and interests whom he could call friends. (Then why did he so seldom come up to London? Surely not from lack of funds.) It was the woman. The type was unmistakable: whatever she was or was not, this was not a woman to efface herself, be at any time unaware of her sex, of her power. Anywhere, she would stand out in the group and know it. It was contrived perfection; obvious that she spent time and money on herself. Yet she was self-effacing now before two men, silent, a little apart from us.

The only maid I had seen waited at table, but it was another who came in later—and another relic. The figure like Mrs. Noah, the mouth like a trap, the kind eyes, the white apron: unmistakably a Nanny out of the Edwardian past.

'Excuse me, Miss Eve.'

Mrs. Manson was on her feet instantly. 'I'll come ...' But Manson was up, too.

'I'll see to it, Eve.'

'No, Richard,' and some of the poise slipped, 'I'll go, of course. You must stay and ... keep Mr. Harkness company. You'll excuse me, Mr. Harkness, I'm the fifth wheel anyway, I'm sure you'd prefer to be alone—it's good for Richard to have some masculine talk once in a while, you know. Please don't bother, Richard, I'll ... ' Dividing a rather taut smile between us, she went out with the Nanny.

I asked politely, 'You've a family?' The fishermen had implied that; now I was remembering what had been said, trying to piece it together.

'A boy,' said Manson. 'A boy. Yes.' He was still looking after his wife, frowning. He said, almost to himself, 'Nightmares—and she spoils him, makes him all the more nervous. Excuse me ... women are usually indulgent with sons, aren't they?'

I remarked conventionally that it was grand country for a boy to grow up in; that seemed for some reason to startle Manson.

'Oh—yes. Dangerous, though. I had the wall made higher, you know. It's a three-hundred-foot drop to the beach. My uncle used to keep a boat—I don't care for sailing. He must be taught to swim. On the other hand, the city might be even worse—traffic and so on.'

An only son (yes, 'that's her fault, the London female'), only natural they would be anxious, overindulgent. I felt brief envy of Manson for son, for family.

'You haven't married again?' Manson was

asking.

'No.'

It seemed a long time ago, these days, Betty and all our plans. Newspapermen are popularly supposed to be libertines; maybe I'm the exception that proves the rule. All I ever wanted was a solid, permanent relationship and a home and family, I expect because I'd grown up in that kind of atmosphere. Well, we had had bad luck. Betty and I had been married for three months, seven years ago, when they found out she had leukemia. She'd lived for ten months. She told me I must marry again, but somehow I'd never come across anyone I wanted to marry since. I'd had a couple of unsatisfactory affairs—well, when it starts out being an affair, so-called, it hasn't much chance of getting to be anything deeper, has it?

The latest had been Vicky Carstairs, who assistant-edited a woman's column on our New York paper. I'd miss Vicky—just a little, I thought...

'You understand how it is, John. Sounds mercenary, I know, but I have to think of my old age.' Her head on one side, watching me. She had not told me the man's name. 'We've suited very well and I'm really fond of you, but marriage—well, it is a woman's goal, isn't it, especially in these times? And I mean to have a good one, you know. I'm very fond of

20

him, too. Of course, if you should duplicate the offer, I might hesitate between you.'

'Well . . .'

'I thought not. You'd be rather old-fashioned when it came to picking a wife. You needn't look so embarrassed, it's all right, John.' Taking the blame to herself, yes, Vicky was a marrying woman, as the phrase went; she just got off to a bad start. I hoped she'd be happy with the fellow, but for me—no, not Vicky, so brittle, so casual.

'. . . A responsibility,' Manson was saying. 'He's seven. A difficult age, you know. And not too strong—nervous.'

A son of Manson's would come by that naturally, and especially an only child, spoiled and agonized over. I wondered idly if the landlord of The Drowned Man was right about Eve Manson. If she was so anxious with the boy, so indulgent, was she as bad a mother as had been implied—not wanting more children? More likely she could not have another.

'Any age is difficult, isn't it?' I answered Manson absently. 'Wait until he's away at school and so on.'

Manson stared at me. 'Oh, we couldn't send him away to school. No, no, out of the question. Not possibly.'

CHAPTER THREE

Despite its situation Poltressor was a well-appointed house. Whether or not the Mansons were accustomed to guests, the room I was given was clean, airy, comfortable. A private electric system, this far from town, but no stinting of lights. The bathroom down the hall was modern.

I'm not ordinarily sensitive to my surroundings. Vague, Vicky calls me—as good a word as any. It's unusual for me to feel atmosphere, but I was feeling it in this house. Something uneasy, just a bit out of true.

It was a well-built house. Passing steps in the corridor were faint. I found there was even an ashtray, sat on the bed in my dressing gown for a final cigarette, and heard the small, distant noises of a house settling down gradually cease. I put out the cigarette; I was not inclined to sleep.

The door opened so quietly that only the movement made me turn.

'Is everything all right, Mr. Harkness?'

'Oh—yes, thanks.' I might have known even her dressing gown would be sophisticated, expensive. So had my first idle conjecture been right after all, the bored wife? But she would scarcely be as crude as that. She came into the room and shut the door. I thought her absolute poise was too studied.

'I hope you'll forgive me—most unconventional, isn't it, and I really do know better, though it wouldn't be a wonder if I had forgotten my manners. Do you know you are the first person—outside person, I mean—to visit us in almost a year?'

'Really?' I said.

'And you look nice and intelligent—I really have enjoyed your columns, you know, I wasn't just being polite at dinner—and so I decided to take the chance and talk to you. I think it's quite possible to get to know a person through what he writes, don't you? Something of himself must get into it.'

'Yes,' I agreed cautiously.

'Do you think Richard looks well, since you saw him last?'

This was rapidly beginning to feel like a scene from *Alice*. Or was it a French farce? 'He's changed very little.'

'Yes. I know. You knew him well at one time, didn't you?' She came farther into the room, stood by the window half turned from me. Without giving me time to answer she went on rapidly: 'I really do apologize—heaven knows what you're thinking of me—but you must understand. No one ever comes—he doesn't care for the few neighbors we have. He seemed so pleased to see you—I thought—you might be able to help.' Her hands twisted together.

Suddenly, as if we had come a physical step nearer, I saw her a little more clearly. At least part of her repressed agitation was due to her awareness of self. It was as much a part of her as eye or arm: anywhere, anytime, she was sex, exuding the atmosphere as naturally as she breathed. She knew it, and here, at least, regretted it; she wanted me to make no mistake.

I felt better for understanding her. 'Anything I can do ...' I began foolishly.

'It's difficult. I don't know—I can't explain. Please believe me, Mr. Harkness, if it wasn't for Jimmy I'd never have ... approached you. It's my own problem, Richard's, none of your business. But I'm afraid—you must understand, I'm afraid for Jimmy.'

'But I'm afraid I don't,' I said. Something was odd, wrong; but where did it lie? Manson, or the woman—or the boy? My imagination, between two breaths, built several plots. Manson mad, keeping them prisoner. The woman a congenital liar, dramatizing, craving excitement. The boy an idiot, and each blaming the other. Fine promising plots, in print. Not hers?

'I know, I know. It's difficult,' she said again. 'I wouldn't blame you for thinking me mad. I don't believe I am, you know, though it's so fantastic sometimes I ... I don't want

24

to tell you too much—I daren't.'

A hand at her mouth; then she sat down in the chair by the table, groped in the pocket of her robe.

'Do you have a cigarette? Thank you. You needn't worry about being compromised, by the way. The servants sleep downstairs, except Nanny, and Richard's room is at the far end of the hall.'

She smoked in silence for a little, as if searching for more words.

'It's Richard I want to talk about, not me, I'm sorry. He was quite like he used to be, tonight—with you. It's bad for him, stuck away here from one year's end to the next. He isn't ... I don't think he's well.'

'Can't you persuade him to see a doctor?'

'Now you're being polite. You don't believe me—or you think I'm a silly woman dramatizing some little thing. It's not that kind of illness.'

I said, 'I haven't seen him for some years, of course, but he seemed quite normal to me.'

'Oh, yes. It's just the one thing. Just that. I don't want to tell you, I don't want to prejudice you one way or the other. Part of it, you see, is that I may be too close to judge myself. You know how these things are ... It's a great temptation.' For the first time she smiled at me. 'To tell it all to someone outside, someone intelligent who ... might ... tell me what to do.' And then: 'I'm

25

making a bad impression—you must be thinking all sorts of things. I'll have to ask you to take my word, for the moment, that Richard is—let's say he has an obsession. Will you do that? Will you believe I'm at least intelligent enough and impersonal enough to have judged that much? Did he ask you to stay on?'

'Yes,' I said reluctantly. 'Yes, he did.'

Manson had, in fact, been very pressing. Love to have you, good to talk over old times, and since you're on holiday—at least over the weekend, please do.

She nodded. 'I thought he might. He might even talk to me now. Will you stay, Mr. Harkness, if only for tomorrow? I'll tell you what I want you to do. I want you to go to church and meet Mr. Silver, the rector. Richard never goes to church, nor do I, so you can talk to him alone. He'll be pleased, it's never a large congregation and he loves to talk. I want you to tell him where you're staying and that you're very much interested in folklore and country superstitions. Please! I know it sounds mad, but you'll see why later... He's a nice old man, you'll like him.'

'And?'

She put out her cigarette with an impatient gesture. 'I'll walk down to meet you at the church at one o'clock. I want to talk to you then. I'll tell you the rest then.'

'You're most intriguing,' I said. I meant it

26

sarcastically, but she flushed and stood up. I realized belatedly that I'd meant it in the other sense, too. 'I'm afraid I don't quite see...'

'I must go,' she said, drawing the robe closer about her. 'I know, I know, I've no right to ask you. But there's quite literally no one else, you see. No family, and Richard's cut himself off from all his London friends since we've been here. I couldn't possibly go to Mr. Silver, and Dr. Dyck—even if they'd listen. Even if he'd talk to them. And I don't know what to do—about Jimmy. Please, Mr. Harkness, will you do as I ask?'

I discovered several facts with interest. That now, as if divining it to be her last card, she was deliberately using her femininity; that I could be all too responsive to it; that she had aroused my curiosity. And that, all her manner notwithstanding, this woman had been under great strain and was nearly at the end of her resistance.

'You can't expect me to leave without knowing the whole story now, can you?' I smiled. But I was thinking her more a candidate for the doctor than Manson, quite frankly. Not a countrywoman to feel content in this remoteness. People said it with conviction, I'd go mad if I had to live in the country. Now and again, it might be true.

She looked at me blankly. 'The whole story?' she repeated. 'Do we ever really find

27

out the whole story, I wonder—about anything? You will stay? Thank you—so much. You won't mention any of this to Richard, please. Just—do as I said. Thank you.'

Now, mission accomplished, she seemed not to know how to leave gracefully. She put her hands into the pockets of her robe, took them out, after an awkward moment ended abruptly, said 'Good night,' and went out quietly.

I sat on the bed and lit another cigarette. My curiosity and interest were increasing rapidly. Not inconceivably, that had been her intention.

I slept heavily but woke at seven. Shaved and dressed, I found it still too early decently to go down; the house was silent. I stood at the window smoking the good first cigarette of the day, contemplating the view. Three sides of the house overlooked the cliff; here, below this window, was a ten-foot strip of crazy paving before the wall and the sheer drop to the surf. It was a pearl-gray morning, clear, colorless, looking cold.

Movement below drew my eyes from the sea. A little foreshortened, directly below, a child appeared around the side of the house: a small boy in khaki shorts and a red sweater. A gamboling red-and-white spaniel followed him. Even from here I could see the boy was hers: dark hair, and probably going to be

28

tall—slender, quick. From here there was nothing of Manson in him.

The boy went straight over to the wall, stretched up to it. He could just get his fingers over the top. He stepped back, spoke to the spaniel which sat down and gazed at him adoringly. He disappeared under the overhang of the house and came back, dragging a large stone from the ornamental rough border about the little rock garden. With the aid of this he began to climb up onto the wall.

I fumbled with the catch of the window, but by the time I had it up the boy was astride the top of the wall, and I hesitated. The wall was not quite two feet wide: not a substantial footing, even for an agile youngster. Now the boy had turned and was standing upright, looking out to sea. Below, the spaniel barked sharply.

I watched in a sudden cold sweat of fear. I've no head for heights myself. I was afraid to call out. A shout from a stranger, even of the boy's name, might well startle him into losing balance.

I could not see her: she must be standing just below my window. Her voice was normal, not raised. 'Jimmy—better come in now.'

The boy turned a shining face. 'I can see miles and miles! I bet I could see clear to China if the sun was out!'

'That's nice,' she said. 'But you'd better come in now, Nanny has your breakfast ready.'

'Oh. All right.' Reluctantly, the boy scrambled down from the wall, dropping lightly; the spaniel gamboled about him. They vanished around the back of the house.

I shut the window and wiped my forehead. For some reason I felt there had been subtle meaning in the little scene that I had not grasped. But one deduction at least could be made. That woman was no hysterical fool.

CHAPTER FOUR

'Of course,' said Mr. Silver a little regretfully, 'there are many similar legends. The sixteenth and seventeenth centuries were full of superstition. But it is interesting— interesting. I have always found such matters fascinating, Mr. Harkness, as showing the endless ingenuities of the human race, and how even a religion as—um—gentle as Christianity can be twisted to show an ugly side. Amazing—and dangerous, of course, under some circumstances. Perhaps the most amazing thing is that even in our own time many people still believe in witchcraft.'

'I believe,' I said with an interest not entirely assumed, 'the principle of

30

autosuggestion...'

'Exactly, exactly. As a man thinketh, you know. That probably accounts for the authenticated instances. Now, let me see, where is old Horder? I was sure—ah, here he is. It is most gratifying, Mr. Harkness, to find someone as interested in these things as myself. Nowadays people are so likely to say—what is that obnoxious term?—so what? And to other matters than folklore, dear me, yes. But I should not want to bore you.'

I reassured him and the old clergyman beamed pleasedly. He was exactly what Eve Manson had called him, a nice old man, with a fringe of silver hair, parchment-wrinkled face, and mild blue eyes like the White Knight. At the expense of sitting through a dull and poorly attended sermon in the drafty (though modern) church at Pentressor, it had been easy to establish myself in the rector's graces. We were now ensconced in Mr. Silver's small untidy study in the rectory nearby.

'Of course, you did say you are interested. While it is not a unique legend, it—now let me find the place, yes, here we are.' He handed over the large tome, heavy as lead, open to the middle. 'Not very good cuts, I fear, it is a Victorian edition, privately printed—but it will give you an idea.'

I looked at certainly a very crude woodcut showing a figure of indeterminate sex roped to a stake with flames dramatically blazing. One arm was raised in theatrical gesture. On the opposite page (and where can you see paper like this now, cream-laid, thick, and those extravagant margins?) ran the bold caption: THE MANSON CURSE.

'That is it. There is a similar legend connected with the Wolverhampton family, except that there it was a dragon, not a witch, who pronounced the curse. And oddly enough, as in this instance, it has occasionally happened that the threat was made good—unfortunately leading foolish people to believe in such things. Yes, yes. Well, so far as the Manson family is concerned, you will find a version of the tale there—somewhat garbled, I fear. As you know, belief in witchcraft was rife at the period—the date is 1693 or thereabouts.

'It was the original Cornish Manson, Amyas, who was concerned. He had acquired the property, a small part of which is still held by Mr. Richard Manson, shortly before. Of course there was a certain amount of local resentment—there would be, you know. Country folk are always so insular. He held the living here at that time, and brought in a new clergyman—a predecessor of my own, eh, ha! ha! Yes. The man was not well liked. It was he who accused this village woman, Tamar Wood, of practicing witchcraft. Apparently, at least according to those who believe such things, the accusation was only too well founded. At all events, she pleaded for clemency from Manson—the ultimate authority in those days, you know—but he sided with the clergy and indeed there is some reason to believe that he was the prime accuser. Perhaps she had offended him in some way. So in the end she was burned, which was rather unusual at the period as perhaps you know, witches generally being hanged—and she pronounced the curse at the stake.'

'And what was the curse?'

'Why, that the eldest son of Manson would die in childhood. That is, of all Mansons. The actual wording ran, "that Manson be cursed with a doom on the firstborn son, generation to generation, even as Herod laid the burden on the children, and so long as tide runs, sun sets, and wind blows, the firstborn son of Manson shall never live to manhood."'

I'd found it in the book. 'Vindictive old lady,' I said. 'I wonder why.'

'Undoubtedly the full story is not there. Probably something disgraceful, you know—or considered disgraceful when old Horder was collecting his family legends.' The rector tittered. 'Possibly the woman had been Manson's mistress—or refused him—or, and this would explain it neatly, you know, she may actually have borne his eldest son out of wedlock and been disgruntled when her

33

child could not inherit the property.'

'That makes a better story,' I agreed.

'So far as I know, this is the only published version of the legend—the book is dated 1843, you will notice—but the country folk about here have preserved it among themselves from the earliest origin. Doubtless Horder had it from some Cornish person. The odd and unfortunate thing is—as I was saying—it *has* happened that the eldest son has died in childhood in some generations, and to this day you will find persons round about who believe in the Manson Curse.'

I reflected that I had met some. This was what the fishermen were speaking of.

'Extraordinary,' I said, 'but when you think of it, maybe not so odd at that. Look at the period. Medical knowledge, drugs, surgery, all practically nonexistent—or at best crude—it wasn't at all unusual to lose three or four children from a large family.'

'Exactly, as credulous people never stop to think. The records are confused, and it is probable that the eldest son did live to inherit in some generations. As you say, it would have been nothing out of the way, at the period concerned—life expectancy was not great. But when such a death did occur it gave credence to the curse.'

'Very curious,' I said politely. 'But Mr. Richard Manson seems to have escaped it.'

'Oh, it would not apply to him, you know.

Another unfortunate instance of—um—coincidence. His father was not the eldest son. The eldest son was also a Richard Manson. He was just twenty when he was killed in France, in 1914, and the present Mr. Manson is the son of his younger brother, James. I expect you could argue, therefore, that the eldest son did not live to manhood in that generation, legally—being short of twenty-one. The present Mr. Manson's parents were killed in an accident when he was only an infant, with his own elder brother.'

'I see. There was a guardian, then?'

'Oh, yes.' Off his main subject Mr. Silver was vague. 'Old Mr. Manson, his father's younger brother—he was not old then, of course—and Miss Belle Manson, his aunt and uncle, supervised the estate until he was of age. Miss Manson was the eldest child, considerably older than his father.' He seemed reluctant to speak of that, or uninterested. 'And even more oddly—the records here, of course, are fairly modern—in the preceding generation there was another instance. The father of the Richard Manson who died in France was not the eldest son. His brother, young James Manson, the legal heir, was drowned in 1889 at the age of nineteen. He kept a little sailing craft. It capsized one day and he was lost. I beg your pardon?'

'I only said, I wonder if the inn was named for him. The Drowned Man?'

'Oh, quite possibly. I really do not know. Only accident, of course—pure coincidence. But some people actually find pleasure in believing these legends. You would be amazed, Mr. Harkness, how superstitious country people are, even in our modern age with decent education and so on. Indeed, I am convinced it is not a question of education at all. They may learn, after a fashion, to read and write, but the principal educating is given unconsciously in the home, and when they hear these things as children—you follow me.

'Why, only the other day I came on one of the Plumm girls beside Pigeon's Pond—that is just the other side of the village, I daresay you would not know it, but no matter—and if you please she told me she was making a charm to discover who she would marry! It seems if one sleeps on a new shilling, rises at dawn and tosses it into the pond, then repeats the Lord's Prayer three times, the image of one's future husband will appear in the water. Of course, I told her it was all nonsense.'

'You'll find variants of that one everywhere,' I said.

'I daresay. Nonsense, of course. Then there is our local werewolf legend—rather more original than the Manson Curse, I hazard—I must tell you about that. I am not boring you? I do not think you will find any country

36

richer in folklore than Cornwall—possibly the Celtic strain... My dear fellow, won't you stay and lunch with me? I see it is past one o'clock. Oh, Mrs. Twelvetrees! Mrs. Twelvetrees!'

'Please don't trouble, sir,' and I began the preliminary courtesies of extricating myself.

Eve was standing with her back to the little church, facing the war memorial. Even a village as small as Pentressor had a war memorial this century; but this one was of the first war. I came up behind her, and before she was aware, and turned, caught a glimpse of the few names set in bronze. Heading the list was RICHARD JOHN MANSON—1894–1914.

'You were quite right,' I said. 'Mr. Silver is a nice old man.'

She did not start. 'Oh, there you are. I expected he'd keep you talking, but you must be starved. I brought the car so we'd be on time for lunch.' She nodded at it, an old Hillman parked at the churchyard gate. Neither of us spoke as we crossed to the car, and I saw that she would not; she was waiting for me. In the car she did not look at me, and made no move to start the engine.

I said, 'He's made quite a hobby of it, hasn't he? Harmless old fellow, but you know, I got the impression—he was a little too vehement about it—he'd like to believe all that nonsense himself.'

'I wouldn't be surprised,' she agreed in a

colorless voice. 'He did tell you about the curse? It's one of the star turns in this part of the country.'

'And what are you going to tell me? You said "the rest."'

She looked at me briefly, started the car, and made a wide sweep in the deserted road to head back for Poltressor House. 'You don't have to ask that, do you, Mr. Harkness? I think you know now. He believes it, you see.'

'Manson? That's absurd,' I said involuntarily.

'Oh, certainly, but it's not much use to say that. We haven't much time, you must forgive me if I say this badly—I know I've not made a good impression.' She spoke a little jerkily as she drove, looking straight ahead. 'When you live close to a thing like this for a long time, it does something to your judgment. Especially when your emotions are involved, too. I'll try to be as lucid as possible. Richard believed all that, about the curse of the Mansons. You're doubting that any intelligent man could. I'll tell you why he does.

'He was brought up here, all his life until he went to Cambridge. His uncle—I met him once, a vague sort of man—he wasn't much of anything good or bad, you hardly knew he was there. It was Miss Manson who took the responsibility. Sometimes I believe she's a witch herself ... she revels in that kind of

38

thing. All of it, any of it, from telling fortunes with tea leaves to the Manson Curse. She believes in it, the way Mr. Silver believes in God. And she had Richard all his life until he was grown. Do you understand what I'm trying to say?'

'Go on.'

'Oh, he got away, of course. He read, he went away to school and then to Cambridge. He never came back after that, until six years ago when his uncle died and she wrote and asked him to come. He'd got so far away he was actually almost violent about denouncing superstition. Isn't there something they call overcompensation? But when he was back and she could reach him again, he ... I believe he couldn't help himself. At first he used to go away, sometimes I'd be with him, we'd go up to town for weekends and so on. And he went alone. Then, a couple of years ago, this got to be an obsession with him.

'Will you tell me something? Mr. Fowler, the publisher, said Richard showed great promise. Was it just the kind of thing publishers say, because the book was a best seller?'

'No. It was a good novel, *Troth*,' I said without much mental reservation. 'Perhaps a little overdramatized, but none the worse for that.'

'I wouldn't know. I just know what I like. That's a cliché, isn't it? He'd begun to work on another book. He's never finished it. The thing's taken possession of him. I've handled it badly, I started off by ridiculing him—all the wrong things, he won't listen to anything I say now. After all, she had him until he was eighteen.'

'This is all rather fantastic,' I said. 'Will you forgive me if I say I sympathize with you, but what is the point? Thousands of people go through life believing that black cats are bad luck or that you can predict the future by the stars.'

'That's the kind of thing I hoped you'd say. Reasonable. So I could set out all my reasons and see how they stand up. You see why I couldn't go to Mr. Silver. Or anyone close. So many people do half believe these things. It's Jimmy. Why should I care, except for Jimmy? It's so bad for him. Can't you imagine the sort of thing Richard says to him? Children—they've no way of judging. It happened to Richard himself.

'The last time he went to London,' she said then, 'he bought Jimmy a ring. He had them make it specially. It's a bloodstone ring. Do you know what magical virtue a bloodstone has, Mr. Harkness? It protects the wearer from all evil enchantments.'

'Oh, dear,' I said uncomfortably.

'I don't want my son infected with all this nonsense.' She was fierce about it.

'My dear Mrs. Manson,' I took refuge in

formality, 'I sympathize, as I said, but...'

'But what's it got to do with you?' She looked at me directly. 'I'm frightened. Now. I thought once of going away, taking Jimmy away. It seemed so silly, such a little thing. Then it wasn't so little anymore. I am almost afraid to say it. I don't believe he is quite sane.'

Her voice shook suddenly. After a moment she added, 'It seemed a godsend when you came—someone from outside.'

'Look here,' I said mildly, 'I quite understand how it is, isolated as you are, but aren't you making mountains out of molehills? After all, sooner or later he will have to admit there's nothing in it, you know. When the boy continues to thrive and eventually grows up.'

She swerved the car to the roadside, braked, turned eyes dark with emotion to me. She said slowly, 'Will he? If ... but just suppose something *does* happen to Jimmy?'

I thought of the cliff and the wall. 'That gave me a few uncomfortable moments this morning. Yes, I saw it, from my window. Boys will do things like that, won't they? But somehow they survive. With ordinary care. Don't you think you're being a bit overanxious yourself?'

'Fond parent, only child?' she countered sharply. 'I don't know. I don't know. It's not as if I didn't want more children, and that's not ...' She checked herself. 'Ordinary care,' and a laugh. 'He had the wall made higher. But everywhere is dangerous—anywhere. The country, the city. You can't tell.'

'If you'll excuse the question,' I said, 'what had you thought I might do about it?'

Lunch was late. Manson waxed satirical about long sermons, then the church, then Christianity, until his aunt reprimanded him in a colorless tone, 'You should not be disrespectful before the child, Richard.'

The boy sat across the table and looked at me with bright, curious eyes—dark eyes like his mother's. He had needed prompting to offer a shy hand and say, 'How do you do, sir,' and did not chatter at the table. It was not surprising that there should be anxiety about Jimmy: a quick, good-looking little boy, good brow, nice eyes. An attractive youngster.

After the old woman's remark Manson fell silent, rather grim. His aunt did not speak again, and Eve only to the boy in a low voice. I was mulling over what she had told, and asked, and scarcely noticed the silence or what I was eating. I was recalled by her formal voice offering me coffee.

'I climbed up the wall,' said the boy suddenly to his father—a private confidence, accompanied by a wide smile. 'Just like you said to. It was nice. I saw miles and miles and miles, clear to China.'

I was watching Eve, and saw her turn dead white. But Manson's voice, quick and loud, took attention from her.

'On the wall? Good God, you might have fallen. Eve, why in God's name can't you look after him better? The wall!' Suddenly he was in a rage. 'As I said, as I said! When did I ever tell you to climb on the wall? I never told you that, why should you tell such a lie? James—answer me, do you hear?'

The boy looked confused and frightened. He whispered, 'I don't know, sir.'

'Answer me! I never told you to climb on the wall, did I?'

'I guess not.'

'Certainly not—do you think I want you killed? How could I have said such a thing? I can't understand why you should tell such a lie. You must never climb the wall, do you hear? I don't want to see you touching the wall!'

'Yes, sir. No.' The tears had started to his eyes, but he bit his lip manfully, repressing a sob.

'Richard, it's just a misunderstanding.' Her voice was quiet. 'Jimmy knows it's dangerous to get up on the wall. He won't do it again.'

'Kindly don't confuse the issue by covering up for him, Eve. I will not have the boy spoiled and cosseted. If he misbehaves he must be punished. If I find you going near the wall again, James, you may expect something besides a scolding.'

'Yes, sir,' said the boy submissively. He bent his head to his plate, lip quivering. There was a small oppressive silence until Eve spoke. I thought she had needed that time to control her voice, maintain poise before the (after all) outsider; and her voice was too calm, too unedged.

'Let's not quarrel about it, Richard. It's all over now, it doesn't matter.' The boy could not suppress a small sob. 'Will you excuse us, Mr. Harkness? Jimmy.' Head down, he got up and followed her from the room blindly.

Manson muttered, 'Women. No use to coddle him, he must learn to take care. Now she's made him think he was perfectly right to do it. The wall: saying I told him. Excuse me, Johnny, these damned family upsets.'

'Quite all right,' I said politely. I wished Manson would not call me Johnny; no one ever had.

The old woman said angrily, 'It may be possible. It may be, Richard, with effort and prayer and faith. But she makes it very difficult. You must speak to her again.'

'Yes, I will, Aunt Belle.' He looked at me. 'Finished? Will you come into my study, Johnny, there's something I'd like to discuss with you. You'll excuse us, Aunt.'

CHAPTER FIVE

'I'll be damned,' said Fowler. 'He made no pretense about it at all?'

'None. Beyond, as I say, finding out if I was sympathetic. It's one of the oddest experiences I remember having.' I lit a cigarette, reflecting on the impossibility of conveying its oddness to Fowler.

I said suddenly, 'I'm a newspaperman and I don't pretend to be anything else. I hope I'm a good one, but I look on it as a trade. Maybe I don't understand what arty people call creative writers.'

Fowler grunted over his pipe. 'Are you excusing Manson or accusing him? Go on.'

I did not, for a moment, remembering Manson, his reasonableness, his practicality. 'When I say he made no pretense that's not quite right. He tried to pass it off as a mild joke, something amusing. He kept saying, "Can't do any harm, you know."'

'So he's going to try to break the curse,' said Fowler with a laugh.

But what exactly had been in Manson's mind that he should speak of it so openly? Was it merely that he was starved for outside company, talk? Or was he trying to justify himself, something of the old intelligent Manson, the man who took a First at

45

Cambridge? Or so I'd heard. Or was it more subtly that he suspected she had already spoken to me?

He had begun by asking quite frankly if the rector had ridden his hobbyhorse in front of the visitor. 'I thought possibly he might have told you.' Aware of the danger of antagonizing him, I had been noncommittal and Manson grew confiding.

'Yes, well, I don't mind telling you it rather worries me. You can laugh. It seems to me the scientists are too quick to pooh-pooh these things. Have you read Seabrook's *Witchcraft*? Extraordinarily interesting, I must lend it to you.' He pressed the book on me then and there. 'Take your time with it. Well, I don't really want to believe it, you know, though according to the available family records the thing has worked out. The fact is, my aunt...'

He broke off, staring absently over my head.

'She does believe it. She has an idea the curse can be broken. She's been after me for years, ever since the boy was born.' I noticed that he seldom called the child by name; it was 'the boy' as if still, after seven years, he was advertising the fact that he had sired a son.

And then he said for the first time, 'Can't do any harm, you know. In case there could be anything in it.'

During that little speech he kept looking narrowly at me, gauging my reception of all this. When I offered no ridicule, maintaining an air of polite interest, he went on more confidently.

'I believe he thought he convinced me that it's entirely his aunt's idea,' I said to Fowler. 'Like everyone who has a bent toward superstition, she's interested in spiritualism.'

Fowler was digging out the bowl of his pipe. 'Are you sure it isn't the aunt? Manson may be credulous, but not the fool his wife makes him out to be.'

'Nothing Mrs. Manson said implied she thinks him a fool,' I said rather stiffly. 'She is obviously an intelligent woman, and under the circumstances surprisingly self-controlled.'

'I'm not doubting you,' said Fowler to his pipe. 'So Manson, or his aunt, or both of them together, have the notion of getting in touch with the witch through a medium and persuading her to recall the curse. Interesting, but a little unsubtle. Not the kind of thing our firm does well with.'

'Damn it,' I said irritably, 'this is real, not a manuscript you're rejecting. I told you the whole thing was mad.'

'With a kind of dark logic to it. I agree, with reservations. You humored him.'

'If I hadn't he'd have shut up at once. Mrs. Manson found that out for herself. He isn't

47

interested in anyone else's opinion.'

'You'd think a clever woman would know that to start with.' There was mockery in his tone; I paid little notice, knowing Fowler for a misogynist.

'She's clever enough, though it isn't the word I'd have chosen,' I acknowledged, 'but she's also, if I read her rightly, extremely emotional and extremely inhibited, if you'll forgive the jargon. My own opinion is that, if it came to a choice, for her it would be the boy before Manson.'

'I wonder,' said Fowler, 'if that's an honest observation or wishful thinking.'

'And what the devil do you mean by that?'

'She's a beautiful woman.'

Fowler said that exactly as another man had said it to me very recently: she is a liar, a cheat, a destroyer. I knew about Fowler: that his wife was also a beautiful woman, who had deceived him for years before leaving him: that perhaps he loved her still as he hated her. But it was conjecturable what had put the venom in Dr. Dyck's tone.

Without replying to that I went on, 'I can see how the situation developed so gradually that she hesitated to do anything. I did think it rather odd that she didn't confide—if she wanted someone outside to know of it—in someone nearby. And as a matter of fact I found out that she did. There isn't much choice, among the gentry, as you Britishers say. There's the rector; the doctor; two old maiden ladies who take in paying guests in the summer; one of those bluff country squires, Colonel (retired) Christopher Bullen, straight out of a bad American novel about the English upper classes; the Trehernes, a nice normal dull county family; and a couple of others much the same. I saw them all at church that morning. With the possible exception of Bullen, who has no imagination at all, all of them would be inclined to think a woman like Mrs. Manson a bit suspect.

'You've met her,' I added, belatedly realizing it.

'Certainly. When we did *Troth*. Suspect because she's good-looking?'

'Not entirely. She always looks as if she were going to a wedding at St. Margaret's, Westminster.'

'A flair for clothes,' agreed Fowler. 'Quite French, though actually she's half Scottish. And never country things, tweeds and so on. I know what you mean. But you say she did go to someone?'

'The doctor,' I said. I took out a fresh cigarette, turned it about in my fingers, frowning. Here in London, in the safe anonymity of a pub, with Fowler's saturnine eyes on me, it was difficult to recapture the atmosphere of Cornwall. I wasn't sure that any of it had happened, that I had not misread the facts, taken too much for granted.

No, damn it, my imagination wasn't as vivid as all that. There was the other thing to think about, too. But surely that was even madder than the business of the curse? Manson saying 'the boy,' which implied such pride of ownership. Ownership? Perhaps that was the key to the whole thing. 'She went to see the doctor,' I said slowly.

★   ★   ★

I had gone to see the doctor, without telling her, because I'm a practical man, whatever else I'm not. A physician is likely to be a realist; and if Manson should be going mad, some competent person within reach ought to have the facts. The local doctor was an obvious choice; doctors are discreet by nature. And I liked Dyck at first: obviously a capable, alert man. In the fifties, stoutening a bit: a shrewd pair of eyes, firm mouth, unexpectedly deep bass voice, thinning ginger hair.

In his office, behind his scarred desk, Dyck listened expressionlessly to a brief recital of the story. I didn't tell him everything in my mind. There were aspects I wasn't prepared to examine openly until I'd given them more thorough consideration myself.

At the conclusion Dyck said coldly, 'That's a remarkable statement, Mr. Harkness. In

50

several ways. I may as well say at once that while I appreciate your motives in coming to me, it's not the first time I've heard of the matter. Nor do I think it's any cause for alarm. Tempest in a teapot.'

'I beg your pardon,' I said, feeling foolish and angry at once. 'I hadn't realized it was common knowledge that Manson...'

'In that sense it isn't, certainly. Mrs. Manson came to me several months ago and told me substantially what you have. Of course, you're only repeating what she's told you.'

'Are you suggesting that it's a lie? Manson himself...'

'Not at all,' said Dyck dryly. 'May we be frank, Mr. Harkness? I take it that you don't know the Mansons well.'

'At one time I knew him quite well. We were both living in London. He was the assistant literary critic on a London paper and I was London correspondent for my own paper in New York. We used to meet quite frequently. But I haven't seen him for several years, and this is the first time I've met his wife, as it happens.'

'I see. Let's be frank,' Dyck repeated. 'The nonsense about the curse...' He gestured, dismissing it as beneath discussion. 'Plenty of people believe such things. It doesn't do any harm except to their reasoning capacity. If Mr. Manson chooses to believe it, that's his own concern. If you'll forgive me, we haven't any evidence, by your own admission, that he's in any way serious about it, that his mentality is affected. That's Mrs. Manson's opinion.'

'Would you mind telling me what you said to Mrs. Manson when she came here?' I asked.

'Not at all—exactly what I'm about to tell you, somewhat more frankly. I think she's exaggerated the situation in her own mind. On the facts it's merely absurd, not the calamity she implies.' Dyck smiled.

'You know, Mr. Harkness, a doctor gets into the way of discounting fifty percent of a nervous patient's report, sometimes more. Mrs. Manson hasn't been accustomed to living in the country, and Poltressor House is isolated.'

'Yes. He's spent a couple of years, I understand,' I said deliberately, 'reading everything ever published about supernatural phenomena. He has a whole filing cabinet of notes.'

'Really. Well, that's a harmless hobby, isn't it? Our rector, Mr. Silver, has a similar one, and I hope you're not going to maintain that it's unhinged *his* mind. As for Mrs. Manson, she's a highly emotional type—restless, impulsive, volatile.'

'I wouldn't quite say that.'

'But you don't know her well.' Only a hint

of superiority in Dyck's smile. 'She's a beautiful woman,' he said, 'and doubtless accustomed to adulation, a round of entertainments, all that kind of thing. She had nothing to occupy herself with in the country. She's imaginative, and she has unconsciously dramatized the situation...'

'To get attention,' I finished. 'I'm afraid I can't agree.'

Dyck shrugged. 'I'm not asking you to. One thing I'll give you—old Miss Manson. She's a strange old lady, but a lot of old ladies I've known have been converts to astrology and spiritualism, all the other claptrap you can think of. I don't suppose she's comfortable to live with, but that's just one of those things,' and he shrugged again.

It was not until afterward that I realized Dyck had made me angriest by expressing some of the little doubts present in my own mind. Whatever prejudices I might have, however, I lacked one which had probably been the main factor in deciding Dyck. There was startling bitterness in the man's tone when he said, 'She's a beautiful woman.' Obviously he disliked her and for that reason alone. How minds, even good ones, get into a jumble like attics in old houses with hundreds of forgotten things locked away in trunks...

Emotional, restless, impulsive, volatile; so Dyck's beautiful woman had been like that, and for him every beautiful woman was the same.

I thought it must have taken courage for her to come and speak to him. I felt she was essentially a self-contained person not given to expressing private troubles, certainly not to virtual strangers. It followed that, rationally or not, she must feel the trouble to be real, imminent, or she could not have brought herself to speak of it.

This I kept to myself; it was no use arguing with Dyck. I said, 'It's quite possible you're right, Doctor. Would you mind telling me something else? I haven't any reason, or right, to ask you. Let's just say it's to satisfy curiosity. Have you ever had the little boy as a patient?'

Dyck looked at me sharply. 'As you say, it's irrelevant, and technically I suppose I'm not called on to answer. However, there's no harm in telling you. Yes, I have. About three years after the Mansons came here. The boy was just past three then. He had a mild case of whooping cough. Perfectly normal recovery. A couple of years ago he fell down the stairs and had a concussion. Last summer he fell off his bicycle and broke his arm. All rather normal accidents for an active youngster.' He was politely sarcastic in detailed reply. 'May I ask . . . ?'

'I see. It doesn't matter. I'm afraid I've taken up your time for no reason.'

'Not at all. As I said, I understand how

you've been misled, Mr. Harkness, and I appreciate your intentions...'

I decided I disliked Dr. Dyck. An opinionated, pompous fool. Also, I felt that he was casting me in the role of the credulous dupe taken in by a silly woman, which was hardly flattering. Ten minutes later, in the car, away from Pentressor for good, I could laugh. But ... but there was the rest of it, that I had not mentioned.

CHAPTER SIX

That I did mention to Fowler, who said, 'Dr. Dyck sounds like an eminently sensible man. It's obvious why she said nothing about her visit to him.'

'Leave Mrs. Manson out of it for the moment,' I said. 'You're confusing the issue, you and Dyck. It scarcely rests on her word, whatever you think of her. It's Manson...'

'He was always nervous,' agreed Fowler, nodding. 'Strange. I wonder how they get along. Odd types to marry each other—I always thought so.'

'You seem to be obsessed with the woman.'

'Oh, not me, John, not me. Not with any woman, but especially not with Eve Manson. You were going to say?'

'Well, I must say I think it's rather a neat

idea. She asked me to locate a spirit-medium for Manson's great plan. He's completely out of touch with anyone in London, and I let him think that if I'm not exactly in agreement with his beliefs, at least I don't openly disagree with them. I could easily write him and mention casually that I'd heard so-and-so was an excellent professional medium. Mrs. Manson's idea is that I find one and brief her of the facts—it's usually a her, isn't it? And that if Manson can be persuaded he's really broken the curse, he'll drop the whole thing and forget about it.'

'Very possible,' said Fowler. 'Curses broken while you wait. Sorry, I don't mean to be tiresomely facetious. But I'm inclined to agree with the doctor, you know. I'm mainly interested to locate Manson. I may get another novel out of him.'

'Not while he's in this state,' I told him. 'He won't work that hard when he doesn't have to.'

'Are you going back to see how the double play comes off?'

'I am not,' I said with emphasis. 'If Manson has lost touch with all his other friends, I've lost touch with him. He used to have a good mind. I'm sorry for Mrs. Manson and the boy, and I'm glad to help her if I can, but it's none of my business after all.

'It's a nice house,' I added inconsequentially, 'to look at. Lovely view and so on. But there's something strange about it inside. Wrong. It's been lived in by a lot of unhappy people.'

'Oh, you're a hard-boiled newspaperman,' said Fowler. 'You haven't any nervousness, any oddities, like other writers. If you change your mind, I'd like to go down with you. I may go anyway... Very fortuitous, your stumbling on Manson like that just when a crisis was brewing—according to what she told you.'

'You're not generally so suspicious, even of women, Charles,' I said a little spitefully. But Fowler seemed not to hear.

'She's a very handsome piece of goods,' and he spoke absently, squinting down the stem of his pipe. 'Ve-ry handsome. You'll excuse the intrusion into your private life. I gather you're still unmarried. Pity.'

'But not your business,' I said.

He grunted. 'Somebody ought to rescue you before you get into trouble. It always surprises me that fellows like you don't know more about women. You tall scraggly chaps with what the women's magazine writers call roughhewn features'—Fowler's tone was only half-mocking; he was shortish, balding, unhandsome himself—'the girls always take to your sort, no trouble getting enough experience. You'd think by this time you'd have learned a few fundamental facts.'

'Meaning?'

'You're a nice chap, John—for an American,' and he grinned. 'I wouldn't want to see anything happen to you. Tell me this. The situation with Manson is strange enough to be interesting. But aren't you so much interested in it—don't say you're not, because you are—because the woman dramatized it that way to you? Because you're interested in her?'

'That's quite ridiculous,' I said coldly. 'It's true Mrs. Manson's a very attractive woman. I liked her. I was sorry for her. But as to anything more—well, I'm no stick-in-the-mud, but she's another man's wife.'

'My dear chap, I wasn't thinking you were planning any actual seduction. Though you probably wouldn't find it difficult. I only want you to have all the facts in hand. Facts are sometimes damned useful, though you romanticists will twist 'em about to suit yourselves.'

'I'm not sure that isn't the subtlest insult you ever offered me. I'm not a romanticist, I'm a news hack, the facts are my business. And what do you mean by facts in this case?'

'You never happened to meet Manson's wife when he was, so to speak, still in circulation, did you?'

'No, I didn't. I knew he was married, I think. I remember him speaking of his wife. But usually when I saw him it was at the Press Club or a pub somewhere. As a matter of fact, now you mention it, I did think it rather odd that he never asked me over or ...'

'He seldom asked anybody,' interrupted Fowler softly. 'I pieced the story together from various sources because I was interested for a reason of my own. You wouldn't call Manson much of a ladies' man, would you? He's not bad-looking, but he's small. Not a man you'd notice in a crowd, not a man women admire. Never was very truly sought after, was he? No. Well, the first great success of his life was his marriage. He married a beautiful, notorious, young exciting woman. And he's been terrified ever since, I think, that he'll lose her. Even when ... but no matter. They lived very quietly, seldom went out, seldom entertained even when he made money from the book. I believe that must have been the principal reason he moved to the country, to keep her away from possible temptation.'

'I see,' I said slowly. 'That does make sense. From the viewpoint of looks they certainly are rather oddly matched, but then so often that ... What do you mean, notorious?'

'Her maiden name was Eve Henrys,' said Fowler. 'Say anything to you? What about Margaret Henrys? The Henrys–Paxton case, January 1946?'

'I do seem to recall.'

'Margaret Henrys was Eve Manson's

mother. Hanged at Pentonville for murder. It was an interesting case. Sordid, but interesting.'

★   ★   ★

I stared at a steel-gray sea visible from the upper windows of The Drowned Man and wondered why I had come back to Pentressor. I had not intended to come, and I felt uncomfortable that it had not been a matter of free will. That, of course, was dodging the issue; I knew perfectly well why I was here, but I hated to admit it. The woman. And other riddles.

I heard Fowler settling himself in the room across the narrow passage: thump of a bag on the floor, muttered curse. Damn Fowler. The trouble with him was that he read too many detective novels. I couldn't very well have told Fowler, 'I don't want you,' when he said, so casually certain, 'I'll drive down with you if you don't mind. I'd like to see Manson again.'

After all, I didn't know these people. Manson—they said you changed completely every seven years, or was that just superstition?—I had known a Richard Manson, but that was in another cycle of life. This was a different man. And the woman I had never known. I had met them by chance, she had asked my help—strange request to make of a stranger, but she had (or felt she had) no one else to ask. Very well, I'd gone a little out of my way to help her, interested because it was a strange story, and that should be that.

I like a good detective novel, I enjoy a ghost story. But only in an idle way, you know, to pass the time. This wasn't my kind of thing.

Fowler said from the door, 'Well, I wonder if Madam Sonia is duly installed in the Manson's guest room by now.'

'Very likely,' I said without turning. 'What the devil are we doing here? Shouldn't have come.'

'At least I have an excuse.' He was cheerful. 'What more natural than to run down to see Manson after all this time, now I know where he is? If they've room we may be invited to stay. They'll know the doubtful amenities of The Drowned Man.'

I said nothing to that. I wasn't anxious to be in Poltressor House again.

A clever idea, I'd said to Fowler, yes...

★   ★   ★

'Don't you see, Mr. Harkness ... oh, it sounds mad, but it's like fighting fire with fire. He believes in it, he's afraid of it, and if he can be made to think he's stopped the danger he'll be satisfied, and forget it. It's the

61

only way he'll feel safe. That would satisfy him, you see, because he does believe in those things. What do you think about it?'

'I think it's quite feasible,' I'd told her. 'And an interesting notion.'

'I've thought it out, since he's talked about it so much. It would be so logical for him and settle the whole absurd thing, you know. I've no idea how to get in touch with one, but neither has Richard. He talks about it a good deal but even he knows that these people are mostly frauds. I wonder . . .' She was using her sex then, playing on me: artful, but with pretense. She was not so helpless. A mature intelligent woman, using me, seizing the chance to carry out a plan in greater safety.

However susceptible and sympathetic I might be, I was not such a fool as not to see that, and to see why. It would be safer that she have no contact with it at all; in the event Manson discovered he had been tricked, no one could prove she had planned the trick. A doubly clever idea, yes. Hindsight? At the time I had felt only sympathy . . .

This playing around with spirits and séances, like adolescents. But there's more to it than that, I thought. This is only the veneer. Very well, bring it into the open and look at it. You are here and concerning yourself with it because of the woman, but not for the usual reason. The part about Manson is odd enough to be interesting, but the woman ... You thought you had her summed up, and now you find you know nothing about her at all and you're curious. Just that. No emotional involvement.

I felt better for admitting that to myself. I was even, for the moment, more kindly disposed to Fowler. 'Madam Sonia,' I said with a laugh, turning. 'My God, what a farce. You can't conceive what a fool I felt.'

★   ★   ★

I'd found the woman's name in the telephone directory. Since these people were all frauds there was not much to choose among them. The address was in Bloomsbury, not far from my own place—respectable-shoddy, an old house cut up into flats. There was a neat sign on the flat door inviting callers to step in please. Evidently the flat was an office. Or did spiritualists keep salons, or studios? Up to then I was amused; Madam Sonia embarrassed me. As I told Fowler, I felt like a fool explaining to her.

She might have been born O'Brien, a large raddled woman. I diagnosed her: unsuccessful music-hall turns, a predilection for gin. But her eyes were shrewd; I didn't have to do much explaining.

'You understand, I never guarantee results. Sometimes the spirits cannot get through.' Whatever original accent it had been, the veneer of pseudo-Mayfair disguised it. 'I hope you wouldn't think that I'd use any tricks.'

I'd forgotten there would be professional ethics to overcome. 'Of course not—' I could not possibly say 'Madam Sonia.' The police were interested in fraudulent mediums. Probably she thought I was the police, looking for evidence. 'All this is quite new to me, but I assure you you're not being asked to do anything dishonest. It's merely that Mrs. Manson is particularly anxious to obtain satisfactory results, and if you should do so she would like to make you a little gift in appreciation.'

Apparently she decided that no police spy, even an American one, would command such delicate language; she relaxed a little.

'Well, it's all in the day's work. I'll do my very best to satisfy.' Was that the suggestion of a wink?

'I'll give Mr. Manson your name, and you may hear from him soon.'

'Too pleased, I'm sure.' Was there any possibility that the woman could stage a performance to convince Manson, who was after all an intelligent man? And just what was I playing at? What was in Eve Manson's mind, to go such lengths in this absurd business? One tenth only on the surface, Harkness.

I did as she had asked: wrote to Manson, thanking him for his hospitality, mentioning casually 'about that interesting business you spoke of.' If Manson was still interested in finding a reputable spirit-medium, I had heard this woman was honest and (what was the appropriate word?) talented.

After that I decided that my part in the affair was finished. It was Manson's move now. And as for Mrs. Manson, speak of wheels within wheels! Why all her concern about an absurd conviction—a quite harmless conviction, yes, of course it was—of her husband's? An intelligent woman. But Manson was intelligent, too. So maybe what it came down to was that she believed it as well, but was one degree more self-conscious than he about admitting it. Or that she half believed it; and of course she would be overanxious about the boy, the only child.

There was also the child to consider. Where did the child fit in?

None of my affair. I went back to the office—not to my legitimate work, but to have all the papers from January 1946 fetched to my desk. And I spent an hour on the Henrys-Paxton case.

CHAPTER SEVEN

All I vaguely remembered of it was that it had been compared to the Thompson–Bywaters case. Murder of husband by wife and wife's lover. Here it was, set out like a serial, day by day, compressed a little by war news, true, but there in detail. Not very pleasant detail. The press had made Roman holiday with it, as is our unfortunate habit on such occasions. Nineteen forty-six—strange how remote it seemed, just considered as a date. I'd been out of the army almost three months, and was just getting back into the routine of my job. Of course, I'd been in New York, and the American papers hadn't made so much of the case.

Margaret MacDonald had been in pantomime when she succeeded in marrying James Henrys. Not under that name, of course: she had called herself Gloria de Vere. The very crassness of that conjured up a picture of her, not at odds with the photographs in the noisier papers. A vain, silly, shrewd woman of poor birth, little education, limited ambition—limited to the obvious. The photographs startled me into swearing. Eve—Eve ten years older, in the clothes of twelve, thirteen years ago. An Eve grown a little coarse, with platinum-dyed hair.

Henrys was twenty years older, staid, stolid, respectable: a youngish widower, childless. And well-off by most standards: a bank manager at Henley, with a tidy private income. Certainly of superior social status to her, and very probably a fool outside of his office. She was twenty-two when they married, and certainly no innocent. It was possible to guess that they had not wanted a child; but perhaps his daughter preoccupied Henrys enough, in the ensuing years, to blind him to his wife's defections.

Several of the defections were present at the trial, willing or not. The star of them was Robert Paxton, twenty-eight, good-looking in a pretty-boy way, former chorus boy, unemployed, son of a tobacconist in Clerkenwell.

It was a stupid crime, but they were stupid people. Counsel could not defend Paxton with any degree of conviction. The cook and the maid actually witnessed the final attack he made upon Henrys, in the sitting room of the house at Henley—a brutal attack with a hammer. The only element of mystery in the case was whether or not the woman was an accomplice. It was an unconvincing mystery, though the reporters made great play about circumstantial evidence. The concrete evidence, aside from the hammer, which belonged to the household, was the packet of letters—incredibly indiscreet letters, found in Paxton's room. Beyond any reasonable doubt Mrs. Henrys had been his mistress for more than a year, had planned the crime and persuaded him to commit it in the expectation of inheriting a fortune, which proved to be nonexistent.

Paxton under examination: You were not the first lover Mrs. Henrys had taken, were you? Objection, unsuccessful. No. To your knowledge, by what she had admitted to you on several occasions, she had been deceiving her husband almost constantly since their marriage? Yes. Strike that from the record as inadmissible evidence.

But the Crown had more to offer. Joseph Reginald Smith, former chauffeur, unemployed. Is it not true that you were intimately acquainted with Mrs. Henrys during the latter months of 1943, that on several occasions you spent the weekend with her at a certain popular resort, posing as her husband? M'lud, I have the hotel records here. Yes, it is. And who paid the expenses on these occasions? Why she did, acourse.

Three Joseph Smiths. (All the Crown had been able to find? Probably not.) Hysterical protestations by Mrs. Henrys. Then the defense's star witness, the daughter. Miss Eve Henrys (seventeen), recent graduate of Woodhill Young Ladies' Academy, in the box to testify on her mother's behalf.

The photographs were bad. I saw the adolescent girl—hating the notoriety, enjoying it, numbed with shock, fierce with loyalty?—impossible to tell from the transcript. To your definite knowledge, Miss Henrys, was your father aware of the prisoner's deception of him? Oh, yes. And you yourself knew of it? Upon what occasion did you learn the truth? I really don't remember, I had always known. Your father was, um, complacent about it? Oh, yes. There was nothing he could do. (Cold, tight little voice because she was controlling tears? But it sounded bad.)

Paxton's counsel put in some strong sly hints to the effect that Mrs. Henrys was sacrificing herself for her daughter. The letters were signed with a pet name. Was it not conceivable ... But the jury put trust in Joseph Smith, found for the Crown, and both appeals were denied. They were hanged on the same day three weeks later. The last photograph was of Eve: key figure in the Henrys-Paxton case leaving court, Miss Eve Henrys, head bent with grief after hearing mother's appeal denied—Mrs. Henrys to hang.

What would that do to Eve Henrys, seventeen? How far did it influence Eve Manson almost thirteen years later? I could only guess.

I had a note from Manson a few days later, thanking me. 'As I explained,' ran the precise miniature script, 'It is my contention that science should investigate these so-called supernatural (I prefer "supernormal") matters; it is possible that laws govern them that we do not yet fully understand. From the way you spoke when we discussed it, I take it you agree, which I may add rather surprised me, in a materialistic American.' (There is something peculiarly irritating about that phrase, and peculiarly obtuse. You'd think Europeans would have grasped by now that if any generalizing can be done about nations, we are a nation of starry-eyed idealists.)

'But it is also gratifying; in this century the essence of modernity appears to be denial of all beliefs and morals which have gone before. That being so, I feel no self-consciousness in admitting to you that I am uneasy about this situation. I am, after all, a rank amateur, a mere player-about with books and words. I had hesitated over any definite action, feeling myself all too poorly equipped to judge the honor of any qualified person I might employ. Your recommendation, of course, is sufficient...'

Finicking, affected, the kind of letter people in bad novels wrote. Something just wrong about it, like Manson's house. But it appeared he had taken the offered bait.

*   *   *

None of my affair. Yet here I was in one of The Drowned Man's two bare bedrooms. I was abruptly aware that Fowler was speaking to me.

'I'd like to sit in on that séance. Had you

thought of calling there this evening? I suppose...'

'No, I hadn't. I don't know what I'm doing here anyway.' I hunched my shoulders angrily. 'Of all the damned ridiculous things.'

The knock at the door was perfunctory. The landlord thrust his bald head round the panel; the pale eyes found me with secret curiosity. 'Beg pardon, sir. There's a tellyphone call for you.'

'Oh?' I followed the man down the narrow stair. The telephone was in the rear passage, no cabinet for it. I had a strong conviction that the landlord was listening behind some near door.

'Mr. Harkness?' Her voice was clear, warm. 'I understand you're back. But how too bad of you not to let us know you were coming. Are you on holiday?' Conventional, casual. Damn the woman.

'Not exactly. Or rather, yes, I suppose I am. How is Manson?' At that irrelevant moment I realized that it had always been difficult for me to use the man's first name. Manson used mine readily enough and other peoples', but I never remembered anyone calling him by his. Something standoffish, precise about him.

'You've been so kind. I can't thank you for what you've done for us.' A tiny pause before the last word? 'I hear Mr. Fowler is with you, how nice. How did I hear? My dear man, you don't know the country! Our maid has a sister who's married to the landlord at the inn. I don't believe you could have arrived ten minutes before Elsie was telling me that "that nice London gentleman as was here last week" was staying in Pentressor ... Oh, no, she is to come tomorrow, Richard's driving into Truro to fetch her. The ... party is tomorrow night.'

'I see.' I conveyed a question in my tone.

'I'm not sure Richard ... well, in any case won't you come and dine with us tonight? No, no bother, of course not. Richard will be pleased to see Mr. Fowler again—and you, of course.'

I swore silently at the telephone as I hung up the receiver. All surface again. Very much the conventional lady. Woodhill Young Ladies' Academy.

I went upstairs to tell Fowler we were invited out for dinner. 'Good,' said Fowler absently. 'I was dreading a meal here. Where'd you get this?' Trust Fowler to find the one book in the room.

'Manson insisted on lending it to me.'

'Humph. Seabrook. Well, he was rather a lunatic anyway, wasn't he?'

'That's just where you're wrong,' I said. 'He was a lot of things, a rugged individualist if you want to be charitable, an irresponsible fool if you don't, a sensualist, an egotist, an odd sort of devil altogether, but first, last,

72

and always he was a realist, Charles. True, he seems to have been fascinated by the supernatural, but he never accepted any of it, you know. He was always insisting on physical, concrete explanation, and he has some interesting things to say.

'He maintains here'—I tapped the book—'that witchcraft is a real force operating on the principle of autosuggestion. That just because there is no supernatural force behind it, it isn't nonexistent or harmless. If you believe a curse can kill you, sometimes it can, just through fear. And that most members of the human race are so strongly superstitious unconsciously— atavism controlling the subconscious—that even people who rationally disbelieve in superstition are vulnerable to ... well, call it witchcraft, generally speaking. He makes out a convincing case.'

'You don't say,' grunted Fowler. 'He sounds like a credulous fool.'

'I believe you've taken against the man on account of his morals,' I said rather maliciously.

'I know nothing about him except that he was American and a lunatic.'

'England, my England. Don't miscall him until you've read him. He may have been completely amoral, but that doesn't argue venality in other fields.'

'Now that's the first time I've heard you

defending loose morals,' said Fowler. 'As long as I've known you you've been pretty old-fashioned respectable about sex. It's a pity you didn't marry again years ago. Whatever happened to that little actress you were going about with?'

I had to think before I remembered whom he was talking about. 'My God, that was before I met Betty. Well, she was an actress. They're bad risks.'

'Grow up, John, grow up. All women are actresses, but the inferior ones turn professional.'

I heard him only vaguely. I stared at the book in my hand, not seeing it or thinking of it, feeling, uncannily, a flash of *déjà vu* that somewhere in that little exchange something important had been said, something relevant. It was gone. With a shrug, I tossed the book aside and began stripping off my tie.

CHAPTER EIGHT

For a moment, after we came into the house, I was slightly surprised that the Mansons were not in evening dress. Then the absurdity of that struck me. In the England of the 1950s one no longer expected it. But it was that sort of atmosphere. From my former visit I realized that they were living almost a prewar existence here, even pre the first war perhaps: the large house, the servants, the leisured isolation. Well, if you have money that sort of life is still to some extent possible, I suppose.

Manson was effusive, welcoming us; for the second time I had the impression that the woman was deliberately retreating into the background. The dutiful wife deferring to her husband? The idea for some reason irritated me. But the ins and outs of this marriage were nothing to me. It was only that my mind automatically went to work on people, deducing, debating.

In the sitting room Manson offered drinks. Was it significant, I wondered, that it should be cocktails? Bad ones, but cocktails instead of whiskey for the men, a genteel sherry for the women. One of the wrongnesses here was that Manson was a city man; he did not fit in in the country.

The sudden shocking crudity of Fowler jerked me from reflection. Fowler was relaxed in a corner of the sofa, swinging one leg over the other, watching Manson with a smile.

'Well, and what's all this John tells me about you, Manson? Living in splendid isolation unscrewed your brain a little, old boy? I understand you've taken up spiritualism. And the family curse—I had a laugh over that.' It was said casually.

Manson took fire at once. 'So you told him, Johnny? I might have known you'd take that view, Fowler. You know what it is? This damned craze for conformity. The so-called modern sciences have got you all frightened to death to disagree with their dogmas. Not that I discount science, I simply believe they haven't done enough research. In time we'll discover that these things operate by natural laws, scientific laws. After all, the theory of the circulation of the blood was laughed at until it was proved. And gravity, and gas warfare, aeronautics, a hundred things we take for granted today. You'll admit that. I maintain . . .'

What had possessed Fowler to come out with that? He had not done so without a reason. Now he was doing more jeering, and Manson was sitting forward to argue excitedly.

'It's like arguing about politics, isn't it?' interrupted Eve Manson's quiet voice. 'Rather silly, because you never get anywhere. Everyone has different values. Don't encourage him, Mr. Fowler, I'm sure you're really bored with it . . . I hear London is full of Americans this year.'

Manson gave her one unfathomable glance and subsided; in decency, Fowler took her lead. The little gray woman, who shared the sofa with him, compressed her lips to a thin line, staring into space silently.

There was another awkward moment during dinner, and what caused the

76

awkwardness mystified me. The talk had been of *Troth*—Fowler asking half humorously when he could expect a new Manson MS, Manson shrugging that off, Eve mentioning a much-discussed recent novel, which precipitated a desultory discussion of modern literature. Through it all the old woman sat silent as if she were chaperoning a children's tea party, resigned to immature entertainment.

'By the way,' said Fowler suddenly, turning to Eve, 'I saw Mrs. Chadwick the other day and she mentioned you.'

'Really,' she returned noncommittally.

'She was saying she'd completely lost touch and wondered where you were living. At the time I didn't know myself, but she'd be pleased to hear from you, I know.'

After a moment Eve said levelly, 'I never knew her terribly well. We were at school together, and both lived in London just afterward.'

'Oh, yes,' said Fowler easily. 'She was still Mrs. Burton then, I believe.'

Her lips tightened; she said nothing and then turned to me. 'Will you have more coffee?' and there was a tense little pause until Fowler abandoned the subject. His eyes were speculative on her, and I thought she was aware of it. Manson did not appear to notice at all.

Later Fowler renewed his attack on

Manson, leading the talk back to controversy, and this time both refused to leave it. A strained line grew round Eve Manson's mouth; Manson spoke more and more passionately, and at last Fowler fell silent, listening.

Manson argued brilliantly; quite evidently he knew his subject. He could not be convincing, since at least where I was concerned he was talking unreason, but that he believed fervently himself was obvious. I did not wonder that they were on distant terms with their neighbors here; if Manson was given to riding his hobby at any provocation, he would have acquired a very odd reputation in the community, and in the country one must conform. Watching Eve's taut expression, I made several attempts to intervene, but in the end it was Miss Manson who succeeded.

'. . . You will never examine the evidence with an open mind. You think you do, but the prejudice is so strong you cannot see the truth. I'm no primitive arguing against scientific advance. Quite the contrary. There are a good many scientists conducting research into various supernormal fields, you know—telepathy, for example. It's early to say what they will conclude, but I believe that everything we consider to be "supernatural" will eventually be found to operate according to natural law. In a more enlightened age . . .'

It was at that moment that the old woman rose. She had not spoken since we returned to the sitting room, and her shrill, agitated little voice was an exclamation point halting all others.

'It's no use, Richard, no use at all. You cannot talk to these materialists! I have told you that before. Dangerous—the Other Forces are jealous and wayward, often destructive, and They resent hearing such crude rejection of Them. You would best take care, Mr. Fowler—you may meet a dreadful punishment! I must ask you to excuse me,' and she made a fluttering exit.

It should have been merely absurd; in fact, it killed the subject effectively and created an oddly sinister silence that grew to discomfort until I made some foolish remark about the weather. That dull safety bridged the gap; but the talk was spasmodic, and Fowler soon made a move to depart.

In the car I asked savagely, 'What in the name of God made you do that? I thought...'

'I was never a believer,' said Fowler, 'in sacrificing principle to politeness.'

'You needn't be so obtrusive about it. Nevertheless you see what I mean about Manson. He's right over the edge on the subject. No pretense about it tonight. A damned strange thing, but in a way I suppose it's understandable. Only the one child. He would be fearful anyway, and when he was

79

brought up believing all that mumbo-jumbo...'

'Was he? Oh, yes, the aunt, of course.' Fowler was abstracted. 'Yes, you were right about Manson.' As we drew up before the darkened inn he added, 'I'm going back to Town tomorrow. To see Manson like that—a good mind, you know, but I'm afraid you're right—he's no use to himself or anyone else in this state. You can drive me to the nearest station if you will, or perhaps you're going up to Town yourself?'

I opened my mouth to say yes, and then did not say it. Suddenly I could not bear the thought of Fowler's company on the drive to London. I was tired of Fowler, yes, the materialist, the cynic. You probably wouldn't find it difficult ... All women are actresses ... Grow up, John. I certainly had no reason for staying here, but I would let Fowler go back to London alone. I said, 'I'll drive you into Truro; you'll be able to get an express from there, I should think.'

We were let in by the landlord. The bar was dark. It was after closing time. At the top of the stair Fowler asked abruptly, 'By the way, did you ever know a chap called Kenneth Templeton?'

'No, why?'

'I just wondered. Doesn't matter,' said Fowler vaguely. 'Good night.'

I was glad to be rid of Fowler. I had lunch in Truro and drove back slowly through the bare Cornish landscape so curiously punctuated with its white clay pyramids and little abandoned mines. I came toward Pentressor from the south-west and so passed Manson's house before entering the village. A little this side of the house I met Eve and the boy and the red-and-white spaniel walking at the roadside. When the car slowed she glanced up and lifted a hand.

'Can I drive you wherever you're going, Mrs. Manson?'

'We're not going anywhere in particular, thanks—just for a walk.'

I looked at the boy, whose eyes were on the car. 'Would you like a ride?'

'Yes, sir.' Shy, but definite.

'In you get, then. Yes, Roddy can come, too—that's his name, is it? And your mother.'

'You may be very sorry about Roddy,' she said, following them both into the front seat. 'Richard doesn't allow him in the car and he's not used to it.'

'He'll be all right.' I had not yet seen her in anything like country clothes. She might have dressed for an afternoon's shopping in London: pale wool frock, silk stockings, shoes low-heeled but fragile, fashionable heels. I was aware of a faint disturbing scent,

81

female. I thought of Fowler saying, You probably wouldn't find it difficult. Last night, now, her cool manner making it fantastic to remember she had invaded my bedroom, admitted me even so far into her private problems. I remembered my awareness of her then; it was the same now, a thing about her perhaps she wished not to possess, but a man could not be near her and not feel it. And I thought, the mother: the same with her, but no principle, no honesty to balance it.

'Don't you mind dogs in your car?' asked the boy. He had been studying me soberly, his narrow bulk between the two of us.

'Not in the least.' The boy was Eve, only Eve: dark hair and eyes, pale skin, the small elongated bones people called aristocratic. A boy often looked like the mother.

'Oh. Well, I wouldn't either if I had a car, but father does.' After more study, 'He's gone to the railway station to meet a lady who's going to help us about the witch.'

Involuntarily I stepped hard on the accelerator and took the curve much too fast. I was startled and disgusted. The casual tone told me it was no newly imparted tale to the child: it was an accepted piece of his small world. No longer a mere adult eccentricity, it took on sinister aspects.

'That's just a story Father likes to tell,' she said quietly.

'Yes. I guess so. Mother doesn't believe in

the witch, but I mustn't say so to Father, it makes him cross. Is it all right to say it to him?' Belatedly anxious, he indicated me to Eve.

'Yes,' said Eve. She did not sound certain about it. A kind of slow, deep anger rose in my mind. The child. A crime against the child. The sins of the fathers.

I said at random, 'Fowler has gone back to London, by the way. He had hoped for another book, you know, but evidently there's no prospect of it.'

'No. No, I don't think so. In that case'—she hesitated, glancing at the child, but went on—'I don't think Richard would mind if you joined us this evening. If you'd be interested.' I was not; normally I would recoil from the very idea of a séance. But her voice said, please come.

'I'd like to very much, if you want me.'

'Yes, I wish you would. You're staying on. Why?' And now she was saying, to interfere in my affairs?

'Oh, gathering local color.' Would she know that for an excuse? That 'local color' was a layman's phrase? 'It's an interesting landscape, isn't it? Bare, but rather fascinating somehow.' Damn it, I sounded like a guidebook. 'Do you like living in the country?'

'Not especially. I don't really mind.'

'Where do you live, sir?' asked the boy.

Had I thought last night, prewar? Someone had taught the boy almost Victorian manners. Eve? I wondered.

'I'm living in London now, Jimmy, but really I live in New York.'

'Oh. I was born in London but I don't remember. Oh, look, Mother, there's fishing boats!'

'And do you like living in London, Mr. Harkness?' Subtle mockery in her tone.

'Sorry, did I sound inquisitive? Well, it's town, isn't it? I'm afraid I'm urban by nature. I was brought up in the country, but I'm very bad at all the things you're supposed to do in it—hunting and shooting and fishing. My family gave me up as a bad job and were quite resigned when I turned out to be an effete newspaperman.'

'Oh, look, Mother. They're mending nets.' A little crowd of men on the beach, where the slope of the cliff was shallower here. I slowed and stopped. 'May I go down and watch?'

'Be careful,' she said. 'Take Roddy with you, and don't go too near the water.'

'Yes,' obediently. We watched him across the road, the spaniel running circles, and down the pebbled track to the shore.

'I try not to be too strict,' said Eve suddenly, angrily, 'not to be at him every minute. What are you going to do? They've got to be warned. It isn't that I want to frighten him.'

84

'I know.' Manson, accusing her of frightening the child? Manson! 'And it's none of my business,' I said almost violently, 'but that is criminal.' She knew what I meant at once.

'Do you wonder that it worries me? I knew you thought I was exaggerating. Dr. Dyck told you that, too, didn't he?' She smiled tiredly. 'Oh, I knew. You can't take a step in a village without everyone knowing about it. Anyone would think that on the face of it. So fantastic—a little joke. Did you know Manson believes in witches? Now perhaps you see. Is she very awful, by the way?'

'The . . . woman? Let's say,' I temporized, 'that you wouldn't invite her for the weekend ordinarily. I hope it won't be too difficult or embarrassing.'

'In a way it's all rather farcical. I hope to God she puts on a good show for them,' she said then viciously. 'Convinces them, so he'll drop the whole thing and let us forget it. I haven't had a chance to thank you properly, it was good of you. I'd have found it difficult to make the arrangements.'

I made the obvious reply to that. On the shore, the boy was watching the fishermen, standing quite still at a respectful distance. The dog nosed about at seaweed. 'I hope you didn't think I was interfering, going to see Dyck. I only thought . . .'

'I can guess what you thought, thanks. No,

as he told you, I'm sure he told you, I had gone to him, too. It was a mistake. Do you mind if I say something rather rude? How on earth did you and Richard ever happen to be friends? You're quite opposites, aren't you?'

'I don't know,' I said vaguely. 'You don't choose acquaintances, do you? Proximity. Any more than you choose families.'

'Any more than families,' and at the repetition her mouth looked drawn and tired. 'No ... It's odd how life always turns out so unexpected, anyway. None of the things you thought would happen.' She took the cigarette I offered, suddenly smiling. 'Fifteen years ago I had it all planned so neatly. I was going to have seven children.'

'What, no husband?'

'Oh, the husband to start with, of course. I thought a titled one would be nice, with a country estate.'

'Mhmm. Twenty years ago,' I said, 'I was going to be a famous playwright. I was also going to marry a rather plain girl who lived across the street—I didn't think she was plain then, of course—and buy a very expensive sports car and a silver cigarette case and perhaps a yacht. I've forgotten the rest.'

'Aren't we being obvious? And I have achieved ...' she nodded at the small red-sweatered figure below.

'And I a temporary editorship,' I laughed. 'Not the girl across the road?'

86

'No, another one.' I told her about Betty very briefly.

'I'm sorry,' she said.

And I said quite honestly, 'You needn't be. It's six years, and we didn't have much time together. I've got over it now. One does.'

'Yes.' She gave a sharp small sigh. 'I think I'll ask you to take us back now.' She leaned from the window to call the boy. 'You'll come tonight? For dinner, too. I have the feeling it will be rather a difficult evening.'

I wondered what she would answer if I said what was in my mind. May I ask rather a rude question, lady? How on earth did you ever happen to marry Manson, and why?

Then she turned, tugging at the door to let the child in, and in the narrow seat there was all the femaleness of her close, and I wasn't thinking of anything but that.

CHAPTER NINE

It was obvious that it would be a difficult evening. It could never have been anything else. Madam Sonia (recalling by mere absurdity of contrast a woman who had called herself Gloria de Vere, but there were probably inner similarities at that), painfully conscious of manners and accent, in a nondescript, shoddy, black flowing garment.

87

Manson, pale, excited, eager, asking questions. The little gray aunt darting curious beady looks at the guest. Eve authoritatively lovely in lavender silk, and in her eyes alternate amusement and dread.

'Of course you understand, Mr. Manson, I cannot guarantee you will obtain what you desire. Sometimes there are barriers the spirits cannot get round.' It was perilously near 'rahnd.' The Woolworth rings gleamed as she lifted her cup, little finger consciously crooked.

'Oh, yes, I realize that. But I'm anxious to get in touch. We must go on trying until something comes through. It's so extremely important to make the contact, you see.'

'Please, Mr. Manson.' The rings gleamed again as a queenly hand lifted. 'I would prefer to know nothing about it whatever. If we do obtain results, I should not like it to be thought as I'd used any tricks.' She was in a position to play that strong card, having all the information; I wondered how she usually managed.

'Oh, I see, of course.'

Miss Manson said almost cordially, 'That is very honest of you, Madam. Do you go into trance very easily? I have heard sometimes it is a terrible ordeal.'

'Awful. Simply tears me to pieces sometimes, my dear. But when one has the power one must use it to help people,

88

shouldn't we, and I always say I owe a duty to one's public.' But it was worse than farcical, it was—it should have been—merely funny, yet I didn't feel like laughing. I thought it was unfunny, and the woman's crudity was passing unremarked, because the evening was growing toward the unknown. At least two of us at this table, I thought, are rank unbelievers and yet we are feeling this uneasiness, so strong is the hold Neanderthal still has on the little dark bottom of our minds. There are no spirits, but we are about to meddle with them and we are a little afraid.

I sat on the sofa with Eve and watched the preparations curiously.

'Oh, I'm afraid that table would not do, Mr. Manson. The spirits are not very strong.'

'She looks strong as a horse,' whispered Eve with a nervous giggle. She was feeling my own compulsion to register irreverence. Manson was offering a card table, unfolding it, bringing chairs from the dining room.

'Excuse me, ma'am, were you wanting coffee?' The maid's eyes were bright with curiosity. Manson snapped at her.

'No, no. And you will not disturb us unless I ring, do you understand? Shut the door, please.' There would be avid discussion of this in the kitchen; by tomorrow it would be all over the village, one of they spirit-trickers down from London, funny doings at Poltressor last night; and Dr. Dyck would tighten his tight mouth fastidiously at Manson's childish (but harmless) hobby; and the county people would agree that the Mansons were rather odd, I always thought so, my dear, fancy spiritualism; if this was summer and the Misses Paget's house full of paying guests, it would provoke a lively discussion among them.

'That will do very nicely, Mr. Manson.' She was enjoying this, a novel windfall. She would live on it, financially and otherwise, for months. All expenses paid and a visit to a gentleman's country estate. The tale would grow in the telling, to impress other clients.

'We'd better arrange ourselves. Where would you like to be, Madam?' Absurd title easy on his tongue. 'I thought just the firelight. You did say no lights at all? Well, yes, I understood that was ... You sit here, Eve. Aunt Belle...'

'I'm not a member of the family,' I said. 'Perhaps I'd better not join you.'

'Oh, yes, you must be in the circle—everyone. Not at all, Johnny, you're an interested party, aren't you?'

I supposed you could say that. I sat between Eve and the medium. The other woman was beyond Eve, then Manson. 'Will you distinguish the lights, please, Mr. Manson?'

'Dis ... oh, yes, certainly.' In the dark Manson could be heard taking his chair. 'We join hands, don't we?'

Eve's hand was thin, flexible, in mine, and rather cold.

'There must be absolute silence, please. We must not move until the power comes onto me.'

Sitting in the dark, a silly children's game. The hand in my right hand was dead, cold, limp. I thought it was one of the woman's stage props, leaving her own hand free for tricks. More props up those loose flowing sleeves. A silly game, the most credulous believer would not be taken in. And Manson had read widely, he would not be deceived by the obvious.

It was very quiet and very dark. I stopped feeling quite so much of a fool in the anonymity of dark and then things began to happen to me. I could hear Eve breathing, light and slow, and Manson, unevenly, across the table. We must have been sitting here for half an hour. No, not that long; I was only just beginning to feel the disturbance set up in me by the hand. The slim, warming hand. I could feel her bones, the wires of nerve and muscle, the essential Eve-ness of her in miniature as it were, lying in my own hand. The hollow of my hand. Not grasping, not reluctant, only being. I felt the awareness of my own muscle and nerve like wires running down arm and finger, establishing contact (never mind the padding flesh) with those other wires. It was intolerable, it was ridiculous. I couldn't bear it any longer, how many hours had it been now? I must drop the hand, break contact, or get her closer, all of her, hard and hot. This woman, this damned woman, you could not hold her hand without . . .

The low moan made me start involuntarily. A theatrical hollow moan. Eve's hand jerked in mine and I pressed it slightly. The show beginning, that was all. Curtain going up. The voice was hollow, too, deepened. 'We are waiting for someone to guide us. We are waiting for the spirit guide.' After more silence she repeated it several times.

There was a sharp rap on the underside of the table, and it lifted jerkily. At the same time a tiny white circle of foggy light appeared above the medium's head. No dark is complete; now I could make out very dimly her figure slumped in the chair, head down. The light grew and then took form. It was a small ghost-hand hanging in the air. My heart was beating rather faster than usual. A good show, perhaps she would put up a convincing show after all. All the tricks of the trade. There was a breathy exclamation from Miss Manson.

Another voice spoke, high, shrill, malicious. 'I'm here, I'm here, I'm here. What do you want, what do you want?'

'We wish to be guided to the Other Side.

We wish to speak with someone on the Other Side.'

Manson moved sharply; he said in a strained voice, 'The name is Tamar Wood. We must speak with Tamar Wood.'

Silence. The hand disappeared. Then there was a white ghost-face instead, very cleverly done, perhaps phosphorus, in the dark effective: it's only the Neanderthal in you that is a little frightened, Harkness. A hoarse cry, apparently from above the medium's head. The shrill voice: 'Difficult. It is a long way to go. A very long way, but I will try.'

Abruptly I felt better. She could not disguise the accent entirely.

And Manson burst out again, 'It is important—try, try! We must get through.'

His aunt said, 'Richard,' in a whisper. If you believed it were you frightened all the more, or not?

The voice, wordless, rose to a hoarse shriek and my pulse jumped again. The white face vanished and the hand reappeared, this time above Manson's head. Another hoarse cry.

'You must try, you must reach her,' said Manson.

The voice cried, 'She will come, be patient!' and for me whatever half spell had been cast was broken. This could not deceive Manson. Children, yes, not an adult. The woman was only superficially clever at changing her voice.

It did not deceive Manson. She had begun to speak again when he sprang up and his chair went over to thud on the carpet. 'It's a trick!' he exclaimed furiously. 'A fraud!' and he plunged for the light switch by the door. Light assaulted us, showed Eve pale, strained; the old woman exactly as usual; the medium hastily adjusting the sleeves of her gown. Showed, nevertheless, the tiny white-painted ghost-hand, fastened to a long handle, fallen on the floor, and the woman swooping after it.

'You damned fraud!' cried Manson.

Her mauve-powdered sagging face went ugly with fear. Safe from search, from proof, she might have blustered; she could not now. Manson began to swear; he was white with rage. 'Damn you, you cheap lying fraud, to trick me, try to play your dirty little games! Get out of my house, I won't have you in my house!'

'Can't throw a woman out this time o' night, sir,' she was panting. Now it was funny: pathetic.

'Richard. There's no need to make a scene.'

'By God, I'll make a scene if I please! Bringing her here in good faith ... ' he swung to me, 'I might blame you, but I daresay you were taken in as she's probably taken in others. These damned harpies, victimizing honest ... You heard me, you can fetch your

94

things and go!'

'Richard. You promised her twenty pounds.'

'Do you think I'm going to pay to be cheated, to listen to her ridiculous lies?'

'Sir . . .' she quavered.

Manson was shouting for the maid. Not only Elsie but a manservant appeared. Evans the gardener-handyman, it would be. 'Very well, Eve, for God's sake stop it! I want her out of my house! Thinking I was that sort of fool, to be taken in by tricks that wouldn't deceive a child! Evans, I want you to drive—this woman—to the station. Go up and fetch whatever you have here, I'll give you ten minutes.'

'Sir, you'll not . . . I'm a poor woman, sir.' All pretense gone now, whining.

'Oh, my God!' ejaculated Manson. 'I don't give a damn about you—prosecute? You'll be caught soon enough. Advertise the fact that you tricked me even so far? Get out, that's all I ask.'

There was frustrated disappointment in his eyes as well as anger. He flung away across the disordered room, to stand with his back turned, shoulders tense.

She scuttled for the hall without argument. The servants were looking excited. I thought Eve was dangerously near to tears. She murmured, 'But I suppose she must have something—not fair,' and turned to follow the woman. Miss Manson was standing motionless in the centre of the room, and her voice was placid. 'Are you sure, Richard? Are you sure she is a fraud?'

'For God's sake! Cheap childish tricks.' He was containing rage coldly; I would not have been surprised to see him kick over a chair, like a child in a temper. There was a tense wait then, when no one spoke, until the woman came down, with the bag, a faint smile on her mouth now. Eve would have given her money, and this was a long way from London, she need not tell the true story.

'Get out, get out,' said Manson in something like a snarl, not turning. The man had brought the car round. When the front door had shut Manson went on, 'God—all no use, no good at all, with a woman like that! And so damned many of them like her. How would you ever know? Never be sure if it was a trick. Like a fool, thinking I could stop it that way.' He turned, passing a hand across his face; he was very pale. 'It's no use,' he said, speaking to his aunt.

She put a hand on his arm. 'There may be a way, Richard. We can try again. We must, to save the boy.'

'The boy,' said Manson, and was echoed from the door.

'The boy? Miss Eve ...' The Nanny was there, the relic from the past. 'Miss Eve, I'm sorry, is Master Jimmy down here with you?

I went in just now to see was he asleep, all the noise downstairs, and he's not in his bed, Miss Eve.' Her eyes were frightened.

I thought I heard Eve breathe, 'Oh, God,' as she turned. Now this, it said; then concern for the child put energy into her voice. 'Not in his bed? But...'

'I've looked upstairs, I was thinking perhaps—but he's noplace, Miss Eve, and just in his little nightgown, we don't want him taking cold again.'

'Oh, dear, oh, dear, we must find him,' said the old woman. 'You don't suppose he has wandered out of the house? Oh, mercy, in the dark? Richard, call the servants; Richard, you must do something.'

'He must be somewhere in the house,' said Eve shakily. 'Go and look again, Nanny. He wouldn't go out, there'd be no reason. Jimmy! Jimmy! He may have come down to the kitchen to see Evans, he did that once. Jimmy!'

The faint 'Yes' so near startled us all. He was there, at the door just open of the little coat closet set in the angle of hall and sitting room. He took one hesitant step away from the door; his thin body was trembling violently, his eyes blank. He said in a whisper, 'I saw the witch. It was the witch, wasn't it, Father? That was why you sent her away.'

'Oh, my God,' said Eve under her breath.

She was kneeling, arm tight around the small figure, but her voice was even. 'It doesn't matter now, you mustn't think about it now ... get you to bed, so cold, darling. It's all right, you're quite safe now, don't think about it.'

I had thought, it might deceive a child. What would it do to a child, the dark, the hand and the face and the voices? What had it done? I was furiously, helplessly angry, with nowhere to direct my anger. And then Manson moved, to look down at the child. He did not reach to touch him.

'So you sneaked down to spy on us. I told you to stay upstairs, didn't I? I told you I would see to it and make it all safe. Now it's spoiled, it's no use at all.'

So there *was* a place for the anger. Telling the child. Frightening the child. Irresponsible—unimaginative. Taking it so deadly serious himself that he made it real to the child.

'Didn't the charm work?' asked the boy weakly. His teeth were chattering. Suddenly Eve rose, lifting him with her, and turned on Manson. There was in her eyes, in her voice, the terrible contempt, the necessity at all costs not to alarm the child further, not to make a scene.

'You see one result anyway, Richard. That is the last time you will ever do such a thing while I'm in this house. We'll talk about this later. Meanwhile, will you please call the doctor to come out. Dr. Dyck. I don't want him, but he's the only one. Will you call Dr. Dyck, please, now.'

'There's no need for that,' said Manson. 'The boy may have had a little fright, but he'll be all right, won't you, James? Nothing to make a fuss about. I'm sorry, but it wasn't my fault.'

'Mr. Harkness, will you please telephone the doctor for me? I won't argue with you now, Richard.' She turned for the stairs, carrying the child.

Manson swore in a whisper. 'Damn' nonsense ... spoiling him, he'll be all right. Can't coddle them—entitled to the truth.'

'Will you call the doctor or shall I?' I asked evenly. It had been years since I wanted to hit a man, as I wanted to assault Manson now.

'Richard,' said his aunt timidly, 'perhaps you'd better. Such a sensitive little boy. He was frightened. I ... I was frightened myself. perhaps you'd better call Dr. Dyck.'

'Oh, for God's sake. All right, all right.'

CHAPTER TEN

I heard the receiver bang down, but Manson did not return; he stalked down the passage to the study and shut the door. Miss Manson

99

murmured something about helping dear Eve and took herself off. I lit a cigarette and stood looking rather blankly at the disheveled room.

No reason to stay. Difficult evening: what an understatement. She would not want a guest underfoot now. Nothing I could do, none of my affair. Better go. Absurdly, I felt guilty. If I hadn't taken the trouble to find the woman—but it had, at the time, seemed so Gilbertian.

I should go. But I stayed, and presently a car drove into the yard. The man would have left the gates open, of course. I went to the door before the bell sounded.

'Good evening, Dr. Dyck. If you'd go right up, Mrs. Manson is there somewhere . . . I'm afraid the household is rather upset.'

Dyck gave me a sharp look and went upstairs without wasted words. Now certainly no reason to stay. Absently, for want of other occupation, I carried the chairs back to the dining room, folded the card table, emptied the ashtrays into the dead hearth. Harkness the housewife. Down the passage from the study drifted the B Minor Mass. Manson and his phonograph. It was a large expensive machine, the kind that took a stack of records at once. Rather odd that Manson should have such a passion for music? Stranger still that he liked Bach.

Above everything else, whether or not you

like it, there is something so essentially sane about Bach. Sane like the sanity, the utter stark integrity, of double columns in a ledger neatly totalled and balanced at the bottom.

He must have the volume turned up. He seemed to be playing the Mass right through. There was no other sound in the house.

I found my hat and coat in the little closet. But I was not at the door when Dyck came down the stairs with Eve. She looked white and tired.

'. . . Which is all I can do,' Dyck was saying. 'You might keep him in bed tomorrow if he seems at all feverish, but on the whole better not make any more fuss than necessary, to impress it on his mind.'

'Yes, I understand. Thank you.'

'And if you think it necessary you have only to call me.'

'Thank you,' she repeated. 'Oh, Mr. Harkness—I thought you had gone. I should apologize for all this.'

'That's hardly necessary. I feel I owe you an apology instead. I hope everything will be all right.'

'Good night,' said Dyck, clapping on his hat.

But when I came out to the curving drive the doctor was still there, motionless beside the dark bulk of his little car drawn up behind the Morris. The night was clear and cold, moonless, but the reflection from the water made small unearthly light in the walled courtyard. Dyck's voice was cold and clear, too. 'Can you tell me any more about that bad business?'

'Probably no more than Mrs. Manson told you. Except,' I said deliberately, 'that I wish Manson was not half my size so I could reason with him a little without being called a bully.'

'Ah, that,' said Dyck. Some of his professional manner had slipped. 'God forgive me, I said it was a harmless hobby. With a child in the house.' He banged one fist on the car door. 'A child,' he said. 'The most important thing, the most valuable thing. The way they will be so careless. "I never thought. I'm sorry," they say. Afterward.'

'I hope you're not thinking Mrs. Manson is to blame.'

'Blame?' said Dyck; he made it sound like a curse. 'What the hell does it matter who is to blame, when the thing is done? I see them. They're brought to me afterward. "I never thought he could reach the stove, Doctor." Go through life with a scarred face. "I never dreamed the water was deep enough, Doctor. I was only gone a minute." Bad enough, bad enough. But the others are worse maybe, the inside scars. People!' said Dyck, and drew a breath as if on the worst oath he knew, and said again, 'People!'

'Yes.' I was surprised at Dyck (everyone vulnerable somewhere). I liked him better, but I said, 'Mrs. Manson was just as upset. It was only an accident.'

'My God,' said Dyck impatiently, 'that's a useful word! Only an accident!'

'The boy—he would have been badly frightened—how is he?'

'I don't know. Nobody knows. I can set a broken arm, I can sew up a cut. He's a sensitive youngster and imaginative. You don't know with children. Sometimes a thing like this you would think might stay with them all their lives, they'll forget tomorrow, and some little ridiculous thing you hardly noticed yourself will give them nightmares for years. You never know. He was frightened. In shock. I gave him a mild sedative, which was all I could do. What did you people think you were playing at in there? Spooks and spirits?'

I said slowly, 'I'm not sure even Manson knows that. I don't really know, Doctor.'

And you don't know all of it, the worst of it. And I am not going to tell you. That whole ugly fairy story, to frighten a child. I thought of Manson's first words to the boy, and a small piece of the puzzle clicked into place. All to capture the boy? You are in deadly danger, but Father will save you, Father the all-powerful, the deity. Yes.

'I get upset, I'm sorry,' said Dyck. 'People!' He jerked open the car door and set his bag inside. He said, 'All this damned mess we're in. War, peace, taxes, the incurable diseases, the dictators and the damn' fools and the criminals. Everybody worrying about next month, next year, the whole future. So busy worrying they throw the future away. What the hell is the future but a child?'

He got into the car and slammed the door. 'Excuse me, I get upset over these things. Should remember my blood pressure.' He clashed gears savagely as he swung the car around for the gate.

* * *

I woke late. Last night I'd thought today I would leave. There was nothing for me here. For the first time in years I thought, what is there anywhere? I'd gone along in life contented enough, but around my age a man starts to realize that if he has any concrete ambitions he'd better begin doing something about them. I was sufficiently happy in my work, I knew I could look forward to promotion, and I'd probably end up in twenty years holding down an editor's desk and annoying my juniors as, God knows, I'd been annoyed. It was my personal life that was a blank. I put the mood down to Manson and Dyck, and Eve. Once I had envied Manson the child, the woman. (That way around, Harkness? Be honest.) Manson, who was blindly destroying what he had.

So by the time I'd argued myself out of unaccustomed gloom, shaved and dressed and had breakfast, it was too late to start for town unless I broke the drive overnight. I debated about that over several cigarettes, and it was later still when I was called to the telephone. Her voice over the wire was abrupt, businesslike.

'Good morning, Mr. Harkness. Though it's almost too late to say that, isn't it? I wonder if you would be very kind and do something for me this afternoon. That is, if you haven't any plans.'

'I'd be glad to do anything.'

'Richard has gone off in the car and I have an appointment in Truro at two o'clock. Could you possibly drive me in?'

'Certainly.'

'In half an hour then, thank you so much. It's too bad, you got into all this just by accident, didn't you? Yes, well, half an hour then.'

I called for her at the house a little less than half an hour later. She had been waiting, and I wasn't out of the car before she came.

'This is very good of you. Richard must have forgotten I wanted the car. I hope I'm not putting you out. You hadn't meant to leave today?'

'Not at all.' I never knew how it would be. One moment a friendly, ready intimacy, the confidences she had made, the emotion she had shown me, and the next this wary formality warning me, not too close. She should not maintain it this time. I said, 'That was a nasty business last night. I was very sorry about it. How is Jimmy?'

'He'll be all right. I think he'll be all right. Thank you. I've left him with Nanny,' she said suddenly, 'he'll be quite safe with Nanny Edwards. She was my own nurse, you know. She was with me until I was nearly ten. Richard says she's really too old now, but that's nonsense. I'm so glad to have her for Jimmy.'

'I see, of course.'

'I don't know what I'd do without her. I'm sorry you had to be there. I'm afraid it was rather a scene.' Apologizing for making it, the well-bred lady, a horror of scenes.

'They're inevitable sometimes, aren't they?'

'I didn't mean to snap at him like that. But Jimmy ...' And there was the anger in me again, for something different now. So this was a little more of the true story. She loved Manson and loved the child and was torn between, the loyalties conflicting in this instance. Was she looking tired and ill today because of a quarrel with Manson or worry over the child?

Manson wasn't worth it. Damned fools, women, never seeing a worthless man for what he is. My own reason mocked me on that thought. Very well, I had once thought Manson almost brilliant; but I'd been young then ... and people change. Anyway, whatever was between them was none of my concern.

After a silence she said, 'I thought it was such a good idea. If he could convince himself that the danger was past, he'd leave it alone, forget it. Let Jimmy forget it. Funnily enough, I never thought of its turning out like that. But I might have known.'

'I feel it was my fault at least partly... That woman.'

'Oh, no. No, it would have been the same,' she said, 'whoever it was. I see that now.'

In town she asked to be let off before a large draper's shop. 'It's too bad for me, using you as a chauffeur. I'll only be an hour.' She did not say if it was dentist or dressmaker. 'Could you find something to do, and meet me?'

I smiled at her. 'I haven't explored Truro, but I hear one should see the cathedral. I'll go and look at it. Shall I meet you here?'

'That would be fine, thank you.' Unlike so many women she knew how to say good-bye firmly and promptly, no dawdling. She walked away from the car rapidly, not looking back, trim and tall and—what was just the right word?—svelte. Yes. I'd never known any woman before who justified the word.

I went to look at the cathedral, and

wondered again why Christian builders saw fit to create places of worship so remarkably like prisons, lest a little light and air creep in to corrupt the congregation. I'd come back to where I had left her twice, and been moved on by a traffic officer, before she returned.

'I've imposed on you dreadfully.'

'Not at all. It's a little early, but couldn't we have tea somewhere before going back?'

She glanced at me, subtly withdrawing. 'No, I ... it's very kind of you. But I promised Jimmy I'd be back to have tea with him.' And as if aware of impoliteness she added, 'If it wouldn't bore you, won't you come and share it?'

I thought, it would be a very good idea, Harkness, for you to get away from Pentressor and from Cornwall and from the Mansons entirely. To go back now to your comfortable London flat and your circle of friends, some of them dull and some of them strange, but not as strange and dangerous as all this is. A very good idea. Because while you don't pretend to be a model of virtue, you do have certain standards and as yet you have never been involved with someone else's wife. And when you find yourself sufficiently interested in a woman to seize an invitation to a nursery tea simply because she will be there, it is time to run, Harkness, and not risk anything more.

'... You probably wouldn't find it

difficult...' Who the hell did Fowler think he was, to say a thing like that? Only because of the mother? Or did he know something else? There could be nothing else to know.

Aloud I said, 'I'd like that very much, thank you.'

CHAPTER ELEVEN

As we went up the stairs in the silent house (Manson evidently still out, sulking to himself after the fiasco last night?) she said, 'It's so bad for him, I know that. We've lived here almost all his life. He's never known any other children; scarcely seen any except the fishermen's children in the village and Richard won't have him playing with them, even if we lived close enough. All Jimmy's ever had is Roddy. It's bad for him. You've got to learn to get on with people. What's going to happen to him if he ... when he goes to school, once he's old enough to be out by himself?'

'It's difficult, I know, in the country, but surely he has lessons somewhere now?'

'There's a grammar school in Pentressor for the smallest children, but Richard doesn't like it. That kind of thing's only for children like the village children, he says. I don't know, it may be all right, but I don't think

Miss Carter is awfully fond of children, though she may be a competent teacher. I've been teaching him myself, but it's not right, you know. He'll be eight in November. He ought to go to a proper school next term. But not boarding school. I wouldn't want that.'

'You are rather isolated here.' I answered the thought instead of the words.

The room was out of Kipling, I swear: a Victorian nursery right down to the Nanny. 'Mr. Harkness is going to have tea with us, darling, isn't that nice?'

Rather flatteringly, Jimmy seemed to think it was.

'So we'll mind our manners and not have the gentleman thinking we're a little pig. We've had a nice nap, Miss Eve, and a nice little read.' Oh, straight out of Kipling.

'I've been reading *Alice* again. Did you ever read *Alice*?'

'I forget how many times.' I was given the largest chair by an approving Nanny, and as I thanked her, surprised such a shrewdly speculative look in her eyes that I was startled. And what are you after? it said. I heard myself going on mechanically. 'I had an older brother and sister and by the time I wanted to read *Alice* she was all torn and pages out of her, and my father bought a new copy. And then by the time my younger sisters wanted her, there had to be a third copy because I'd read mine so many times.'

110

'Oh. Which pages were gone out of the first one?'

'The father William bit, I think.'

'Oh. What were your brother's and sisters names?'

'Alexander and Cecily and Marjorie and Anne.'

'Oh. How many times did you read it?'

'Twenty,' I said. 'I rather think you're going to grow up to be an Oxford don.'

'Good heavens,' said Eve. 'Why?'

'Passion for exact information.'

'I don't think I'll grow up to be anything,' said the boy casually. 'I think the witch won't let me unless Father thinks of a charm. He knows lots of charms.'

I opened my mouth on angry words and then did not speak.

Eve said, 'That's only a story, darling, not anything real. A story like ... like *Alice*. Like "Jack and the Beanstalk."' And there was confusion in the dark eyes so like her own. How helpless one could be with a child. There were no sharp edges for a child, between real and unreal. And you could not say, a lie.

'I saw her,' said the boy.

'Don't think about it now. Here's your tea. Thank you, Nanny.'

'We were very wicked,' said the nurse severely, making a clatter with the tray, 'to get up and sneak off downstairs like that.'

And Eve was silent. I would have expected the quiet words, 'It doesn't matter now,' meaning let him forget it, don't remind him. But she said nothing, and then she spoke, surprising me again, almost as if forced by something outside herself to say the words.

'Nanny's right, you know. You deserve a scolding for it. We're sorry you were frightened, but you shouldn't have come down.'

The boy looked embarrassed, resentful, bewildered to be corrected before a stranger and this long after the event. 'But I didn't mean to do anything wrong,' he muttered. 'Father said to. Well, I guess not exactly, but he said ... I didn't mean to.'

'Now there,' said Nanny, 'that'll be a fib, and a wicked one.'

'You know Father couldn't have said that, Jimmy.'

'I ... guess not. But he ...' The boy gave it up. Too intricate to explain to grown-ups. He was near tears now, the adventure of a stranger to tea spoiled, and he looked at his mother as if she had betrayed him. She sat motionless, staring at her plate, and her hand shook on the spoon that was stirring her tea.

Cold moved up my spine briefly and my mind split in two directions. The top half went to the boy, and I heard myself begin to talk easily, genially.

'I did that once and got a scolding, too,

Jimmy. I was just about your age and there was a party going on downstairs. I got up and went to the landing to watch and my father saw me and sent me back to bed. I'd never seen him in evening clothes before, and he looked so different I was almost frightened of him.'

'Oh, did you? Was he awfully, awfully cross, sir?'

'Awfully, but not with me. Mostly because he hated dressing up and dancing. He liked horses and dogs better than people, I think, except his family of course, and he just thought I was very silly to want to watch a lot of people in fancy clothes talking to each other.'

'Oh. Did ... did you have a lot of horses and dogs? What kind?'

'Lots,' I said, 'and all kinds.' I went on talking about our old house in the little Pennsylvania town and the animals, and the boy listened, the moment's tears forgotten.

*　　　*　　　*

When we came to the top of the staircase, the phonograph was audible below. It was Wagner now. She had not spoken since we left the nursery; now she said, 'Richard's home. You're sure you won't stay?'

'No, thanks, but...' No excuse. However, she did not seem to expect one.

'Thank you for being so good with Jimmy. He doesn't often take to strangers—not that he meets many.'

'He's a nice youngster.' All this mouthing of conventionalities! For once now, I wanted only to be away. I felt obscurely frightened, as I had felt watching the child climb the wall. Vicariously, I felt the ground unsolid beneath me.

And Manson must have been listening in spite of the music, for he had come to the foot of the stairs. Hands in pockets, he watched us down with a little fixed smile.

'Hello, Johnny. I hear you've been playing friend-of-the family today. Sorry about the car, Eve. I had quite forgotten you said you wanted it. I felt like a drive. But what a bore for the man, to impose on his time like that and then drag him to a nursery tea. You'll need a drink, old man. Come into the study.' There was no humor in his eyes at all.

'No, thanks, really...'

'Nonsense, come along.'

Unwillingly I followed him down to the small cluttered room at the end of the passage. Manson turned off the phonograph impatiently. 'Very good of you to look after Eve. Tell you the truth, I felt like the devil. Had to get off by myself. That hellish business...' He stopped, shaking his head, and measured whiskey neatly into glasses. 'You're thinking me a fool,' he said

114

unexpectedly. 'Don't deny it.'

'Not at all.'

'Ah, but you are. I suppose I'm not very clever about people. It surprised me you should be so patient, listen to me. I assure you, I'm quite used to the kind of reception Fowler gave me about it, you know?' Manson wandered over to the window, glass in hand, standing profile to me. 'She had spoken to you, hadn't she? It worries her. I don't know why. After all, it's like any other kind of belief. Nothing you choose deliberately, it's there or not there. Just because I happen to believe... No, no, I won't argue about it.'

'That's true, certainly,' I said cautiously. But when we grow up we stop believing in fairies—and ogres, Manson.

'You aren't really interested. Eve asked you to find that woman. I know. It doesn't matter, don't apologize.' He gestured rapidly. 'As a matter of fact I'm glad it happened that way, you know. I'd been planning that for some time. It seemed the most logical defense against it. Fire with fire. Now I see it isn't possible. We should never be sure, never. No way of proving that it wasn't a clever fraud. I'm afraid my aunt would be easily taken in, but I have made a more serious study of ... and there is nothing else I can do, nothing. You do see that.'

'No,' I said.

'Yes, yes, you're dropping pretense. You

don't believe in it. I wish *I* didn't.' He finished the whiskey in one swallow. 'Don't look so embarrassed,' he said softly. 'I'm not holding you responsible. Even for the pretense you put up. Eve dragged you into it willy-nilly, didn't she? She makes such a fuss... Women, they never can live and let live. Always must be their way, good or bad. Good or bad ... I've been thinking it over, trying to decide what can be done. There must be some way, some better, surer way.'

I sat very still, watching him. Any pretense Manson had made was gone now. It was no longer a little joke, an old woman's foible only half accepted.

'And as to that, you needn't think me so much of a fool. I've another reason besides blind belief. I'll tell you something I've never told anyone, if you'll promise not to tell Eve. She mustn't know, of course. Women get upset so easily. I wonder if I'm what they call psychic, because I felt it at once.

'You saw some action at the end of the war, didn't you, Johnny, in your own army? You remember how it was. On patrol, I mean. Not knowing where they were, expecting it from any direction, watching and listening and waiting and never knowing.'

'Yes, I remember.'

'But some of us had a kind of extra sense about it after a while. It might come suddenly, but a second beforehand we'd

116

know, it'll be over there. Like a private radar beam. I suppose you could call it psychic. I felt that about the boy, you see, from the first. Another? Sure?' He splashed more whiskey into his glass. 'Perhaps because she wanted a child so much. I never cared one way or the other—no compulsion to bring another life into being—the most obvious form of vanity, isn't it? But Eve... We'd been married almost five years, then, you know. We were still living in London but I'd come down here that weekend, my uncle had just died. They sent me a telegram from the nursing home, that it was a boy. And I knew right away. I'd thought it before, she wanted it too much. Dangerous. Something always happens to things you want too much. And with that telegram in my hands I knew, just the way I'd known when a German patrol was near. That she wouldn't keep him. That she couldn't keep him.'

'You're talking damned nonsense,' I said coldly, furiously. 'No one can know a thing like that.' This coddling of Manson, that was the wrong way. Pretend sympathy, pretend not to notice. It was time someone talked straight to him. 'If you don't mind what people say about you, you might give a little thought to your wife and child for a change. I've no right to say that, but someone ought to. Very well, I'm not pretending any longer. Nonsense is the mildest word I can think of for it.'

I shut my teeth on more words, and the voice in my mind said, oh, fine, Harkness, brave, bold, speaking out on a matter of principle, and if you had no personal interest what would principle matter? You don't convince people, change them, by talking. It satisfies the ego, that's all. Gives an illusion of action.

And Manson laughed. 'You don't understand. What else am I thinking of? No, I knew what you thought. I could guess. I couldn't explain it to you, if I wanted to try.'

On the whole I was relieved he wasn't going to try. I'd had enough of Manson. Quite enough. Useless to expend anger, much less argument, on what you could do absolutely nothing about. I finished my own drink and got up, the anger a hard core in me.

'Well,' I said abruptly, 'it's none of my business.' You never spoke a truer word, Harkness. 'If you want to expend all this agony over a problem you've created for yourself, there's nothing anyone can do to stop you.'

I came away gladly. Each time I had left this place I had thought it was for the last time. Now it was, it had to be. When I stepped into the one long room of The Drowned Man, as if to point up the working of destiny, the same five men were there as on

118

the first day I entered the place: the three old men and one young one at the same table, the publican leaning on the bar with his secretive eyes fixed on space. This time their eyes went to me with a little indifferent speculation. Not an outlander now, but accepted associate of local gentry. Their talk shut off, and I wondered if it had been about me.

It did not matter. I said to the landlord, 'I'll want my bill in the morning, please.'

CHAPTER TWELVE

I came back to London telling myself it was a little vignette ended. I attended to the conventions of ending it. I wrote the Mansons a polite note thanking them for hospitality, and, the gracious gesture, bought and sent a book to the youngster. The note did not call for reply and I had none; but I did have a creditable little note from Jimmy, thank-you-very-much-sir. That tied up the loose ends.

Manson was just another former friend, like Cunningham, Adams, Wakefield; you knew them, you drifted away, and later, meeting them, you found nothing in common any longer. So you did not press it, you let it go.

I'd allowed myself to get involved only

because it was an odd story. But be honest, Harkness: the woman? All right, damn it, the woman. I was sorry for her, but it was her problem, she was married to the man.

I'd called myself a hack to Fowler. But I suppose the one quality any writer has to have in some degree is the thing called empathy. More than imagination, it involved me with people unbidden, sometimes unaware. Here I was only unwilling.

I felt I was not done with Manson, and the thought—yes, it was not too strong a word—frightened me.

I settled back into my London routine. It was about two weeks later that Vicky Carstairs showed up. I wouldn't bring her into this story at all except that unwittingly she contributed a little to it. She'd been in Paris and Italy covering the fashion shows and said she was treating herself to a month in England before going home. Vicky loves England; I think it spells elegance to her. She belongs to quite a wealthy New York family and had several society seasons in London before she decided she wanted a career, so she still knew quite a lot of people there. Much more respectable people than I knew; the kind who'd been on top before the war.

Well, I saw her, of course; and equally of course the thing between us was dead. I liked Vicky well enough, but I had never (to be frank) had any emotional interest in her, and

120

the physical interest had disappeared.

She called one afternoon and asked how I'd like to take her to tea. There's not much a man can say to that but yes, and I said it. She looked very smart, I remember, very American. Little and dark and vivacious. Somehow, I don't know, she seemed a bit too vivacious.

I found out why when I asked when the wedding was scheduled. She said brightly, 'Oh, that's off.'

'Oh?' I said.

She stopped smiling for a minute, and then she looked tired and older. 'Maybe I was overanxious,' she said with a little grimace. 'It's kaput, anyway.'

'I'm sorry.'

'Oh, so am I. But tell me what you've been doing with yourself, John.'

'I *am* sorry,' I said, feeling uneasy. 'I hope it wasn't . . .'

'Don't flatter yourself. And do you mind if we don't talk about it? I've been feeling rather a fool and it's never pleasant. Especially for a woman with plenty of natural ego, hmm? What have you been doing?'

'Nothing much. Nothing really.' And later on I took her back to the tiny cluttered flat where she was staying and waited while she changed and we went to dinner. But it was a waste of time, it was like reading the same page over in a book. No matter how good it was, what satisfaction and pleasure you had from it the first time, it is never the same at a second reading.

I didn't know what she expected; over the coffee I said, not knowing how else to say it, 'I don't want to make you feel a fool all over again, Vicky, but ... it's no good anymore.'

'All right,' she said. 'All right, John. I didn't really expect it would be. Things come to an end. But we don't have to stop talking to each other, you know. Damn, it's no use—you do make me feel a fool. "Run away and play, child, I'm busy now."'

'I didn't mean ...'

'No, no, I suppose not. Men do that sort of thing. Did you think I was trying to entrap you? I don't believe it could be done.'

'I wonder,' I said lightly, 'if that's intended as a compliment or an insult. Don't tell me I'm supposed to be the worldly-wise rake.'

She laughed. 'That's really funny. You? You're a nice respectable upright family man, darling, only just like me, you took the wrong turn awhile back. The war sent a lot of us down the wrong road ... well, a different road, anyway. You couldn't be a rake if you tried—know why? You haven't any sense of sin. I mean, you don't enjoy sex just because it's immoral. You don't think it is.' She patted my hand. 'You're old-fashioned enough to believe in the double standard, so you can give your whole mind to sinning without worrying about impressing the girl or boasting about it to all your friends.'

'I'll take that as an intended compliment at least.'

'I always suspect real rakes,' she said. 'Self-advertisement never turns out to be true, you know. I've known quite a few of them, and that's why I appreciate somebody like you. Take a man like Mark Forsythe or George D'Arcy. Did you know Mark was actually born Benjamin Smith? It's a fact, and I'd blackmail him except that too many people already know about it. Or Kenny Templeton . . .'

'Who?' I interrupted sharply, before I realized why the name was familiar. Fowler had said it, said it without explanation, as if thinking aloud.

'Kenny Templeton. Did you know him?'

'Who is he? The name seems familiar. Perhaps I met him somewhere.'

'He's dead. He was killed in an auto accident six or seven years ago. But talk about a womanizer . . . that's funny. I never realized it before. You look a little like him.'

'Do I?'

'But I was going to say . . .'

★   ★   ★

I took her home much later and came back to my own flat. For some reason I was wakeful;

I wandered the rooms restlessly, leafed through a few magazines, uninterested. At last I went to the shelves for a book which might prove soporific. And the first title that leaped to my eye was *Troth*. Barclay, who had also known Manson, would have a copy, of course. It might be interesting to glance through it again.

An hour later I roused myself to make coffee, open a fresh pack of cigarettes. What had I thought about second readings, in connection with Vicky? Yes, well, sometimes, too, you found things you had missed the first time.

I'd read the book when it came out. It had attracted a lot of attention. Fowler told me later that Manson had casually shoved the manuscript at him one day and he'd read it out of curiosity. Reviewers seldom perform well as novelists. I remembered thinking at the time that the book was better than I would have expected from Manson, though I understood some of the cynical reviews it had. It was, well, let's say made for Hollywood, where it ended, of course. But that was eight years ago, and maybe I wasn't quite the same man now.

Reading it again eight years older, eight years more experienced, I thought of Eve saying '... quite possible to get to know someone through what he writes.' Possibly a fallacy with a professional, but *Troth* was an

124

amateur's novel, a novel written (how had I missed seeing it before?) to prove that Manson could write one.

I thought, forget you know him. Think about the man who wrote this book. This clever, cynical book that is only an intricate plot, peopled by two-dimensional cardboard puppets. The puppets speak clever, cynical dialogue; the whole thing is brilliant prose if not strictly good technical fiction. What of the man?

The book is full of sex, I reflected, and it was written by a man to whom sex is disgusting. He writes of the amoral, the lecherous, the perverted—and there is too much sex in the book for balance—but not casually, like the faithful reporter, or mockingly, like the cynical commentator, or even severely, like the would-be reformer. He is like a man with a horror of blood and mess watching a surgical operation, unable to look away, fascinated with loathing.

I shut the book toward the end without finishing it. All that I had not found in it before: was I finding what was not there now, reading too much into it?

Gray dawn was beginning to light the windows; and now I could sleep. Instead I picked up the book again, searched for that first description of the puppet Manson had named Lilith, the lovely, lying, loose-moraled Lilith.

'Of diminutive stature, more plump than slender, she was a natural blonde ... her blue eyes set a trifle close together ... She had small fat hands, a penchant for heavy antique rings to make them look smaller, fatter. A narrow small mouth was enlarged cleverly with paint ... girlish voice sweet as honey could rise to shrillness in emotion ... the honey-blond curls usually untidy ...'

I read it over twice and was speculating on it even as I fell asleep, with the rising sun in my eyes.

CHAPTER THIRTEEN

Once or twice a year Fowler, carelessly punctilious, repaid the most pressing of his social debts at one large dinner. He had kept his house in Mayfair, too big, old-fashioned, probably out of perversity, living in it alone with a series of today's difficult-to-find servants. 'I'm too old to turn into a cliff dweller. Somebody else can cut it up into flats when I'm dead.' Even at those dinners there never seemed to be enough people to fill the rooms. It was a ghost, a house that had outlived its time.

I was invited there in the following week; as usual I found myself one of a motley company, people Fowler knew in business, in

society, in a dozen milieus. I had not seen
Fowler since I got back to London, and
deliberately arrived late to avoid private talk
with him.

I was introduced to half a dozen strangers,
the names slurring over one another; it was
only at table that necessity forced me with an
effort to connect my right-hand companion
with a name. She was a plumpish blonde with
a good-humored expression and shrewd eyes,
pretty in conventional fashion.

'... And I'm just dying to get away for a
holiday, but Harry keeps saying we can't
afford it, business is so bad. Have you
managed to get out of town at all?'

'Oh, yes, for a few days. What is Mr ...'
Damn it, what was the name? '...
Chadwick's business, then?'

'The City.' She noticed my hesitation with
an amused smile. 'Don't apologize, I'm awful
at names myself. I wouldn't be able to
remember yours if I hadn't read some of your
articles. Where did you go for your holiday?
Harry says I've a middle-class taste,
personally I like Bournemouth, but Harry
says...'

Chadwick, good God, yes. Even as I
answered I had a recurrence of the
uncomfortable sensation, destiny propelling
me: no free choice. But I had free choice at
least in not pressing it. I was not the detective
in a crime novel. I hadn't planned to say it,

and heard myself with something like anger for unwarranted interference.

'I've been to Cornwall, staying with some people called Manson. Near Truro.'

She was delighted. 'Not really? Then perhaps we've mutual friends. Would that be Eve Manson and her husband? Fancy. Cornwall! I'd love the address. Eve and I used to be great friends but I've lost touch. Fancy Eve in the country, right off the map like that. Do you know them well?'

She was the type that needed only a word to set her off on irrelevant gossip, but there was some innate caution there, too. OK, now you've committed yourself, Harkness. Playing the detective after all, and a fine mess you're likely to make of it. At least do it thoroughly.

I said easily, 'I'd never met Mrs. Manson before. I knew her husband fairly well once, but hadn't met him for some time.' That amounted to a green light, for a woman like this one.

'Oh, I see. Well, when I say Eve and I were great friends, she's not very easy to know. Didn't you think so? We were at school together.' Woodhill Young Ladies' Academy, yes. 'You can understand it, I suppose, knowing who she was ... Eve Henrys—you remember that awful murder, after the war, her mother ...'

The murder took us through the consommé

128

and wilted salad.

'Personally I was frightfully sorry for Eve, but my people were quite horrified at my knowing her. It was only a year or two later when I was married to my first husband, you know, and on my own, that I saw anything of her. Of course we knew lots of people and went out quite a bit and when Eve got married, too, I—you know—tried to draw her into our crowd, because I *did* feel sorry, but Bob, my first husband, just couldn't bear her.

'They were married the year after the trial, you know, she was only eighteen, though why I should say only, when I was married the same year myself, but, you know, I always thought she married just so she wouldn't be Eve Henrys any longer. That's a funny thing to say, but I do. Personally, I could understand it. She came in for a lot of publicity, you know, testifying at the trial and so on. And then she was so extraordinarily good-looking. I wonder if she still is. The boys were always round her like flies, even when we were at school, and she did enjoy it. She was clever with them, too, knew just how to handle them, you know. Some women are born with that.

'And the mother, well, I don't want to sound malicious, but you can't get away from it, she was her mother after all, as far as I can gather just a cheap tart who tricked an old man into marrying her. A lot of people took it for granted Eve was the same sort. Not that I believe altogether in heredity or anything like that.'

'But where did Manson meet her?'

'Now that I couldn't tell you. I expect in London, on leave. I think he was still in the army then. Of course I never knew him, I just met him a few times, that's all. Eve was rather funny about it, and I always wondered—oh, well, I shouldn't say that.'

'But now you've aroused my curiosity. Do go on.'

'Oh, well, it was just that I invited them to join our crowd somewhere, oh, heaps of times, and she always made an excuse when it was couples. I mean, if it was just the wives, she'd come, you see. Personally, I began to wonder if she was ashamed of her husband or something, you know? And then after I divorced Bob, she never accepted any of my invitations at all. Well, I'd thought we were friends, you know, and I expect I'm funny but I do like to know where I stand with people. So one day I called her and just asked her straight out if I'd, you know, done anything to offend her. And she told me she didn't approve of divorce! Well, really. I mean, we're all supposed to be civilized these days, aren't we? And it wasn't long after that I heard some gossip about her and some man, so it just goes to show. No, I never heard *definitely* who it was, but I could make a guess.' A small titter. 'It doesn't matter now, he's dead. But one couldn't help wondering, you know, knowing what her mother was. Bob always said she was probably just the same kind, only clever enough to cover it up better. Oh, dear, I shouldn't say that either, I don't really know. She was never awfully friendly at school. She isn't the kind of woman who's friendly with women, if you see what I mean. But you'll be thinking me a terrible gossip, only you did say you didn't know her.'

'No.' I'd have to make some excuse if she asked for the address. Unthinkable to let the woman loose on Eve.

'Personally, I always suspect people who pretend to be prudish. You know? But here I am gossiping again, it's awful, I know.'

I found I had lost appetite for the excellent casseroled chicken.

However, there was no longer any mystery about Eve's polite reluctance to claim Mrs. Chadwick as a friend. Personally, I thought with an inward grin, the mere fact that Mrs. Chadwick was in London might be sufficient to send me into the wilds of Cornwall.

Fowler's dinners never encouraged much jollity; by eleven o'clock people were beginning to drift away. I was thinking of it myself, and looking about for my host, when Fowler put a hand on my arm.

'Stay and have a drink when these people

are gone, John? I was rather looking for you when you came back to town.' Yes, to hear about Manson. I hadn't wanted to discuss him with Fowler; I had found Fowler's comfortable cynicism annoying. Why? All right, admit it. I didn't want to think Fowler might be right about Eve. Which was foolish and dangerous, when you find yourself dodging facts to maintain a prejudice; play detective if you like, but an honest one, Harkness. And in any case, of course, there was nothing in it. Fowler's own prejudices were behind his cynicism.

I had thought, a thing ended, where I was concerned. Life might be stranger than fiction but it lacks any dramatic unity; you come across these strange stories, these strange people, never knowing the beginning or the end; you move on—not your story— wondering casually, that's all. Yet ever since I'd been back in London the thing I had found out had been teasing at my mind.

I wanted now, suddenly, to talk about it to Fowler; quite possibly I had read too much into it, which would collapse of its own absurdity once it was openly spoken.

'Yes, I'd like to, thanks.'

'Why don't you go down to my study and wait? Half an hour,' said Fowler, glancing about the thinning groups. 'Whiskey in the cupboard and ... John...'

'Mhmm?'

132

'You'll find a letter from Manson on the desk. You might be interested.'

*　　*　　*

'I want,' said Fowler when he came into the study some time later, 'to hear about that séance. Were you admitted, and was it a good show?'

'Yes and no. About as bad as it could be.' I told him the story briefly, absently; I was thinking about Manson's letter. 'You called it a double play,' I said. 'I think it was a triple one. Unless I'm an overimaginative fool, Charles, or maybe over-Freudian, I've found out something, and frankly it scares me. You don't expect to meet case histories from a psychiatrist's notebook in real life. Let me tell you what happened afterward, and then you can tell me I'm seeing ghosts in daylight.'

Fowler listened, pouring a drink for himself, tilting back in the desk chair, half smiling. When I paused expectantly he remained silent.

'What do you make of it?' I asked.

'You're doing the analysis,' said Fowler. 'You're the expert on human relations. Go ahead and expound your theory.'

'All right. I'll tell you what I think, fantastic as it sounds. Manson wants that curse to work, Charles. He's expecting it to work. It's—what's the word?—what your

133

Freudians call ambivalence. He doesn't know it himself, of course, people never do. He's not what I'd call an affectionate person, but even he would feel some hidden jealousy. According to the psychiatrists, at least, that kind of thing's quite common. I wouldn't know, they could well be right. But it isn't anything as relatively open as that.

'Start out with the fact that he believes in the curse. Believes fervently, as he was taught to believe, in all the abracadabra of superstition. It's like religion—not a rational thing. He tells himself and everyone else he's afraid of the threat to the boy, and he really thinks he is. But everyone else has ridiculed him so much, and his belief is so strong, that actually he—how shall I put it?—he would like to see himself proven right. I think he was pleased when that woman turned out such a palpable fraud. Logical, yes, if he could call off the curse by supernatural means, that wouldn't be denying its reality. But so tame compared to a ... a dramatic tragedy that would prove its existence. To him anyway. Oh, damn it, it sounds like nonsense put like that.'

'Not at all. I agree with you,' said Fowler unexpectedly.

'She knows it. Perhaps not realizing it consciously, but it's what worries her about it. I think she was trying to tell me that, see I knew it, too, but perhaps it's all unconscious

134

for both of them.'

I got up restlessly, paced the room as I talked; I was arguing as if Fowler had taken an opposite stand and must be convinced.

'Look at the way he treats the youngster. He said to me, children are entitled to the truth. My God, frightening a child that way, but it's all part of it, you see. I can imagine exactly how he talked to the boy. The main reason for that is probably to build himself up in the boy's eyes; you know, Father will protect you. It's devilish, but there's a kind of logic behind it. He would have told him about the woman coming, what they were going to do, aroused all his curiosity, and then warned him specifically not to come down to watch, putting the idea in the boy's mind whether or not it was there already, you see? And if you asked him he'd deny it, say he'd done nothing of the sort, and he doesn't realize, of course, that he did, or why he did.

'It was the same about the other thing—you never heard about that. The boy climbed up on the wall. He said Father had told him to, and Manson had a fit, understandably. It's a three-hundred-foot drop, and rocks below. But I can guess that the boy thought he was telling the truth. Manson would have said something like, you could see much farther from the wall, putting the idea there again, you see. Not knowing why he did it. Unconsciously, he would be

135

thinking of ways the curse might work out, and that would be one way, but he'd never realize why he said those things, it's buried too deep in his unconscious mind.'

Fowler sat up with a jerk. He said, 'You've been reading Adler again. Tell you the truth, I go just so far with the psycho-johnnies. Maybe it's old-fashioned of me, but when they talk about phobias and neuroses I'm inclined to call it plain original sin. No, I'm not disagreeing. I think you're quite right, but for another reason.'

'I was going to say,' I said reluctantly, 'that there's something else behind it, too. I'm afraid it is rather Adlerian, or Freudian. I've just reread *Troth*, and I found a few things in it that I didn't stop to analyze the first time. It's an amateur's novel. Manson's on every page of it.'

'Careful,' said Fowler, leaning back and shutting his eyes. 'Professional jealousy, John. You've never held much brief for the slick modern approach. I know.'

'All right, all right, discount half of anything I say. I'm not a novelist myself, but to use the old bromide, I know what I like. It's well written but it's not good fiction, and you know it as well as I do. He's not a writer, he's a man who once wrote a novel. You can't say, about a professional novelist, that he's a man who once wrote a novel. You can't say, about a professional novelist, that he's immoral because he writes about immorality—maybe he just found out it sells. But in *Troth* you can deduce something about Manson because he's not a professional. I think you'll agree with that.

'And the first thing that's really obvious is that he's a puritan. Dyed-in-the-wool. The mere fact of sex disgusts him, but he is under compulsion to examine it clinically, as it were. No, that's not quite right. He's not the little boy fascinated with dirty words, because he doesn't get a thrill from it. Quite honestly it nauseates him. The whole novel is packed with sex, but not for any of the usual reasons. The common one, of course, you get with novelists like ...' I mentioned a few names, and Fowler nodded. '... The immature attitude. Sex to them is something to snigger at in secret. Fascinating because it's forbidden. Immature is the kindest thing you can call them. And you always get that atmosphere in whatever they write, the little boys chalking words on fences.

'But at least there's no rejection of sex there, as there seems to be with Manson. All through the book he is saying, look at the absurd antics of these human animals over this loathsome and overrated function.'

'Not the perpetual undergraduate,' murmured Fowler, nodding, 'or by any means the effeminate cynic. A kind of neuter intelligence.'

'Yes. But along with it is something a little closer to the flesh, and that's a real feeling of enmity toward women. Did you get that, or is it part of the other, I wonder? All the women in the book—and if you'll remember there isn't one who can by any stretch of the imagination be called an admirable character. Every one of them he really hates as he's writing about them. And the major feminine character . . .'

'Yes?'

I said slowly, 'It's rather interesting to analyze the description. Perhaps I'm being too clever. But I think the woman in the book is meant to be Mrs. Manson. The physical description is so painstakingly just opposite. Lilith—Eve. In Rabbinical scripture Lilith was the first woman . . .'

'I am familiar with the Apocrypha,' said Fowler, eyes still shut.

'The fictional woman is blond—small, plump, untidy, and so on. Every quality you can name exactly opposite. *Too* opposite, as if he was conscious of the identification himself and went out of the way to make it impossible for anyone else to suspect.'

'That's clever. I can't say I thought of it, but quite probably you're right. As I say'—Fowler sat up again and began to fill his pipe—'I'm an old-fashioned man. I happen to be nervous about little boats, but I'd have a laugh at the psychiatrist who told me it was because of an unhappy memory of floating around my mother's womb, when I know it's because I fell out of a fishing boat and damn' near drowned thirty years ago.

'In other words, after all your fancy talk, and I agree with most of what you say, substantially, has it occurred to you that there may be some plain down-to-earth everyday reason for Manson being what he is? Aside from all your deductions about the state of his subconscious mind. I think it's time I justified my curiosity about the Mansons to you. I don't ordinarily poke and pry at people this way. You've reason for being interested. So have I.'

Fowler eyed me through a blue cloud of smoke. 'If there was no other reason for claiming man is simian, it would be sufficiently convincing to point out that both species conduct perpetual mating seasons,' he observed dryly. 'Let it go. That's my reason, too, then, after my first experience with the Mansons. Get yourself another drink if you like.'

CHAPTER FOURTEEN

'When Manson brought *Troth* to me and we decided to publish it,' Fowler said, drawing on his pipe, 'I knew him only casually, mostly through his reviews. He was a cocksure, rather cruel critic, as you'll remember. Well, of course, afterward I got to know him a bit better, but I didn't meet his wife for a long time. She didn't seem to go about with him at all.

'About that time, you may recall—no, you wouldn't, you're not a crime fan—it was about that time we were doing Prentice's collection of Modern Murders, and included in it was an account of the Henrys-Paxton case. Prentice had done some research on it, of course, and he happened to meet Manson in my office one day, and afterward he mentioned that Mrs. Henrys' daughter had married a man by that name. Well, I daresay it was rude, but I was just curious enough to mention it to Manson next time I saw him, and he got quite upset. I could have understood it if he'd been ashamed, or belligerent, or even embarrassed. The only way I can explain it is to say he was defiant and proud at once, like a schoolboy who's got involved with a barmaid. Something occur to you?'

'Just corroboration,' I said. 'Self-advertisement. I'd seen that about him before, when I first knew him. Very young men who play the sophisticated cynic are usually covering up a lack of self-confidence. Sorry to inflict psychiatry on you again, but he probably started out with an enormous inferiority complex, when you come to think of it. He's small, he's rather insignificant-looking, he'd lived in the country most of his life, he hasn't any great talent or personal charm. He was—he is—a man who's overcompensating all the time, proving himself. The reason he did so well at the university, had to make up for his littleness, be better than anyone else. And possibly the reason he married her, Charles? Yes, you said something like that. It couldn't be an ordinary woman, not for him.'

'Oh, yes, I guessed that, so many writers are like that,' said Fowler with a half grin. 'Some prima donnas, some fussy eccentrics, some who pride themselves on being oh-so-normal, but essentially they wouldn't be writers if they weren't overcompensating for inferiority complexes. You see I know the jargon, too.'

'I thought the basic theory was that the creative imagination consists of surplus sex drive. A slightly more flattering idea—but go on.'

'Well, they were living in London at the time and I saw something of them, eventually, in a very small way. He had to make some show of repaying invitations. But usually I saw Manson alone, just as you said was your experience. It rather puzzled me, you know, because Mrs. Manson is obviously not a retiring woman. You'd expect her to be

141

quite competent socially.

'One afternoon I happened to meet Mrs. Manson in the street and purely on impulse had tea with her, at a Lyons Corner House, as I recall. We couldn't have been in the place above half an hour, and anything less like an, er, romantic interlude ... you take my meaning. Even,' said Fowler humorously, 'disregarding my lack of romantic propensities. Manson came round to the house that night in a fury and accused me of seducing his wife.'

'You must be joking.'

'As a matter of fact I was rather flattered,' said Fowler thoughtfully. 'It's not often a man of fifty-three with a face like the back of a cab and no money to speak of is accused of seduction. I'm afraid I laughed at him. He let me give him a drink, and then it all came out.

'Perhaps he'd had a few drinks beforehand; he was rather maudlin. He started out cursing her in a feeble kind of way as a damned whore, and then degenerated into self-pity. It was just as embarrassing as it sounds. He did apologize for what he'd said to me, excused himself by saying the damned woman had him where he didn't know right from wrong. There were so many, I might easily be one of them, and now and then he made a fool of himself trying to do something about it. "More of a fool than she made of me perhaps," he said. I was rather disgusted with the man. I told him he needn't advertise the fact. If that was the case he'd much better be rid of her.'

'You believed him, of course. Of course.' Fowler of all men would believe that, having been through something similar himself.

'Prejudice?' Fowler cocked his head. 'Pot calling the kettle black, John. Who would know better than the husband? And can you conceive any man, even with drink in him, telling a mere acquaintance a thing like that unless he was certain, unless he was so certain that it was killing him? You don't know. He talked about her mother, said you might expect it after all, there was bad blood, and he'd been a fool to marry her.'

'Heredity!' I said, and laughed.

'And environment. She was raised in the same house with the woman. I'm not making a case, I'm telling you about Manson. He pulled himself together after a bit and apologized. Whatever else you can say about him he's ordinarily reserved, you know, not a man to make private confidences of that sort even to men he knows well. Which was the reason . . .'

'But it wasn't the only reason you believed him, Charles,' I said coldly.

'Maybe not,' said Fowler, looking away. 'I can't say I liked him—a strange, nervous little chap—but I felt sorry for him. He believed it anyway. What disgusted me was the way he

143

took it. No backbone. He kept muttering something about scandal, publicity. I gather he couldn't face the prospect of divorce, with all the attendant fanfare. I told him...'

'I can guess what you told him. I never heard such damned nonsense in my life. Do you think I don't know a—a loose woman when I meet one?' Unconsciously I was reverting to the terminology of my Presbyterian boyhood.

'Not when you're attracted to her romantically,' said Fowler. 'I haven't finished, so don't swear at me. You know you are, and you're not the first by a long shot. She's a beautiful woman.'

'You can't tell me that that woman, the way she is with the boy, anything more normal and right...'

'Even the psychiatrists have never been able to trace any connection between sexual morality and mother love. Well, naturally I never mentioned it again to Manson, or anyone else. We weren't on those terms. Nor he to me, after that night. But I was interested.' Yes, Fowler would have been interested for his own reasons, identifying himself a little with Manson. 'About a month later, Templeton was killed.'

'Now we come to it,' I said, sitting up. 'Who was Templeton and what's he got to do with all this?'

'Templeton was a bastard,' said Fowler. He

144

seldom used profanity; the word was spoken in cold judgment. 'I don't say that because my wife happened to be one of those he victimized—God knows it was any man's choice between them. Templeton was a professional womanizer. Anyone was fair game to him, bored wives, debutantes trying to be sophisticated, casual women of his own type, anything female. You can use your psychological jargon on the type. I'll call it just plain irresponsible wickedness. He was charming, of course, to women. Half the husbands in London had good reason to murder him, but he saw to that himself, with a racing car he had. Took a blind curve too fast and smashed into a lorry, and probably went straight to hell.

'I had some people here a couple of nights later, the Mansons among them, and the Chadwicks—I think you met them tonight.'

'I did indeed.'

'And at the table Mrs. Chadwick started to talk about Templeton, such a tragedy and such a charming man and so on. Evidently Mrs. Manson had not heard about his death. It was rather embarrassing. She went white as a ghost. I really thought she was going to faint. No one missed it. She made a gallant attempt to behave naturally, but it was obvious she'd had a frightful shock. Not only embarrassing for the rest of us but for Manson, more so, actually.'

'If you're basing an assumption on such flimsy evidence as that—'

'I'm not making an assumption. Manson did that. And, in that particular instance, everyone else, too. I heard a certain amount of talk about Mrs. Manson, among people who knew them, after that. About a year later they left London and I lost touch with Manson entirely. In the light of what's happened since, as I said before, I think he must have had some idea of keeping her out of circulation, so to speak, away from temptation.'

I said again, 'I never heard such nonsense in my life. They went to live in Cornwall because his uncle died and there was no one to look after the estate. The old aunt is probably incompetent legally. Maybe they thought the country would be healthier for the boy.'

'What sort of youngster is he?' asked Fowler, prodding at his pipe.

'A very nice lad, actually. Intelligent, good-looking, well brought up, as they say.'

'Does he look much like Manson?'

'No. No, he looks like his mother. Boys often do.'

Fowler grunted. 'Not always. It'd be a joke, you know, the curse of the Mansons, if the boy wasn't his at all. Interesting to speculate on. Just occurred to me.'

'And I thought *I* was talking fantasy,' I

said.

'I see I'm not convincing you. However, my point is this. Whether it's so or not, Manson's conviction about his wife has left him only the boy as an emotional interest, that's obvious. I agree with you that at least part of his fuss about this curse is an effort to build up his own power in the youngster's eyes, win him over from the mother. And can't we say, too, some of it is just contrariness, because she's so dead against it?'

'Yes,' I said unwillingly, 'I'll grant you that. But I can't believe...'

Fowler pointed the pipe at me accusingly. 'You're a romanticist. All Americans are, they can't help themselves. Because a woman is good to look at and behaves like a lady in public, you don't want to believe a word against her. Tell me this. Whatever she is or isn't, don't you think she knows what her husband thinks? And if it wasn't true, if he was mad or malicious or only oversuspicious to that extent, do you think any self-respecting woman would stay with him? But a woman forgiven and offered another chance ...' he shrugged.

'And what the hell does it matter?' I asked. 'All right, I'll stop arguing with you. In either case, it's nothing to do with you or me. She's Manson's wife.'

'And better leave it that way. I thought we agreed it was just curiosity. I,' said Fowler with a mirthless smile, 'am womanproof. But you're at a dangerous age, when a man begins to feel nostalgic for lost opportunities, or for somebody to fetch his slippers in the evening. For an American you've very little caution. Did you find Manson's letter?'

'Yes. Some people,' I said absently, 'and Manson is one of them, write letters as if they expected them to be published for posterity. Yes, I see he mentions that Mrs. Manson's coming up to London. I wonder why.'

'Woman has to replenish her wardrobe sometime. I don't suppose she patronizes provincial dressmakers. I just thought it was a good opportunity to warn you.'

'Warn?' I smiled. 'Now you're flattering me, Charles. Granted you're right about Eve Manson—and I don't think you are, not at all—were you afraid she'd make a play for me? I haven't anywhere as much money as he has.' Childish, as if to say, there, I can be just as cynical as you.

'All right,' said Fowler equably. 'Play it as you like, so long as you know what you're doing.'

CHAPTER FIFTEEN

Very definitely, of course, my connection with the Mansons was slight. I did not intend to encourage it into anything more. So she was coming up to London (Manson writing casually in a casual letter to Fowler). Well, it wasn't likely I would meet her, and I was far from sure I wanted to. The whole affair had been nonsensical from start to finish; beginning like an old-fashioned ghost story, degenerating into an ill-conceived modern novel. I had plenty of work to keep me occupied.

But somehow I felt restless. I got bogged down on those damned columns, couldn't settle to work properly. One afternoon in the next week I surrendered to impulse—or was it destiny again?—and called Vicky. She sounded pleased.

'I should pay you out by having another engagement. Actually, I'm at loose ends. I'd love to have dinner with you. Sevenish? Are we going anywhere that calls for my new dress? Scarlet, darling, and it rustles. Great, I'll expect you then.'

I took her to Charlot's, feeling reckless. It was one of the new smart places, all very modern and expensive: the kind of place Vicky liked. As we were seated at our table I was thinking: and perhaps afterward, we...

Then I saw Eve Manson at a table across the room. She was alone, but she would draw glances for another reason. Quite suddenly, and apart from any other emotion, I found Vicky a little tawdry, a little too obvious.

149

Every other woman in the room faded a little. Eve was in something dark with a touch of white at throat and cuffs, no exposure of shoulder or breast, and I thought I'd never seen her look more beautiful. Never? How many times had I seen her, how well did I know her?

She had not seen me. She was sitting very still, with a half-finished cocktail before her. I could sit with my back to her, here, and she would not see me. I would not be called on to make even a little polite talk with her.

So of course I said, 'Excuse me a moment, there's someone I know. I must ...' I felt Vicky's eyes following me as I crossed to the table.

'Good evening, Mrs. Manson.'

She looked up startled, smiling involuntarily. 'Mr. Harkness.'

'I heard you were coming to town.'

'I came yesterday,' she said. 'The first time I've been in London in three years. Isn't that shocking? Won't you sit down?'

'I'm sorry, I'm not alone, I ... Shopping?'

'Just a holiday,' she said. Her brief animation had died.

'How is—Jimmy?' I'd begun to ask for Manson; but I did not care how Manson was. She smiled again.

'It was very kind of you to send him the book.' But it was absurd, after confidences between us, this painful politeness. I thought

150

she looked tired.

'Manson?' I asked abruptly, almost angrily.

She lifted a hand, let it fall. 'There's no point in talking about it, is there?' Now, in a more formal milieu, she was regretting that she had admitted me into private places, wanted no reminder of it. Of course, in any case, we could not talk here, now. At the same time there came into my mind all that Fowler had said, and an extraordinary familiar emotion flooded over me. Emotion is not quite the right word. Sensation. A primal thing. I identified it between shame and speculation. A basic thing. The line down the middle, good this side and bad that, and an automatic reaction to each. With the one, a kind of mechanical censor, shutting off awareness of her as female; with the other, the available woman, you found yourself noticing, judging, anticipating. I had said to Fowler, don't you think I'd know. But would I? A woman of education, intelligence, it would not be obvious, and I did not know her well, of course, of course. This woman, this elegant beautiful woman alone.

'I see.' She had discovered Vicky at the table behind me, probably watching.

'Where are you staying?' Only a casual question, it did not imply that I would make use of the information.

There was an odd little pause. She looked at me straightly and I saw her make the

151

decision. Her shoulders lifted in a slight shrug: what does it matter? There is no harm. As clear as if she had said it, and the hesitation betraying that she felt it, too, that this marked subtly, irrationally, a step forward in the relationship. 'Benton's Hotel. Perhaps you don't know it. It's a little private place, just off St. John's Wood. About a week, I think, I don't really know. Yes, Richard's fine, thank you. I mustn't keep you.' Her eyes went back across the room.

'I hope you'll enjoy your holiday.' Nothing more, at the moment, to say to her.

I went back to apologize to Vicky.

'Who's your film-star friend, darling, or shouldn't I ask?'

I shrugged. 'Acquaintance,' I amended. 'Her name is Eve Manson. She's up from the country.'

'She doesn't look country. That's a smart frock. Mrs.?'

'Mrs.,' I said, and knew I emphasized it for myself as well as Vicky. I set myself to entertain her, to forget the woman behind me there across the room.

★　　★　　★

I called the hotel the next day; she was out. Not often one has the chance to reconsider. I had wished, the moment I heard the voice at the other end of the line, that I had not called. So I didn't leave my name, and I would not call again.

But what did it matter? I was the one making mountains out of molehills now, and why? Only because of Fowler, damn him, Fowler and my own imagination. These people had had me as a guest, and whatever my private feelings about either of them it was only courteous to offer some nominal hospitality in return when the opportunity arose. Do that, have it over, then forget it.

I called again that evening.

'Oh, Mr. Harkness. I thought it was probably you who called.' Reserved again.

'I thought perhaps you'd let me give you dinner one evening.' Careful, casual, sounding like the stock man-about-town out of a slick magazine story.

'Oh, that's very nice of you.'

'Tomorrow?'

'That would be nice, thank you.' I had caught her off guard; she had no time to formulate an excuse.

'Seven o'clock,' I said. 'Is that all right?'

'Yes. Seven. Thank you so much.'

So quite obviously it was a case of mere courtesy on both sides. I felt absurdly relieved.

The cab driver had some trouble finding the hotel. It was a dark old building hidden away on a back street. Inside it was old-fashioned, respectable, dull, with an aged clerk at the desk and stuffed figures about the lounge. Figures out of Kipling again, surely: one stout, mustached old man who could be nothing but a retired Anglo-Indian major, nondescript elderly females with knitting. She was waiting for me there. A good number of the guests here would be permanent residents, and in any case she would attract attention. I saw curious, speculative glances as she came forward to meet me.

'What a relic,' I commented in the street. And what an odd place to find you.

'Isn't it? My father used to like it. It's been there forever, I think. He had an old uncle who lived at Benton's. So respectable and quiet, he used to say. It's that all right. I haven't been near it for twenty years, and I never stayed there, but it was the oddest thing—when Richard asked where I'd be, I said Benton's, as if I came up every week and always stopped there. I didn't even know if it had been laid flat in the Blitz or not.'

She was in the same dark dress, without a hat. 'Did you care for Charlot's? We could go there.'

'It's all quite American, isn't it? If you don't mind my saying that? I felt rather a fool—alone.'

'I don't like it much myself. Some place a little more dignified, hmm?' And as we got into the cab, 'I don't want to be . . . to seem to interfere. How is it about that business

154

now?'

In the dark I couldn't read her expression. She was silent, and then said abruptly, a thing to say and have it over, 'You're not interfering. After all, I invited you into it, didn't I? And now I'm feeling rather a fool about that, too. I said to you then, you lose perspective on things. Don't you? It was just, I felt it was so bad for Jimmy.'

'Yes, of course.'

'I suppose I'd built it up in my mind, with no one to talk to, into more than it is. When you came that time I'd just got to the place where I had to tell someone, and there you were. I'm sorry. You were very nice about it, but it was all a bit unnecessary and silly, I think.'

I started to speak but she went on quickly, determinedly. 'After that happened, I had better tell you frankly, Richard and I quarrelled about it, more than before, I mean. I thought perhaps I'd been making a thing out of it, more than it warrants. If I got away a bit, away from the country, I'd get a clearer perspective on it. That's really why I'm here. But please, if you don't mind, I don't want to talk about it.'

'Then we won't. I quite understand. Did you say the first time in three years? That really is shocking.'

'I know. Richard doesn't care much for London. He didn't want me to come. There's

155

really not much reason to come up—I've lost touch with most of the people I knew.'

'What are you finding to do with yourself—shopping?'

'No. No, actually—not much,' she said vaguely.

We went to Simpson's in the Strand, where you are left alone to enjoy an intrinsically British meal in peace without a band. 'This is nice,' she said. 'Marvelous how they've managed to keep it all practically unchanged.'

'They had a couple of bad hits in the war, I believe. Yes. But they never let the food standards slip.'

I wished to God I could stop thinking of what Fowler had said, what Fowler had said Manson had told him. And of Manson himself, the man who had written *Troth*, who, whatever else there was to know about him, good or bad, would not be, surely, an accomplished lover. It was an oddly juvenile sensation, akin to that of the very newly adolescent—self-consciously speculative, only for the one thing, about every woman and every married couple encountered. Manson, and this woman.

I went on feeling adolescent, but remembering that it was an atmosphere she created. A romanticist, Fowler had said. Nothing romantic about this, something much more primitive, but it was nothing she said or did, nothing intentional. I

156

remembered how it had been to hold her hand in the dark, during that silly affair; and she knew it, she must, for now she was withdrawing again, her little smile fading. Only me? No, it would be the same with any man.

'Would you like a drink?' I sounded brusque.

'No—yes, I will.' Her tone was faintly defiant, not of me. 'It's so long since I've been out, as you might say, socially, I'm afraid I've forgotten my manners. You'll have to overlook it. But just sherry, I think.' And when I'd given the order and the waiter was gone, 'We don't entertain much, even. When we were first there I tried to get acquainted with people, but it's been difficult. Nobody's fault, I suppose. The Paget women are a little strange, and the one time we had Colonel Bullen to tea he kept patting my hand and saying "little lady" and Richard was furious. You know the type. They don't mean anything, but... And then the Trehernes got offended—you know how important church is in the country. Not necessarily attending, but recognizing its prestige.'

'Yes?'

'Richard is an agnostic. I suppose I am, too, in a mild sort of way. There's no sense arguing about convictions, and it's bad manners with people you don't know well. But he's ... you've probably met other

157

people like that. They're tempted to take the opposite side just to, to stir up the conversation, you know? They always say, better to discuss something important than gossip about the neighbors. But it never is a discussion, it always turns out to be an argument. It was the time we had the Trehernes to dinner. He's orthodox High Church and he got quite angry at some of the things Richard said.'

'I see.'

'So...' She broke off with a small shrug as the waiter came back.

'One of the disadvantages of the country,' I said. 'In the city you can be a nonconformist in comfortable anonymity.'

'And I wasn't going to talk about it, any of it. Not exactly entertaining for you, and that's why I came to town, to get away from it for a bit.'

And then a silence fell between us. It was at first the comfortable silence of people in accord; it grew to awkwardness. Civilized people are afraid of silence, I thought. One more proof of our simian ancestry. It was absurd that I should feel this shyness, this self-awareness. I hunted for something to say. It was, I remembered suddenly, like the first time I'd taken a girl out, the same awful unsureness. Twenty years later: absurd was no word for it.

She was looking remotely over my

shoulder, but she was aware of it, too: wires between us, little nervous thin wires carrying emotion along. She said, 'Shall we play Humpty-Dumpty's game and take turns choosing subjects?' And the wires broke, we were only two near strangers sitting together, and I was thirty-six again and safe. I laughed.

'It might be a good idea.' And she answered the thought instead of the words.

'Awkward, I know. When I've—what's the phrase?—washed our dirty linen in front of you.'

'Well, I wouldn't say...'

'That it was very dirty? Perhaps not. And I *will not* talk about it. I'm sorry, I seem to...'

'King Charles's Head,' I said.

'Or Looking-Glass Country,' she smiled.

We both recovered from self-consciousness (if that's the word for it) after that, and began to talk sensibly. It was the first time we'd really talked together. And I began to feel more and more uneasy. Frightened, perhaps.

This was the first time since Betty I'd felt so interested in a woman, so—concerned, I think is as good a word as any—with a woman. Not in the way of a little light entertainment, but for something real. And she was someone else's wife and, damn Fowler, I thought she was a good wife.

Well, we talked. She asked questions about America and about my job. And presently we got on to books, for she said there wasn't

159

much else to do in the country but read, and it was lucky she was a reader anyway. I wasn't surprised to find her better read than I was. She said the difficulty was finding something new, and stupidly, not following her thought, I said, 'I suppose there isn't a very good library nearby.'

'Oh, I didn't mean that. I meant most fiction is so much alike. The same people and plots. You know the story from the first chapter, if you've read much.' And then she laughed. 'But, of course, there are only a certain number of basic human motivations to make plots, aren't there? I suppose, whether we like the idea or not, we're all types of one sort or another.'

'Yes. To some extent that's so,' I agreed. Only a certain number. Love, hate, lust, jealousy, greed, that was about it. 'Yes,' I said again with a smile, 'I sometimes think the largest part of a novelist's work must lie in covering up the fact that he's writing a novel that's been written a thousand times before. It always amuses me, that little announcement after the title page that these characters bear no intended resemblance to any person living or dead. What's the use of writing the book or reading it if that's true? Of course, it isn't, it can't be. However bad a novel may be, it must be based on life.'

'Sometimes the announcement is quite right, though. You wonder if the author has been living on Mars, to think people behave like that. There's . . .' she mentioned a recent widely discussed American novel condemned for obscenity, praised for frankness. 'Presumably, the man has met a few women, but the women in his book are ridiculous, impossible. No woman since the beginning of time felt such things, did such things, for the reasons he describes. Women simply aren't like that.'

'I agree with you there, but other parts of the novel are extraordinarily good. No writer can see clearly into everything and every type of character. Something of himself gets in, not necessarily in his characters or plots, but the kind of thing he chooses to write in the first place.'

'Yes, of course, I see.' She was interested, suddenly smiling, half mischievous. 'That's true. A writer tells more than he knows, or intends to, about himself sometimes. You're an idealist, for instance. It comes through every word you ever write. Did you know? Funnily enough, so is the author of that rather disgusting book we just mentioned. Even though you know better intellectually, so to speak, you want to believe that people, especially women, are essentially good and kind.'

'Oh, I don't think you can judge about me,' I said, slightly embarrassed. 'I don't write fiction.'

'Only *he* is young enough to get very angry because they aren't always, and you're just, oh, gently resigned. The difference probably is that you have a sense of humor.'

'Why "rather disgusting"?' I asked, ignoring that. 'Because it's full of frank talk about sex? Censorship is an insidious thing. Begin by censoring out the words you see chalked up on fences, and before you know it the censorship's extended to politics, religions, and every other controversial subject there is, if there are any others.'

'Oh, yes, I agree with that in theory. I didn't say disgusting because of the sex, of course,' she said thoughtfully, 'but on account of his preoccupation with it.'

'Oh, but that's not him,' I said. 'It's the set of characters he was working with. You can't hold the writer responsible for the behavior of his characters. His job is only to report on them.'

'I can hold him responsible for the kind of people he chooses to write about,' she retorted. 'And it can be argued, you know, that he's preoccupied with sex himself or he wouldn't write about characters who were, too.'

'Well, you mentioned the few basic motivations,' I reminded her. 'You can hardly deny that that's one of them.'

Her silence before speaking again suddenly broke the impersonality of discussion; both of us were abruptly aware of ourselves once more, our separate entities and the joint entity created briefly between us, and suddenly the repetition of the one word loomed monstrous, suggestive, a genie over the table.

'Oh, yes,' she said in a subdued tone. 'Yes, it is the biggest basic thing, after all, of course.'

CHAPTER SIXTEEN

The little constraint was somewhat dispelled by the waiter, who was assiduous. Gradually, perhaps from the small glow of sherry or only that she was dining out in London after the years of country, she was gayer; our talk was more spontaneous. I was startled at myself, later, to find I was talking to her about my home, my family—reminiscing, maudlin, eager; I did not remember how or why I had begun, and apologized.

'But why? So you're what's called a second-generation American, with your father emigrating there. I've never been in Scotland, but...' And then she checked herself.

I just saved myself from finishing the sentence for her. 'Yes, your mother was Scottish, wasn't she?' And what would she have said or done if I had said it?

I began hastily, at random, to talk about a new play. She said, 'It's been years since I saw a play,' and then I found the thoughtless easy words on my tongue, 'Wouldn't you like to see this one? Perhaps I can get tickets.' It brought me up short; she was not any woman, without bonds, I might be taking to dinner; it was, it had been, a matter of returned courtesy, oh, yes, but she was not any more Eve Manson there across the table. She was Manson's wife.

And available? No, damn it. I didn't believe that. But the small devilish doubt and curiosity stayed at the back of my mind, I'll admit it. It was that, and neither impulse nor thoughtlessness made me say it after all, say it deliberately, later when I had taken her back to the hotel and we stood at the door making polite good nights.

'If you haven't an engagement, couldn't I try to get tickets for *Ashes of Roses*? Tomorrow night, perhaps.' So never afterward could I say, it was not my fault, I never thought, it was only accident. I had thought before speaking (but perhaps incoherent a little? Perhaps).

She had her hand out, to leave me. There in the stuffy respectable lounge of that stuffy respectable hotel (the Anglo-Indian and the knitting ladies had disappeared upstairs) she looked at me. Nameless knowledge went between us. It was her decision and the answer she made would be a definition of relationship, now and to come, as my question had asked. No, you're very kind, but I have an engagement. A lie; I did not think she had any friends here now, any plans for any day. The formal euphemism for, I think no further, under the circumstances, or, I'd love to, of course.

Once again, I'd taken her off guard. She hesitated. As if to gain time she opened her bag, groping for her key, for a handkerchief. The usual feminine jumble. I saw a little folder of snapshots, the child and the dog. She said, head still bent, 'I don't think—' and then looked up again with odd defiance in her eyes and defiance not for me. 'Why not? Yes, why not?' That was half to herself. She put out her hand.

'Thank you, I'd like that very much. Good night, Mr. Harkness.'

'I'll call you and let you know. Good night.'

I took her to the theater the evening after that. It was as if, I thought afterward, her one decision absolved us both of all future hesitancies. The first time had been perfectly proper by most standards, the returned courtesy; anything more was not. But having overstepped bounds it seemed that tacitly we had taken the decision for all other times as well as this one, and it was casually I asked her, 'What about a drive down the river tomorrow? We could fetch up somewhere for tea.'

And her reply as casual, 'That'd be nice.' We were standing in the lobby smoking between acts; she was glancing about the crowd. 'You know, I feel like a country cousin after so long away ... the clothes.'

'You'll do very nicely. Do you mind if I say how refreshing it is to see a woman who doesn't seem to be trying to dispense with everything but the legal minimum of clothing?'

She laughed. 'Only the young ones, you notice, in years or mind. The rest of us know that a little mystery is far more provocative. Besides, so few women have really good—mhmm—points to expose, you know. Something ugly about shoulders, I think. They're always too fat or too bony. In fact, very few women are lucky enough to achieve the happy medium anywhere, in that respect. Look at that dowager over there, she must be seventy at least and her gown was designed for someone seventeen. And all those diamonds.'

'Perhaps she hopes the diamonds will attract if the flesh fails. She seems to have a faithful swain anyway.' The dowager was attended by a tall fair young man, assiduous.

Suddenly, watching them, Eve shuddered strongly. 'Something walking over my grave ... Yes. So that's what it comes to. Always.

You can't have the real thing, and you take the substitute.'

'Perhaps it's her son.'

'No.'

I was sorry about the play. It was an unfortunate choice, the heart searchings of a woman torn between loves for child and lover. But there was a vein of sentimentality in it which kept it from utter realism. We came out to a damp late mist, the little flurry of the few available cabs, and the laughter and talk of the theater crowd dispersing. 'Rather disappointing,' I ventured.

'A little. She's a very good actress but even she couldn't make the final choice convincing.'

'You think a woman would naturally put the child first.'

'I think *that* woman, the woman she was suppose to be, would. It would depend on the woman and the child, too, of course. Oh ...' She glanced round, and I stopped. A street singer had mingled with the little crowd in hopes of a few coppers; perhaps only an enterprising beggar, he was singing lustily in a reedy unsure tenor. 'Bee-leeve mee, if ahl those en-dear-ing yahng chahms...'

I laughed. 'That's something you don't often see anymore.' The handsome young man with the dowager was producing a coin while she beamed fondly, clinging to his arm. The singer doffed his cap and bowed.

167

Looking at Eve in the half light I saw tears shining wet on her cheeks. 'I'm sorry.' She was fumbling for a handkerchief. 'So silly, old songs always make me want to cry. I'm sorry, it's stupid of me.'

I took her arm. 'Even sung like that?' I asked lightly. 'Perhaps you're part Celt, like me. We always respond to bathos.'

'That's not bathos really. Simple sentiment.'

'Well, Moore was a simple sentimentalist. Would you like some supper?' Not, I thought, a place with a band, dancing, cocktails. Not tonight. That, perhaps later . . .

And that night I had ceased to be so aware of the situation between us, so nice about conventions. There passed vaguely across my mind, as I climbed the stairs to my flat, the memory of Manson saying 'I hear you've been playing friend-of-the-family.' Perfectly easy, a little amused. That was all. Quite an acceptable thing. Even if it was rather recent I supposed it could be said I was a friend-of-the-family; no reason I should not be friendly.

I came into the flat. Mrs. Bunch had been cleaning again; a lampshade was crooked and some of the books in the case were upside down. I was only amused to see *The Collected Works of John Donne* standing on its head. That lively old clergyman would not mind. But I turned *The Golden Bough* right side up,

168

restoring Frazer to his accustomed dignity. I wandered into the bedroom and began to undress, whistling softly to myself.

That little defiance in her eyes ... defying Manson, or only the dull quiet years in the country? She would never fit in the country. Something too elegant, too smooth, for the tweed existence. And yet not all sophistication either, not by any means. Old songs always make me want to cry ... not bathos, simple sentiment. Moore. Celts, I had said: not altogether. She was right in a way. What was called good music—that was an expensive hotel, excellent service, everything smooth and right. The old songs—that was home. Interesting metaphor, I must remember it. And abruptly, appropriately, I recognized the tune I was whistling, the doleful little minor tune out of the past.

Roy's wife of Aldivalloch, Roy's wife of
    Aldivalloch,
Ah, that lass, she cheated me as we
    came down the braes of Balloch...

My father used to sing it, along with others he remembered from his Lowland boyhood.

She vowed, she swore she loved me
    best, she said she loved me best of
    ony,
But ah, that faithless fickle quean, she's

169

ta'en the carl and left her Johnny!
Roy's wife of Aldivalloch...

It was obvious, of course, that Fowler had
been talking nonsense. Only because a
woman was beautiful. So very beautiful.
Nothing in it at all, except perhaps that she
was lonely a little. She would be, of course.
Country. Manson not the kind to be
companionable with a woman. A little holiday
in London. You came up to town expecting
to see friends, go about with them.

And ach, she was a canny quean, and
    weel could dance the Hieland
    walloch...
Happy I, had she been mine or I been
    Roy of Aldivalloch...
Roy's wife of Aldivalloch...

I took her along the river that next day,
idling down the Thames valley, a pleasant
drive through the soft green country, the
pretty miniature villages. We stopped in one
of them for tea. Today there was another
subtle change in her, in the quality of
exchange between us; I thought we shared a
sense of freedom. For a while we were
escapees from the order of things, and
unbidden there was guilty gaiety in our
behavior.
    'This is ridiculous, you know. You come to

town for urban atmosphere and I take you into the country.'

'But it's the thing to do in London. Besides, this isn't country like Cornwall, not wild. I can't imagine it ever was.' Then she exclaimed, 'Oh, but how hideous!' There were rows of new housing just beyond the village to the left, smug, ugly developments, the houses cheek by jowl with each other.

'Don't be a snob. Think of all the people who are desperate for places to live.'

'But it's so shortsighted of the government. Think of the American tourists. You'd think there could be some concession to esthetics. They needn't put up corrugated-tin garages.'

'The government,' I said, 'isn't interested in esthetics, only efficiency.'

'The Socialist trend, I suppose. God knows we hear enough about utility. Am I treading on your political convictions, by the way?'

'Ma'am, I was raised by a country-gentleman landowner with strong Presbyterian principles.'

'Oh, good. Did someone say that Socialism is the panacea of little men, or did I make it up?'

'I don't identify it at the moment. My father used to say that Socialism is like the single standard of morals. It sounds like a wonderful idea but human nature being what it is, it never works out in practice.' She laughed delightedly at that.

We came back to London through beginning dusk and dined at an odd little place in Soho. And when I drew up before the hotel I said, 'Shall we go to the opposite extreme tomorrow? Something very city? Dinner and dancing?'

'Wonderful.' And that marked another change. Just possible, an afternoon drive in the country with a friend, but this somewhat different, somewhat more. At the moment it did not matter. A logical process of events. Nothing in it at all, of course.

But that next night, when I came back to the flat, very late, my reflection in the glass faced me accusingly as I emptied my pockets of silver, cigarettes, keys, unknotted my tie. Well, Harkness, how long ago was it you were boasting you'd never got yourself involved with someone else's wife? Not what you'd call involved, is it? And my mind retorting defensively: no question of anything like that. Really, Harkness, these euphemisms. Are you telling me you feel nothing but friendship for the woman? Friendship! No, I can't honestly say that, of course. Exactly. You're not in polite company now, you can be honest. Or can you, Harkness? You want that woman, don't you, you want her like hell. I will not be cross-examined like this. Certainly. Of course, she's a lovely woman. I'm not senile, am I? Any man. Purely primal instinct.

172

Freud's Id saying, 'I want.' Film stars, professional beauties, any good-looking woman. It means nothing. We are civilized self-controlled people in this century, aren't we (some of us anyway)? We can't help the first primitive reaction but that doesn't mean we *do* anything about it.

Oh, I see, you took her out to dine on Monday and driving Tuesday and dancing tonight perhaps thinking familiarity would cure you of desire. Correction: not exactly dancing, to a restaurant with a band. Oh, I see, a good deal of difference there, of course. You needn't be so damned sarcastic. Well, you danced with her, didn't you? That was very helpful, wasn't it, as a cure. Having her close against you that way and her mature red mouth so close and her scent (something musky and elegant) and her hand warm and slim in yours. Will you be quiet! Was it helpful, Harkness? It must have been, or you wouldn't have suggested meeting tomorrow. You wouldn't have dared.

I turned away from the mirror angrily and stripped off my jacket, but the voice went on mockingly in my mind.

Always been a respectable character, haven't you? No mess, no entanglements. Always women like Vicky if you looked around. Pleasant women, single women who take an adult view of it. Adult. Never quite got rid of that Presbyterianism, have you,
173

Harkness? You still put them the other side of that line along with the harlots. Victorian of you, isn't it, but you can't help it. You know what it is about this, don't you, if you will for a moment be honest and stop shutting your mind to it. Why you deliberately got involved—because you needn't have, you know. It's what Fowler said; still that hopeful curiosity at the back of your mind (yes, I said hopeful) that just maybe he was right and she does belong that side of the line. And in that case...

Well, she doesn't. Don't you think I'd know by now? But you're not sure, either way. She needn't be either, you know. Dangerous. And you both know it. Not right. And you both know it. It's too bad, Harkness, but you can't help being respectable. She is another man's wife. Manson's. Manson is an irritating little neurotic. Manson and his damn' fool witch's curse, when he is married to a woman like this one. Well, he's had her for twelve years; the first fine careless rapture might fade a little in that time. It never would, with her.

But—but, Harkness? She needn't, tonight, have been so provocative, so deliberately inviting. Oh, just the nuance, just the hint, but it was there. So perhaps, after all...

So what do you do about it? Try it out? Chance it? That's a fine idea, respectability your middle name when you think about a

174

thing like that, the wife of an old acquaintance. What a nice tangle that would be, either way ... yes or no. But you're trying to look at it as if there were no more than that concerned, no emotion but the one crude emotion. Not true. Not just a married woman: Eve.

You know another thing. She was quite right. You *are* something of an idealist. You want her, but you would be a little disappointed to find you could have her. Afterward, anyway.

'Oh, damn,' I said aloud. I got up, switched on the light, and went to get something to read.

CHAPTER SEVENTEEN

And that next afternoon—I was really skimping my office work scandalously—we went to an exhibition at a dealers' gallery, admired a little, said irreverent things about the abstractions, and had a leisurely tea at a ` place where the atmosphere, intensely antique, relied on high-backed settles and dim lighting. And there in the intimacy of what the settles made a private enclosure, once more small constraint grew between us. I had asked casually, 'Where shall we have dinner, and is there anything you'd like to see or do?' and then suddenly I was thinking, but that is what I might have said if we were husband and wife sitting here: a thing taken for granted, we are together. Her silence told me she heard the same tone.

Gaining time again: 'I'd like to go back and change.' A decision, suddenly, to make over again; we were back at the same place as five nights ago. No, not quite the same place, for now there was familiarity between us of gesture, laughter, turn of phrase. I wondered if she felt it too, if there came a time in the growth of every such relationship when one was at once familiar and strange. The impersonal wonder, how did I come to be here, this place in time, with you? No going back, and for us, above all, no admitting that this was anything out of the way.

There had been no mention of Manson's name or the child's, no reminiscences but those of childhood, little talk of our real selves; as if time were suspended for us a little and we were the only people in this part of it. Now for a flash the outside crowded in on us again and, whether she felt it too or not, for a panic-stricken instant we were venal wife and deliberate philanderer.

Then I said, 'All right, I'll leave you at the hotel and come back about half-past seven, and we'll have a fashionable late dinner—Ransome's again? And go on somewhere else.' She nodded, smiling, and the moment was gone, but a faint shadow lay across her expression and the returned uneasiness stayed in my own mind.

We went on from the restaurant to a new supper club on the way to Richmond, where there was an American band and a bad cabaret. We did not stay long. 'It's another thing you're supposed to do in town, but like you I don't care much about it. Such a waste of energy, I always think. Look at them, the entertainers working themselves to death and the customers doing the same thing to pretend they're being entertained.'

'Helps them avoid thinking,' I agreed. 'And always a few objectionable drunks. Let's go. We'll take a long way back, it's a nice night.'

And on the drive back in the dark, after a little, silence fell on us again and constraint, so that when I stopped the car before the darkened hotel neither of us spoke for a moment or made a move to begin good nights. Without volition I dropped my hand from the wheel and covered her right hand. It was cold, and it trembled a little. I knew the feel of it, I had held it before, slender and soft, and I knew the look of it now, white and smooth with rose-pale nails. I heard her breathing quick and uneven: still the silence held. I let go of her hand and turned and pulled her hard against me, bent and found her mouth. And this was the reason for all of it, Cornwall and seeing Manson again and that whole silly business of Manson. It was the reason and the question and the answer at once and all that was important now or forever.

*   *   *

Her mouth moved under mine and moved on my name. She was straining up to me desperately, fiercely, her arms tight around me. I did not know how long I'd been kissing her or how often, only that we had not spoken nor had breath to speak. Her whole body was pressing on me, demanding, offering, and I thought I must take her now, here, insofar as I could think at all, such a fury of desire possessed us, twin hungers that must be fed, and no time to ask why, nullifying all the centuries of civilization in a breath.

Through a dull roaring of silence in my ears, as our mouths broke apart then, she was murmuring, I felt the words against my cheek, pushing me a little away.

'No, no, better not here. Oh, my God. Listen. Listen to me.'

'Yes.'

'Five minutes ... follow me in. If anyone asks—the clerk—you're a friend of Major Blount's. It's the first room on the right, the second floor.'

And the straining hunger again until she

178

pulled away panting, whispering, 'Oh, God, oh, God, I can't ...' and fumbled the door again. 'Soon ...' and then she was gone and I took hold of the door and found I was shaking violently. Nothing like this had ever happened to me before. My mind was quite blank for what seemed a long time and then it said to me slowly, something you thought, about civilized self-controls: never found out altogether—like this—what a very thin veneer it is, and it is now time to follow her in.

I got out of the car and remembered to lock it. It was very dark in the street. She had left the door a little ajar for me; if there was a night clerk on duty he would not see it, might even be asleep at the desk. I went in quietly.

The clerk was not asleep. He was standing behind the desk, a look of concern on his face. And Eve was leaning against the counter, head bent.

'Are you all right, Mrs. Manson? Dear, dear, I am so sorry, they rang up just after you'd gone out.'

She raised her head and saw me then. She was very white. My mind began to come back to me a little and I went up to her.

'It's Jimmy,' she said numbly. 'Richard phoned in a message. Something's happened to Jimmy—he just said an accident—hurt—hospital—I must come.'

And suddenly, with that, everything dissolved into normality; it was weirdly commonplace. I heard myself say, 'A train, I'll drive you to the station.' The clerk clucked commiseratingly, groped under the desk. 'I've a schedule here somewhere, sir, what a pity, Mrs. Manson, which station would it be? Oh, I'm afraid there's not a train this late from Paddington, it'd have to be the seven-forty A.M., Mrs. Manson.'

'I must go,' she said. 'I must get back to him. I was such a fool to leave him. Such a fool.' She took hold of my arm and there was nothing any more of passion in her touch, only another kind of desperation.

'John, please, help me to get back to him, now.'

'Of course, I'll drive you down,' I said at once. It was lucky, I thought, I had stopped to fill up the car on our way home. No London garage would be open this late at night. 'Are you all right to go upstairs and pack? We can make it by late morning. Can you do that?'

'I'm quite all right,' she said, stepping back from me. 'Thank you. I'll go and pack. I won't be ten minutes.' She did not take the lift, but hurried up the dark stairs.

'Dear, dear,' said the old clerk. 'Is that her little boy? I do hope it's nothing serious...'

I sat down in the chair by the desk and got out a cigarette. I was hot and sweating in my coat, but my fingers were icy. I took off the coat. I had not experienced anything to kill the passion in me at one stroke, as the news had done for her; it took discipline of mind to put it off from me, and I sat quiet, forcing myself to finish the cigarette, vaguely aware that the old man was talking, my own voice answering, while my heartbeat slowed to normal. It seemed a very short time later that she came, with an old-fashioned large suitcase; I got up to take it from her, waited while she paid her bill, and then we were in the street again and alone but there was nothing of the same feeling. That might have been ten years ago. This was a different place in time.

I said as I started the car, 'I'll stop by my flat and pick up a few things. Is that all right? Ten minutes.'

'Yes, of course,' impatiently. I glanced at my watch in the dim light; it was just half past twelve. 'I shouldn't have come away,' she said. 'I shouldn't have left him.' She was sitting upright, tense, staring ahead.

I almost snapped at her, don't be a fool. Overanxious silly mother. Plenty of people to look after a child, and quite as competent as you. Yes, the inevitable resentment now: deprived of something I wanted. I said nothing, and then, 'It's no good to think that or get into a state about it before you know what's happened. You're not doing any good that way, to him or yourself.'

'No.' But she did not relax.

'Didn't the message say anything definite?'

'Just an accident. The wall,' she said. 'The road, people always drive too fast there.'

'Now stop that. You're only tearing yourself to pieces imagining things.'

'I know. But he's all I have,' she said. 'All I have in the world.'

Neither of us spoke again for some time. I drove across town to my flat, said, 'I won't be long.' She only nodded. When I came back some minutes later with a hastily filled bag she was still sitting erect, tense, facing ahead.

I got into the car beside her. 'You can't go on like this all the way to Cornwall, you know. There's no sense in it. Sit back and relax.'

'All right.' But she did not, immediately. She took the cigarette I offered, but continued to sit forward, smoking rapidly, while we wound our way out of the city. There was little traffic at this hour, but the narrow streets and turnings slowed our pace. Then at last we began to draw away from the suburbs, and were on the westward road, dark and open, and I could drive faster; and then she gave a sudden long sigh, leaned back in the seat, and began to talk in a low dreamy voice.

'I think I owe you an apology,' she said. 'I don't know. I wonder if I would have, if I could have. I'll never know now. But I don't think so. It was like that the other time, all

182

the other times. You don't know how to bear it but somehow you do. Somehow.

'I remember when I first read the *Decameron*, I thought it was such an odd phrase to use, maybe the translation isn't literal, I don't know, but one of the elegant euphemisms in some of the stories is that they solaced themselves with one another until the morning. But it's quite right, solace. It means comfort, sympathy, help, doesn't it. Something given when you need it so desperately, so damnably ... but then you find it's something you can't take. Like dying of thirst and someone giving you a glass of water and knowing there's cyanide in it.

'I wish to God I was like her. No, I don't, it's only those bad times. I was so afraid I was like her, that was it, I thought it was true. But, you said it, tear yourself to pieces over imagining things, it isn't people like her who do that, it doesn't worry them at all because they're—what's the word—amoral. It's the rest of us who do that. Caught between the front and back gates to hell. Did I read that somewhere? It doesn't matter.

'You know about her, don't you? About my mother. I thought when I stopped being Eve Henrys nobody need know, who would connect me with her, but it's odd how a thing like that follows you. They hanged her but she's not dead, she'll never be dead while I'm alive. I know you know. Most of the people

183

who know me know. It hangs on. And I have never talked about it to anyone before. I didn't think I could. I don't know why I am now.'

I said, 'Talk about it. Say it all and be rid of it.'

'I never knew her well. It wasn't that. She used to come into the nursery, when I was little, once in a long while, I remember. It was exciting, she was so beautiful. I couldn't understand why Nanny didn't like her. When I was ten and Nanny was let go and I was with my father more, I found out about that. And that all mothers weren't like her, just coming to see you once in a while.

'It wasn't that he didn't mind. The lawyers said that sounded bad, at the trial, but I didn't know how to explain. He loved her. But he knew someone had to look after her. She wasn't a wicked woman. Something worse, something commoner. Irresponsible, weak. For nearly thirteen years I have hated my own face in every mirror because it's like hers. She was a beautiful woman, they said. I don't know, only that I have hated to be like her. It's your face and your body, and if you're a woman there's a million years of instinct to look after it and make it attractive—it's your capital. If I dared, if I had the courage, I would let it go, even make myself ugly. They wouldn't look at me then the way they do. Men. Perhaps if they didn't

184

it would be easier. No, I don't think so, it's a thing inside.

'It didn't mean much until I went away to school. Until I wasn't a child anymore. And then I was just finding out about myself, and liking it. When it happened. Liking myself, I mean; I did then. For a little while. I wasn't good with people, I was too shy and self-conscious, but I was finding out that I was pretty. One of the ways you learn, that isn't so much fun, is that other girls don't like you. Perhaps they thought I was snobbish. I never could talk to people. I was shy, and that always looks like rudeness.

'Of course, I knew. I said that at the trial. But she was like a stranger until that happened, and it didn't matter. Then it did, because she was my mother after all. As if I'd just realized it. And I might be like her. I was like her.

'He was afraid of that. Things he used to say, the way he looked at me sometimes. I loved him, him and Nanny. Always so kind. He smoked a pipe, and he liked to play at bowls. He belonged to a local club. He used to call me Pet when I was little. She thought he had much more money than he had really, that was why. I believe she'd forgotten about me entirely. But that was when I really remembered about her. That I was her daughter.

'I thought then I was like her. That I might

185

be. Little things, by then I'd been kissed a few times, and the way I felt, the things I thought about, wanted to do ... I'd thought I was in love once and then I met someone else and was in love with him. Oh, I was like her. I was her daughter.'

The straight black ribbon of road was rushing at me too fast. I slowed a little. My voice was angry. 'For God's sake. For God's sake. You were eighteen.'

'Oh, I know now. It was then. And everyone looking at me and wondering. The lawyers. I saw it in their eyes. Those men of hers at the trial. *Looking* at me. And afterward. There wasn't anyone I could go to. They wouldn't take me in any of the jobs I applied for, I'm not trained, and I'd got run down. And there wasn't much money after all. So I married Richard. That was really why.'

'What the hell do you mean by that?'

'He was there,' she said. 'I was so young. Oh, my God, I was so young.'

For a little then she was silent, and I did not speak, fearing to remind her too forcibly of my presence; it was as if she was talking to herself in the dark there beside me.

'I didn't know. How could I know? He was there, he wanted me, I thought. I thought, escape, and I would not, I would not be like her, I would not let myself. There'd be a home, children, to save me. I didn't know about Richard. That he had a reason, too.'

And almost in a whisper, coming closer to the core of this thing now, afraid to startle her into silence, I repeated, 'He had a reason, too?'

'He had to prove he was normal,' she said. 'That's as good a word for it as any. He was twenty-four and I don't think he had ever... Sex isn't anything to him. One way or another. No. He resents its being there, because it belittles him, because he can't always. And that's what he found out. I don't know why, there'd be some reason a psychologist could give, about that. I don't know. Just how he is.'

Oh, yes, there will be a reason. Brought up mostly by a strange, probably prudish spinster. Tremendous lack of confidence. And that deep inner resentment against women: and that all the deeper because women are no use to him, or he to them. Yes, I thought, a reason, all right.

'Once in a long while,' she said. 'It was all he wanted, be able to say my wife, pictures to show. So everyone would know he was a man among men—with a wife. A pretty wife. But that's all. The real part of it, only once in a long while. Not since Jimmy was born, now. Just enough, you see,' and her voice dropped lower on that, 'just enough, just at first, so I ... could guess, about myself. To put me between those two gates, and so after a while

187

I began to think all over again that I was like her.'

A faint, late sickle of moon was showing now. We were long out of Surrey, and the road was turning truer west; it came rushing at me like a thin black arrow out of the dark and I dared not look at her.

'There were other men—always there, looking at me. I was frightened. If I'd had a child—I kept hoping for that. I wanted it so much. Something real, something important to *be* for. It wouldn't be enough, but something, a good deal. But then, the very worst thing happened. I fell in love with someone—really.'

CHAPTER EIGHTEEN

I could no longer listen to her too-calm voice, disembodied, telling a stranger's story unasked, perhaps unaware. Nightmarishly, I wasn't sure I was there at all, that this was not a thing in a dream sequence, tearing through the dark and a ghost talking beside me. I said sharply, loudly, 'That was bound to happen. Bound to. People do.' And I knew the name. I almost said it.

'He was no good. That was the difference. After a little I knew that, but you don't stop loving like turning off a tap. I was so frightened, so frightened. She has haunted me for thirteen years, shaming—even when I knew what he was, I wanted him so terribly. And nothing, no one to hold me from it if I wasn't strong enough myself. Like her, only she had no moral sense. It was easy for her. I must have that from him, and all the rest from her.'

'You're talking nonsense,' and my voice was still loud, indignant. 'Heredity! In a thing like that? It's meaningless. You've carried a burden of guilt too long, for something not your fault at all. For God's sake, get rid of it, talk it out, forget it. A perfectly normal woman. It's him, not you. Only normal, natural. Only one of those things. It happens. You've let it haunt you as well. Stop it now, while there's time and you still have your sanity.'

'I know. I try to think that. Most of the time I know it. I lose perspective. The bad times, when I try to describe it, the way I might put it in a book, you know, I say it's wanting. I find all sorts of phrases for it: desire, I say, passion. But it's not like that. That's not the worst. It's the terrible wanting to give, the need to give, and nobody at all to give to . . .

'He was killed then, in a car accident. That was bad, too. I kept remembering, I kept feeling, but then I knew there was going to be a child, and that helped. It was all right then for a long time. More than all right. Ever since it's been the one thing.'

I stopped the car, not even troubling to pull to the roadside, turned and took her by the shoulders hard. 'Like a cancer inside, growing and eating at you,' I said angrily, 'because you've kept it inside, this absurd guilt, this absurd fear. Don't you see you've created it all yourself?'

But she was not listening or looking at me. 'Where have we got to? It looks like the end of the world.' The dying moon showed the land desolate, colorless all about. We were, I saw, somewhere in the middle of Dartmoor.

'Listen to me, don't you see? You must break out of it, you should have done that long ago. All of it is essentially his fault. There's nothing with him for you, for you or the boy. Leave him, for God's sake, get yourself away from him, into life again, the only way you can be free...'

'Will you let me go, please,' she said remotely. 'Please, may I have a cigarette?' In the little flame of the lighter her face was calm, cold, white. 'We had better get on, hadn't we?'

I started the car again, not trusting myself to speak.

'That's a thing I can't do either. I know that now. And because of her, too. I came to London to be away from him and decide. Not the first time I'd thought about it, but this time, longer, more. So I came away to think it out. We'd had a quarrel. We don't often. I don't quarrel easily. But there's a kind of block—that's the right word, isn't it—against all that in me somewhere. The mess. The legal tangle. The talk. It would all come out again: Margaret Henrys' daughter in divorce court. And more than that. It isn't just for fun,' she said, 'this business of being here. Not just to please yourself. It's got to be for something or there isn't any meaning in it. There was a woman I knew like that. Others, too. Too many people. But I always think of Alice Chadwick about that.'

'A malicious bitch,' I said.

'Oh, you've met her. She's not really. I liked Alice. I used to. But she left her husband, divorced him, just because she was bored with him—he wasn't fun anymore— and married someone else. And I never could feel the same about her, anyone who did a thing like that. Like my mother, irresponsible. It's not all for fun, icing on the cake. You've got to have something solid. I've got that, I've got Jimmy. That's my icing, and the rest of it, too. You can't walk out on a way of life just because you don't like it. You're there, you've got a job to do there. You're not a child to say, I'm tired of this, and go away and do something else just for fun.'

'Guilt, guilt, guilt,' I said, striking the

191

wheel in futile gesture. 'Turning you into a masochist now: my life's a failure, it must be all for the child, penance for sin.'

'Oh, no,' she said tranquilly. 'I don't think so. I came to London thinking I might. It would have been difficult. I've only about a hundred a year my father left me. And Jimmy. But I thought perhaps ... I tried to think it out, but you didn't give me a chance. I don't think you meant it, you're not that kind, are you? Women, but not someone else's woman. I shouldn't have gone with you, I knew that. It was the other time all over again, but better. All the other times. I'm not even sure why I did go with you. Being angry at Richard. Thinking about it. Yes, liking you, too.

'But now. Just now, I see it isn't possible, because it isn't right, and if it isn't right that makes me into her, just as I was always so afraid of, and I'd have nothing anymore at all, even what I've got now, because I'd have lost myself and any integrity I have.'

I said nothing for a very long time, to discipline the anger in myself. When I could speak objectively I said, 'As long as you are thinking so unselfishly, a kind word for it, why not consider Manson, too? He is just as unhappy with you.'

'Oh, no. He doesn't know at all. It means nothing to him, I told you that.'

'Don't be a fool,' I said roughly. 'He

192

behaves that way, but that inability strikes at the core of a man, whatever kind of man he is. Without you to remind him . . .'

'It's none of it Richard's fault. He can't help it. It would be turning my back on him only because things hadn't come out quite as I expected. Nothing he's done or not done, of his own will. More my fault than his, because I never loved him. Never. I married him to have a home and children, to build a life for myself, something to *be* for, some solid center to life. So it was my fault to start with. I cheated him you see . . .

'I have never talked to anyone like this. Too late to be sorry now, but I am. We've said all there is to say, and we'll never mention any of this again, please.'

'I'll keep on saying it,' I told her grimly. 'Surely you know that he believes you have been unfaithful.'

'I wonder what makes you say that. No, I'm afraid Richard is only impatient with me and sometimes, worst of all, amused. The way he is, he can't understand. And that doesn't matter either.'

I swallowed quick words; she did not know, how could she not know? But I could not tell her.

'Don't,' she said. 'Don't talk anymore. I've finished. I can't go on about it any longer, there's nothing more to say. Only—I'm sorry.'

No, there was nothing more to say. Around and around. Foolish, generous, self-sacrificing woman.

'I'm sorry. All I'm thinking of now is Jimmy. Please, can you drive a little faster?'

Neither of us spoke again until the sky was paling with gray dawn, and through the mist ahead pierced the square pointing finger of a tower, and she asked, 'What's that?'

I said briefly, 'Truro Cathedral. Forty minutes.'

*   *   *

I had not, under the circumstances, given any thought to how it would be, meeting Richard Manson again.

I stood in the middle of his sitting room and debated with myself. She had said nothing more to me at all; the sleepy maid admitting us, she had hurried off upstairs at once. Curiously, I didn't resent it. The maid had vanished, too, presumably to dress. I was tired, but not sleepy; I fumbled for a cigarette and wondered if I had not better go to the inn. Every time I'd come here and gone away, thinking it was the last. No reason to stay. Every reason to go.

The room was chilly, no fire laid so early. I kept my coat on. I sat down in the largest armchair, yawning. I would finish this cigarette and then leave, go down to The

Drowned Man and see if they could give me breakfast.

I woke abruptly, startled awake, and Manson was standing above me. Manson in a wild-patterned silk dressing gown, smoking a cigarette, smiling slightly, and every hair in place, freshly shaven, neat. I sat up with the instinctive resentment of a sleeper observed, feeling foolish, unkempt and dirty.

'Good morning, Johnny,' said Manson. 'Nice of you to run Eve down from London. There wasn't a train? Or maybe you were out with her when I rang up?'

'I ... no,' I said. 'Or rather, yes.' Damn him. I stood up. 'She was worried about Jimmy.'

'Ah,' said Manson. He strolled over to the nearest chair, sat down, deposited ash neatly in the clean ashtray beside him. 'I was sorry to interrupt her holiday. The boy's all right now, but at first we weren't sure, you see. Dyck was afraid of pneumonia, complications. And he kept asking for mother—James, that is. I thought I had better.'

'But what happened?'

Manson frowned, as if he had to think, as if the question interrupted another train of thought. 'Pigeon's Pond. He got into Pigeon's Pond. My aunt was out with him walking. The dog went in after a stick or something, and the boy went in after the dog. It's quite deep. My aunt loses her head in a crisis, but fortunately there was a fisherman passing on the road. He came up and got the boy out. He had a bad wetting and a little fright, but he seems quite all right now, though Dyck said to keep him in bed.'

'I see.' Several layers of thoughts were in my mind, one above another, simultaneous. Running a hand over my jaw: dirty, disheveled, ought to shave. Manson so damnably smooth and clean. But, might have been a real tragedy, the boy. Yet he was not now indulging in any self-blaming anxiety. Because it was all over? Eve. This man: no, not even that.

'You'll want some breakfast, Johnny,' said Manson. He sat, legs crossed, smiling, swinging one foot negligently. And now, of course, it was catching up with me, the rest of it, and a hot wave of self-conscious embarrassment was flooding over me. Still quite respectable, Harkness, after a fashion, when you cannot look a man in the eye because you have kissed his wife.

'No, really, I can't trouble your people at a time like this. I was going in any case. Please don't feel ...' Babbling, and Manson so at ease, cool.

'But you must stay. No, no, I insist on it. We want you to stay. The boy's quite all right, I said that. Really extraordinarily kind of you, Johnny, to take so much trouble for

Eve. I appreciate it,' said Manson gently. 'Of course you'll stay, now you're here. I was sorry you couldn't stay longer the first time, you know. You've no idea how good it is to have an old friend to keep me company. That's the worst of the country. If you don't happen to care for your neighbors, well, there's no one else, is there? Not like London, where I could hop into a cab and go to see you, or Fowler, or Brownlee, or Mercer, or Templeton—any of a dozen friends I might...'

'I beg your pardon,' I said meaninglessly.

'Advantages, too, of course. But I can't let you run away the minute you've got here. Eve would say the same. And you do need breakfast after that drive. But first a bath and rest. Come upstairs. We'll find you a room. Elsie! Damn the woman. Never about when you want her... You must have made good time. When did you leave town? Oh, really. Very good indeed, considering.'

I followed him unwillingly as far as the hall. 'Really, I feel I'm imposing.'

'Nonsense, old boy, how could you do that? Did you come away without a bag? I can lend you ... oh, in the car. Elsie, there you are. Will you go and fetch Mr. Harkness's bag from his car, please, and bring it up. The same room you had last time, that'll do. Imposing? Of course not, you must stay as long as you can this time.'

I gave in for the moment. There was nothing else to do. I would be glad of a bath and rest, but even more immediately I wanted to be rid of Manson, his voice at my elbow, neat nervous little man being friendly. Friendly?

But Manson did not leave me at the bedroom door; he came in, wandering over to the window, lighting another cigarette. I stood waiting for him to go away. And now Manson stopped talking and stood with his back turned, smoking rapidly. The maid came with the bag.

'You're thinking I'm taking it too casually,' said Manson suddenly. 'I wasn't last night, believe me. My God, what a time. We couldn't reach Dyck. The boy had one chill after another. I really thought ... Ironic, you know, a senseless little thing like that, Pigeon's Pond. He's never been strong, of course. Sometimes I wonder if he has good sense, too. Said he thought the dog would drown and went to get him out. A spaniel.'

'A child wouldn't know,' I said. It was evident that Manson was not going to leave immediately. I began to unpack the bag, took out my razor, sponge, a clean shirt. I felt an irrational, dreamlike conviction that the rest of my life would be a procession of arrivals at Poltressor House, unwilling, unavoidable, uneasy. I remembered then that the last time I was here I had nearly quarreled with

Manson, called him a damned fool for his superstition. No hint of memory of that in his manner now. And considering everything, why? Manson, speaking those names precise and soft. And she did not know.

'I didn't mean that,' said Manson. 'Of course. He's all I have, the boy, you know. The one thing. I suppose I seem foolish about it, obsessed. But I do believe it's a real danger. I've been experimenting, by the way. Must tell you about it. I may get results yet. You can't just sit by and do nothing.' His voice was strained.

I draped my jacket over a chair, began unbuttoning my shirt. And Manson turned to face me. He watched me undressing, and a little one-sided smile grew on his mouth; under his gaze I was swept again by embarrassment. More reason or less this time? I could not look at Manson. I knew too much about him. I knew the one thing about him, and it was suddenly, absurdly, impossible to be naked before Manson. I put on my dressing gown over my trousers.

'Bothering you with all this when you must be exhausted. You know where the bathroom is, of course. Breakfast when you come down. I'm a late riser anyway, it's never until nine. Just half past eight now. But take your time.'

'As a matter of fact, I'm not so much hungry as sleepy.' Both lies, but anything to get rid of Manson. 'I'll just...'

199

'Suit yourself.' Manson put out his cigarette, went to the door, his gaze still fixed on me, and what was in his eyes? An indefinable expression. 'Carte blanche,' said Manson, smiling. 'You must feel quite at home, you know.'

In the bathroom I faced myself thoughtfully in the glass as I shaved. Just what would it do to a man, that knowledge of himself? Every time he looked in a mirror, looked at another man. And she said, it means nothing. And damn it, Harkness, it means nothing to you. Allowing yourself to get involved with these two tiresome people. Two masochists (to use the jargon again); yes, that's part of the trouble, of course. Manson, raging at Fowler (Fowler!), but eight years ago. Manson, now, torturing himself pleasurably, dwelling on the other men. Putting my name there, too, wrongly (but only by chance, that). Five names he'd said. Templeton, yes; the others? What did it matter, five or fifty? She was Manson's wife.

Manson, of course, with those deviling twin knowledges in him, obsessed with the child, all he had. As she was, but for another reason. Not a very bright prospect for the boy.

Manson, looking at me ... I had felt indecent. Eve ... Well, some excuse there. With some women, it would not matter. Eve ... I felt her close again, warm, yielding, and

200

behind us in the glass saw Manson watching us with a little smile.

Something wrong with this house, I had thought, and no wonder. The sooner I was out of it the better.

CHAPTER NINETEEN

I slept heavily but woke comfortable—and ravenous. It was half-past twelve. I dressed and came out to the passage. Eve was just coming out of the room opposite, the nursery. She stopped when she saw me, and in the tiny space before either of us spoke another and worse awkwardness lay between us than ever before: the embarrassment of people who have shared secret confidences and primal emotions at the necessity of somehow getting back to a surface relationship. And we never could. Whether I went or stayed, whatever happened or did not happen between us, we knew each other too well now, and the awareness of it would underlie all our conventional words. I saw her reject one phrase after another, and her left hand went to clasp her right wrist in a gesture I knew, a gesture that meant she was uncertain.

Out of my own embarrassment I said the first thing that came to my mind. 'How is Jimmy?'

'Oh.' She began to smile. 'Thank you, he's going to be all right.' With that it was easy; it was with complete naturalness she said, 'Won't you come in and see him?,' and opened the door.

He was sitting up in bed, seven years old and the secret center of all this, the reason, the import: impatience and pity grew in me, seeing him. (My God, the times Alex and I fell in a dozen streams on an afternoon's exploring!) Then I thought of Eve saying, 'I try not to agonize over him,' and the pity widened from the boy to her. And Dyck saying, 'The one most valuable thing.' But not even a woman could build a life on that alone. Half a life, perhaps. Aloud I said, 'Hello, Jimmy.'

'You remember Mr. Harkness, Jimmy.'

'Oh, yes,' said the boy shyly. 'We had a ride in his car.'

'That's right. How do you feel now? You gave your mother quite a scare, you know.' How much, how uncannily, the child resembled her. Nothing of Manson. Of course. Vicky said, 'You look a little like him.' Templeton. Did that mean Templeton had been tall, or more dark than fair, or blue-eyed, or all those? But the boy was Eve.

'I'm fine now. I fell in the pond. I thought Roddy would get drowned and I went to help him and there wasn't any bottom to the pond. And Dr. Dyck said keep me in bed a day or two, didn't he, Nanny?'

'He did that and that's just where you'll stay. Going into ponds. I thought maybe a nice custard for our lunch, Miss Eve.'

'You ought to learn to swim,' I said. 'Then it wouldn't matter if you fell into a pond.'

'That's what Father said. Do you know how to swim? Father doesn't or he'd teach me, he said.'

'I could teach you, but I don't think I'll be here long enough.'

'Oh. I wonder who taught Roddy to swim. I didn't know he could.'

'Dogs don't have to be taught, they just know.'

'But I don't know if he was hurted,' said the boy fretfully. 'I wish I could see him. I wish he could come here.'

'Darling, you know Father doesn't like dogs in the house. Roddy's all right.'

'I'll tell you,' I said, 'after lunch I'll go and see Roddy for you, and maybe he'll give me a message and I'll come and tell you what he said. Then you'll know he's all right.'

'Oh, would you?'

Nanny beamed at me approvingly. 'There, what do we say to the gentleman?'

'Thank you, sir. But he couldn't give you a message, you know, because dogs can't talk.' A bit superior. I grinned at him.

'Of course they can't. I must have forgotten you're seven years old and know that.'

'I think it's silly Father doesn't like dogs in the house. Don't you think it's silly?'

'Say sir to the gentleman,' admonished Nanny. So that was where the Victorian manners came from; I might have known.

'Well,' I said carefully, 'that depends on the person, Jimmy. Some people don't and some do. I don't mind, but it's your father's house.'

The boy looked dissatisfied with that. 'I'd just want to see him for a minute. Just to see he's all right.'

'I'll come and tell you,' I promised.

Going downstairs Eve said with unflattering surprise in her tone, 'You're very good with children.'

'It's being a perennial uncle. I have several nieces and nephews.'

'Oh.' And in the entrance hall we met Dyck, just admitted by the maid. He gave me a sharp look.

'I'm sorry if it's an inconvenient time, Mrs. Manson. I thought I'd look in and see if there's any fever.'

'That's all right. I'll take you up.' She gave me a smile, turning, and Dyck turned at the landing to look back, and caught me watching her. I went into the sitting room and there, of course, were Manson and the old woman.

*   *   *

204

'It's a talent, unquestionably it's a talent,' said Manson. 'You can laugh if you want to, but some extraordinary things turn up. Of course, the great difficulty is that there's no way to guide it, you see.'

No one commented on that. Dyck, who had somewhat surprisingly accepted an invitation to stay to lunch, ate tinned ham and looked under his eyebrows at his host. I was watching Eve and wondering how it was I had not noticed the patient, strained lines about her mouth when she was here with Manson. They had not been there in London. She looked five years older. Of course, she was tired.

'After that little fiasco—not your fault, Johnny, there's no way to be sure about these people. That's just the trouble, you know—I decided it couldn't do any harm to try myself. After all, I suppose I'm better read on the subject than some professionals. My aunt and I have been sitting every evening, and, as I say, we've obtained some encouraging results. No actual manifestations . . .'

'But I have felt the presence of spirits strongly, very strongly, Richard.' The old woman was eating with little darts of her fork at the plate, glancing from side to side as if fearing too close observation of such a prosaic process. 'It is most gratifying. Perhaps soon you will achieve trance.'

'I wonder if one is conscious of that at the

time. It will be interesting—but I should beg your pardon, you must find all this quite boring. I expect as a medical man, Dr. Dyck, you scoff at spiritualism.'

'Not necessarily as a medical man,' said Dyck; his bass rang solid to Manson's tenor. 'As an intelligent man, emphatically. But I've no wish to offend you. I should, however, like to say one thing.'

'Yes?'

'It's none of my business, Mr. Manson, what you believe. But as a medical man, I should warn you that the effect of such tales on a child's mind may be harmful. I see no reason for inflicting irrational fears on the boy, as I have just been telling Mrs. Manson. The mind, you know, is a part of the body, more truly perhaps than we yet realize.'

Manson pounced on that, frowning. 'You can't mean that the mere knowledge of danger would cause illness.'

'Good God, no,' said Dyck baldly. 'Make him nervous, timid, the rest of his life, yes, possibly. Personally'—and his gaze swerved round the table blandly—'I've never approved of gruesome fairy tales for children.'

'A child is entitled to the truth,' said Manson, but he seemed disinclined to pursue the subject, for once, and Dyck did not answer that, only directing a look of vast contempt at him. An uncomfortable silence held. The old woman thinned her lips and there was startling venom in her eyes on Dyck.

I spoke only to dispel the silence. 'I must be leaving after lunch if I'm to make London tonight...' And instantly Manson pounced on me.

'But, my dear fellow, no! You must stay a few days now you're here—I thought we'd agreed on that. No, no. I won't hear of your rushing off like that as soon as you've come. God knows we see little enough company here. Can't let you desert us, Johnny. Out of the question. I know Eve agrees with me; help me persuade him, my dear, won't you? I know you're just as anxious to have him stay. More. I'm afraid I've been poor company for her lately, you know, busy over these experiments. You can keep Eve amused for me, can't you? If it wouldn't bore you too much. The country that is. Eve?'

'Yes, of course,' she said mechanically. She was staring at him, her color fading. 'Please do stay, Mr. Harkness, we'd love to have you.'

'You see,' said Manson. 'Nothing calling you back to town, is there? For the weekend at least, do.'

Nothing had been said not conventional. It was all in the tone. I saw Dyck's glance veer from Manson to Eve to myself. I said, 'You're very kind,' casting about for the easy excuse, a plausible reason.

Of course I could have pleaded business, and with enough truth. I had fully intended to, and then, when he came out with all that, I didn't. It was partly Eve's expression, I suppose. Suddenly I knew I had to stay, though I think I'd have given my soul to have been free of both of them. All of them, I should say, the child, too.

In a strange way, it seemed tied up with my sense of responsibility. And that was damned strange, too. I had a job in London. I had no business neglecting it. That was my responsibility. Yet I knew I had to stay, for some inexplicable reason.

'That's settled then. Good.'

Dyck, surprisingly again, added his bit. 'You might find Pentressor interesting, Mr. Harkness, historic landmarks and so on, if you're interested in that sort of thing. Our rector, Mr. Silver, could tell you more about the historic aspect. He's quite an antiquarian. I'd be glad to introduce you, drive you in now, perhaps, on my way. You're sure to find him in.'

'Thanks, I've met the rector, but I'm not much of a historian.' I should have been quicker with a lie. She did not want me to stay. And now, at least, she knew what was in Manson's mind. She was silent now in this group, staring at her plate. She had eaten very little.

'Why not do that?' interposed Manson. 'An excellent idea, Doctor. As a matter of fact, I was up quite late, I was hoping to get in a nap, and I daresay Eve is tired, too, aren't you, my dear? Outrageous, Johnny, shuffling you off after urging you to stay on. But you're an old friend after all. Friend of the family, I should say. You might find the church interesting; it has quite a history, I believe. And sleeping this morning you'll want some exercise or you won't sleep tonight, even in our celebrated sea air, eh? Why not drive in with Dyck and walk back for tea?'

'All right.' I was watching Eve. All three of them anxious to persuade me, though she had said nothing. 'I'll do that, then.'

'Good. And I'll tell you,' said Manson pleasedly, inspired, 'you can do a little errand for me if you will. Post a parcel. I intended to get in myself, but if you're going ... it's a manuscript, as a matter of fact. What? Oh, yes, I know I told Fowler I wasn't writing, but just to surprise him with this. I've been working on it most of the past year, actually. Let's hope he'll like it as well as *Troth*.'

'A novel?'

'Oh, yes,' said Manson, and now his eyes were on Eve, too. 'Yes, it's a novel. I rather like it and I'm anxious to hear what Fowler thinks of it. I'd be grateful if you'll see it off for me.'

I excused myself when coffee was served

and went to call the London office. Allen, my immediate junior, was sarcastic, and justifiably so. I reminded him that the traditional British weekend was upon us. There wouldn't be anything he could not handle for a couple of days, but guilt rode me for what I thought of as neglect of my job.

The only excuse I could make to myself, or to anyone else, was that against all reason I felt I had also a job to do here. That's the only way I can put it, and it didn't make much sense to me; but there it was.

CHAPTER TWENTY

Dyck's car was an aged Morris of no particular color. Dyck talked about it as if to get over the first hurdle of conversation, as we got in and he started the engine.

'I daresay I could get my name on the list for a new one, if I had the money. But I don't know that I'd want to. I've got used to this, and you'd be surprised how reliable she is. Much like people: it takes a certain amount of guts to live to seventy, say, and once you've made it you aren't going on out very easily. Old people are the tough ones. It's the youngsters who go out—like that,' snapping his fingers.

I chose to misunderstand him. 'Do you

mean you're worried about the boy? I thought . . .'

'Jimmy? Not the way you mean. To tell you the truth, I wanted to talk to you alone.' Another sharp look. 'Damned interfering of me, and possibly worse. I gather now you're a close friend of the Mansons, at least you seem to visit them often enough.'

'If you mean anything by that,' I said, my temper rubbed thin by Manson's effusive double entendres, 'I can only say . . .'

'What should I mean? Look here, let's have some plain speaking,' Dyck said roughly. 'I was short with you when you came to see me before, and I'll admit I was wrong. I thought Mrs. Manson was making dramatic capital . . .'

'And using me as a god from the machine. I gathered that.' The irrelevant reflection crossed my mind that in this affair I seemed to be leaping to intimate terms with several people at an unprecedented social pace, for me. However, at least I would get no double entendres from Dyck.

'I've never known the Mansons well. Since that business when you were here before, I've taken rather a different view of it. Regardless of what the man believes, to fill a child's mind with that nonsense! If he was feeding the boy arsenic I could do something about it, but this . . . and like most women Mrs. Manson appears unable to cope in any extraordinary

211

situation.'

I was still annoyed. The old feeling of being manipulated, not my own master. 'And just what do you think she could do about it, short of locking the boy away from his father?' His father. Ironic, Fowler had said. It was that: the Manson Curse.

Dyck shrugged. 'That's a point, of course. In any case, whatever damage there may be is done now. I gather it's been a bone of contention. There was an atmosphere today. I've no right to ask, but do you think it's made enough trouble between them, plus other things, perhaps, that there might be a separation?'

... That wasn't atmosphere, Doctor. You're tactful. It was the tone of Manson's voice, the look in his eyes, that said, 'This is a piquant situation, my guest, my wife's lover.' I realized suddenly that I was resenting it more on her account than my own. Ridiculous, considering, but here at least both of us were innocent. And if Manson went on like that before many outsiders...

I said, 'Let's have plain speaking by all means, Doctor. Probably what you mean is that you had no difficulty picking up on Manson's hints. Nor did I. I needn't insult Mrs. Manson by telling you he is, to use a soft word, mistaken.'

'Really,' said Dyck cautiously.

'So far as I know, Mrs. Manson is quite

beyond suspicion in that respect.' Damn it, I sounded pompous, but having gone so far I had to continue. 'And frankly, Manson's behavior shocked me. You don't need to be told either that whatever the truth might be it's scarcely the normal reaction.'

'That,' said Dyck, 'was what interested me.' We were in the village now. He pulled up beside the little war memorial and turned in the seat to look at me directly. 'More plain speaking,' and he grinned suddenly. 'I don't give a damn what the truth of that is. I'm thinking about the boy, and Manson. In my opinion he is not in a normal state.'

'What else did Mrs. Manson try to tell you? Or I, for that matter? Of course he isn't.'

'He's a writer,' said Dyck. 'There are different standards, I realize that.'

'My God, so am I, in a way. Don't identify the man with the job.'

'I'm not basing an opinion on his opinions,' said Dyck imperturbably, 'but on my own observation. The man's as nervous as a witch, can't sit still—probably smoking too much, and not sleeping enough. Whatever the trouble or the cause of it, he's not normal. I hadn't a chance to talk privately with Mrs. Manson. Naturally I shall try to do so, but I thought you and she together might persuade him to consult me.'

I looked down at the parcel on my lap. Manson's neat boxed parcel with the address

213

typewritten. And prominently labeled MANUSCRIPT. I wondered what sort of thing it was, if it was anything like *Troth*. I said slowly, 'I don't think he would do that, and if he did, he wouldn't tell you the truth.'

'Which is?'

'I'm not sure, or sure that he knows half of it himself. I've no right to attempt a diagnosis, as an amateur psychologist. It may sound wild, but I believe part of his trouble is that subconsciously he wants that curse to work, just to prove he's right about it. But he is, of course, obsessed with the boy, and the consequent conflict, probably all unconscious, is behind his conscious behavior.'

Dyck smiled. 'You sound like an American problem novel. Ambivalence, that's the word, isn't it? It's possible. You see some funny things. Just seeing him last night and today, I don't like his looks.'

'When you say he's not in a normal state, do you mean mentally or physically?'

'Perhaps both,' said Dyck. 'Considering his behavior at the table, he may have some reason to worry about his wife as well as the boy, you know.'

'I can only say,' I began stiffly, 'that ...' What, Harkness? Why the pompous defense? I thought you had decided to stay out, and even if Fowler exaggerated a bit he was still right.

'She's a beautiful woman.' If anyone says that again, in that tone... Not blind, am I, Doctor? 'Did you know who she was, by the way? Margaret Henrys' daughter. Remember the Henrys-Paxton case just after the war, some years ago?' Yes, Doctor, and I thought, mistakenly by all accounts, that we had in this twentieth century abandoned the superstitions of bad blood and inherited villainies.

'Would you mind telling me how you knew that?'

'I believe Treherne told me. Someone. Doesn't matter. In any case, she's not a woman I'd think would particularly enjoy the country life. Nor is Manson the type, oddly enough. Well, it's none of my business, except that she ought to think about the child more.'

It is you who are blind, Doctor. Shrewd up to a point, but your prejudice (and I wonder what your story is) blinds you to her or any woman, perhaps. She is thinking of nothing but the child; and that is her trouble. I bit back a retort. I was tired of Dyck, and opened the car door.

'Thanks for discussing it so frankly,' he said. 'Are you staying long?'

'I don't know.' Not any longer than need be. Why so vague? I was in a perverse mood.

★   ★   ★

215

It was my first real opportunity to look at Pentressor. I didn't think much of it. Approximately twenty fishermen's cottages, running in rows down the shallow cove shore under the cliffs, three or four better houses a little distance inland, The Drowned Man, three or four nondescript shops-by-courtesy, one of them housing the post office and the telephone exchange.

At the back of that shop, as I posted Manson's parcel, I noticed a shelf of lending library books and wandered over to inspect them. *Troth*, of course. The jacket dusty; I smiled. *The Constant Nymph*. Half a dozen detective novels, none of postwar vintage. Yes, what was there in Pentressor, if you did not care for your neighbors or they for you?

'Was there anything else?' Contrary to fictional tradition, the postmistress, so far from being a sharp-eyed spinster, was mountainous, supremely indifferent to me.

'Yes,' I said absently, 'have you any writing paper?' I bought a cheap packet, opened it, and on the counter scrawled a message to Fowler. One sentence: 'When was Templeton killed?' signed it, sealed the envelope, addressed it, and gave it to the woman. I stuffed the rest of the packet into my jacket pocket and came out. Before the shop I paused irresolute. I felt no interest in inspecting the church. I found it difficult to

216

feel enthusiasm even for the genuine Norman article, which this was not. Glancing at my watch I found it was far short of opening hours, but I had a notion the publican of The Drowned Man kept a sturdy Cornish independence of such matters. I walked across the road toward the inn, and on the doorstep met the rector.

'My dear fellow! What a pleasure to see you again. Surely you have not been with the Mansons all this time? I should have ... ah, I see, I see. You liked our little village, then? Just so.'

Mr. Silver at least was the very rector one expected of a village. He gave me the comforting sensation that it was curious how the dictates of popular fiction ruled some if not all of one's instinctive reactions. Why should Mr. Silver be typical? Was he the prototype of all village rectors in fiction, or a holdover from the time when a majority of such actual rectors had dictated their fictional copies? I wondered while I returned a suitable greeting.

'I was just about to attempt a violation of the law. Do you suppose the landlord would oblige us?'

'A violation. Oh, dear me, that's excellent, yes. Oblige us? My dear Mr. Harkness, Evan Meeker has never paid any notice to closing hours in my memory. He is a Welshman, you know. It is curious how all the Celts share such irreverence for law and order.'

'Well,' I said, 'for the last few centuries they've been exposed only to English law and order, and none of them has ever thought much of that. A point of honor to defy it, really. I suppose you could say it was bred in the race by now.'

'Quite possibly. In any case, it is the only inn, you know, and we are remotely situated here. I fear Meeker is a law unto himself, though I will say he is a faithful attendant at church. We should miss his bass in the choir. Indeed yes, I shall be happy to join you—it is venal of me, I daresay—in sherry only. Curiously enough, Meeker keeps excellent sherry. It is vexing, you know, to attempt maintaining a choir at all. Always such a sad lack of contraltos and basses. Confidentially, I have had my eye on Dr. Dyck—have you met our good doctor?—for years, but he is, I fear, not a religious man. I see no prospect of capturing him for the choir. A pity.'

The pale-eyed landlord gave us silent greeting, but his expression relaxed a trifle on the rector. 'My usual glass of sherry, Evan . . . I am surprised at you. No whiskey? Mr. Harkness is not a drummer, Evan, or any passing motorist. Fetch him some whiskey at once.'

The landlord gave me an embarrassed glance. 'The only thing I've got is Irish, sir.'

'Any port in a storm,' I said absently. 'Yes,

218

I've met Dr. Dyck and liked him. He struck me as being rather more competent than you'd expect a village doctor to be.'

'Oh, undoubtedly. Abrupt in his manner, and I fear a cynical man, but to understand is to forgive. Poor fellow, he has known tragedy. His wife, you know—an extraordinarily beautiful woman, but also extraordinarily silly—one of those childish, appealing women, quite irresponsible. There was a child, a little boy, I believe, and she let him drown in the bath. A dreadful tragedy, as she could not have another.'

So that explained Dyck. Very neat.

'The poor woman herself took it so to heart that she committed suicide. Dreadful, dreadful. It was all some years ago, but he is still bitter, one sees that.'

'Yes.' I drank thoughtfully, thinking of Dyck, thinking of Eve. I turned and leaned on the bar, surveying the room. I seemed, in this, to be on a kind of roundabout, returning periodically to the same place. Here again were the three old fishermen and the one young one, at the same table, drinking and arguing, paying no notice to anyone else.

'You can laugh, young Jem. The hymn in church book it do say God move in myster'ous ways, and I reckon the devil do that, too. We'll all see it happen, one way or another.'

'I reckon. A pity, him the only one.'

'I heard as he's never been what you'd call clever-strong. It do show.'

'Bloody fools,' said the young man contemptuously. 'Them as say that never laid eye on the lad. So solid and quick as my own Will he be, and a bold one, too. Didn't I fetch him out of the pond? Scared he were but he never yelled, and spoke right up at me, too, and thanked me for it. Not many a lad as'd think to do that. He's a good lad if he is gentry.'

'A pity then, but you can't get from it. Like Jarge say, Manson be Manson and eldest son be eldest son. They'll not keep him.'

'Bloody fools...'

The rector nudged me and said in a stage whisper, 'Just as I told you! They are talking of the Manson Curse. How these superstitions persist—it is amazing. Which reminds me that we never got round to discussing those werewolves. I know you would find it most interesting. But dear me, I should be asking you about the little boy. My housekeeper was telling me of the accident.'

'He's quite all right,' I said. 'None the worse at all.'

'Ah, that is gratifying. The one ewe lamb. I do not like to say anything uncharitable about either Mr. or Mrs. Manson, but it distresses me that they never bring the child to church school. Of course, I understand he is delicate.'

'He's no more delicate than I am,' I said, annoyed. 'Perfectly strong and healthy. Manson is an agnostic; I suppose he feels it isn't necessary.'

'Ah, I see. A pity.'

CHAPTER TWENTY-ONE

At least, I reflected whimsically as I left the rector and set off on the mile's walk back to the house, I had established friendly relations with the publican. Something accomplished. And little good it would do me. I did not intend to stay. The weekend, Manson had caught me for that long, but no longer. And not again.

On the south edge of the village I came past the church, and remembering Manson saying 'an interesting history,' stopped to look at it. Almost new as churches went, and nothing attractive about it. Typical late Victorian, bad proportions. Inside, I remembered, it was bare and cramped. Now I noticed a bronze plaque set into the doorpost, and stepped closer to read the lettering: ST. MATTHEW'S CHURCH. BUILT AND DEDICATED TO THE MEMORY OF JAMES WILLIAM MANSON, 1870–1889. No pious quotation, only the bare statement. I walked on thoughtfully.

It was about half past three when I reached

Poltressor House and came into the walled courtyard. The one manservant, Evans, was laboring in the little rock garden at the side of the house. He stood up and touched his forehead to me.

'Afternoon, sir.'

'Afternoon. That looks like a thankless task.'

'Ar,' said Evans, 'I believe you. There don't nothing grow that you'd want about to prettify the place, this near the water. Rock-stuff is all, like that there. Not what I'd call pretty. Was you wanting anything, sir?'

'The dog,' I said. 'Is he anywhere about? Young Jimmy's worried about him, and I said I'd see he was all right.'

'Oh, ah, the dog. He would be, he's a good lad. Excuse me, sir, he be all right after his wetting? Old Miss Manson, in a rare state she were when they come in. Young Jem Pollock he fetched him home. Such a to-do I never see. I see the doctor come again today.'

'He's quite all right, they think, yes.'

'Ar,' said Evans thoughtfully. 'Let's hope as he keeps that way. The dog, it was about here awhile ago. I reckon 'tis not far. An old beast, it don't stray none, even were the gates open allus.'

'They're generally shut, then.'

'Shut *and* locked,' affirmed Evans, 'and 'special the back one, account of the old path.'

'What's that?'

'The old path? Well, I can show you, sir.' He was gratified at the chance to leave off work. 'You see, right round this way, sir, in the old days there was a deal of smuggling along here. It's a twisty bad coast as you can see, awkward for them as don't know it, rocks and all. The local folk, they'd know just where 'twas safe to run in, and mostly pick a place where 'twould be easy to unload and maybe hide the stuff, see. Coves and such. Mr. Manson could tell you more about it. I reckon whoever lived here them days had a hand in the trade hisself, see. Anyways it were afore they'd cut the steps down to the water. See here, sir.'

We had come to the rear gate, at the opposite side of the house. Evans turned the rusted key in the lock and swung it open. 'There, you see.'

A steep flight of stone steps ran spiral down the side of the cliff to the rocky beach below, but to the right of the small square landing outside the gate was what remained of a path, cut out of the rocky cliff face, winding steep and narrow down to the shore, farther along from the steps.

'Good God,' I said, stepping back involuntarily. I've never had a head for heights.

'Ar.' Evans was pleased at the success of his entertainment. 'You may say so, sir.

Reckon them old smugglers had to be strong and bold, carry stuff up that way. It come right to this here spot, you see, where they alus was a gate. Old Mr. Manson, that'd be our Mr. Manson's uncle, he kept a boat, and built the little old quay out there for her, see, and had the steps put in same time. Nobody's used the old path in donkey's years, but it'll be there a long time to come.'

'It must have been a night's work to get a shipload up this way.' The path was not more than three feet wide and in places sloped nastily toward the far side.

'I reckon. They'd have used donkeys, and men, too, maybe. Ship'd slip into the cove here, unload by night, be off again by dawn tide and none the wiser, see. I wouldn't like to climb that old path meself, less to say with a load on me back.' Evans spat over the edge of the drop. 'Anyways, Mr. Manson be afraid of the boy or someone tummeling over, so the gate alus has to be locked.'

'Very wise.' I was a little relieved to be inside the wall with the gate shut. I looked about again for the dog.

After a pause Evans said, 'Might be Mr. Manson shut it in the garridge. He do at night. It'll be about somewhere, anyways.'

'Thanks.' It did not matter. Little chance the dog had got out. But I went to look in the garage. As if to postpone the necessity for returning to work the man followed me.

'In the little old tool room, sir. Well, I see it ain't. The leash's gorn, though.' Evans indicated a nail in the wall. 'Allus hang there, and it's gorn, so Mrs. Manson or some'un's maybe got it for a walk or some such.'

'Oh, well, it doesn't matter.' I gave the man a cigarette, went on to the house. I was not looking forward to the weekend. I had the feeling that the next three days would be interminable. And not the least of the reason for that was the necessity for facing her in Manson's presence, and Manson in hers.

*   *   *

I came in perhaps too quietly. They did not hear me. Manson's voice was precise and cold from the sitting room. 'There is no point in discussing it further.'

'But we haven't discussed it at all.' Even in the car last night I hadn't heard that note of panic in her voice. Even when...

'Richard, please. Look at me, please. You can't believe that. I never imagined...'

'You are incoherent,' he said softly. 'What are you trying to say, Eve? That you never imagined I knew? That's a little crass of you.'

'Know! There is nothing to know. I don't understand, I can't understand how you could do such a thing. You might as well have said it in four-letter words, before the doctor, before ... No matter why you think such

225

things, how you can, surely you needn't have said...'

'Quite incoherent,' said Manson. 'Really, I don't care to discuss it.'

'Well, I do and we will! I couldn't believe—and then going off like that without a word, when...'

'Kindly keep your voice down.'

There was a tiny silence, as if she struggled for self-control. Her voice was lower, but edged. 'You've never said before, never hinted. What's put it in your mind now? Surely you see I must know, we must talk about it, Richard. Twelve years! You never said. But if it's like that, if you've been suspecting me—for how long, I wonder?—we couldn't go on like that. I want to know why.'

'Why?' And his voice rose a little now. 'Why? You're asking that, after the things you have said to me, the things you've done?'

'I never blamed you,' she said desolately. 'Never.'

One of them at least was probably in a position to see the open doorway; I could not pass it. I stood, uncomfortable, in the hall.

Manson uttered an obscenity in a suddenly shaking voice. It was startling, coming from Manson. I almost exclaimed myself.

'I will not discuss it!' No, of course, discussion implied admission of the fact, and that he could not bear to do. 'Stop talking about it, for God's sake! There's nothing to discuss at all. Did you think I was that much of a fool, not to know? When you are—as you are?' Contempt on that. 'You never tricked me, not for a moment.'

'Richard!' The appropriate horror in her tone. A bit exaggerated perhaps, but on the whole a creditable performance. It's odd in any case how people tend to melodrama in emotion. The deeper the feeling, the more they sound as if they're speaking lines from an old-fashioned tragedy, and with the help of the prompter at that. 'Not true, you know it's not true, how you can—I swear to you—'

'Why do you think I have left you alone? Blame me? Me—for nothing! I have some sensitivity after all. My wife—how could I, a woman like you, whore to any man in the street! Why else would I...'

A little window opened in my mind. Oh, yes, of course, but how logical. An excuse, the excuse he so desperately needs to salvage his pride. Say that is the reason, the whole reason, your fault, not mine.

'Oh, my God,' she said. Horror, disbelief, disillusionment.

'I won't talk about it,' said Manson. I was eavesdropping almost shamelessly now. And then he exclaimed, 'Harkness!' and laughed. 'What is one when there've been so many? And for all I know under my own roof before. It doesn't matter now. I have ceased to let it matter. You will be punished sooner or later,

I know that, for cheating me. Do you wonder, is it any surprise to you, that you leave me only one concern? Only one, the boy, the boy. I've stopped thinking of *you* long ago.'

'I don't believe this,' she said above a whisper. 'I can't. Richard?'

'It was my own fault, I might have known, I should have guessed. What else would the daughter of a whore be but a whore?'

No, I thought, but that is the one thing you must not say to her; she walks with that ghost at her shoulder.

She came out of the room like a sleepwalker, moving stiffly, and never saw me there in the passage. She turned and went up the stairs as slowly as an old woman.

I stayed where I was, not moving to call her attention, but for another reason than that. Such a fury of anger at Manson gripped me that if I had moved it would have been to go in and throttle the man. I stood fighting it down, with my intellect giving me cool advice.

Involved was the word, wasn't it, Harkness? Involved quite far enough now, and you never intended that. (Didn't you? Part of it at least was deliberate.) Fowler saying, you're a romanticist; just because she is a beautiful woman. What is there to choose between? Look at it rationally, man. You thought, these two tiresome people. Never should have been involved with each other, but that is no affair of yours. Be careful. Think—you are using emotion on it, and that is dangerous. Only because (admit it) of a pair of dark eyes, a generous red mouth, a slim yielding body against you. A little too old, a little too experienced, for any such impulsive emotion? Well, no one ever is, but at least you can use what intellect you possess, and what caution.

When she had gone beyond the landing, and no sound from Manson in the sitting room, I went on tiptoe, feeling foolish—a minor character in a bad play, myself—to the front door, opened and shut it rather loudly. I went directly into the sitting room. Manson was standing in front of the hearth, back to the room, wide-legged, hands in pockets, head bent. He turned as I came in. He began to smile. His eyes were very bright, his nostrils flared.

'Well, hello, Johnny. Have a nice walk back?'

He found his cigarette case, opened and shut it several times before taking a cigarette, tapped the cigarette on it violently, snapped the lighter. With the cigarette lit, he went on fidgeting with lighter and case. Nervous as a witch, Dyck said; always had been. Now he put the case and lighter away and went to fidgeting with the contents of the mantel, straightening a pair of Dresden figurines, turning a vase round and round.

'Yes, thanks.'

'Well,' said Manson. 'Well.' He picked up the vase and set it down again in a different place, looked at his watch. 'Nearly four—time for tea, isn't it? You'll excuse me, I'll be back in a moment,' and he walked rapidly out of the room.

I strolled over to the fire, sat down and lit a cigarette. I was thinking of something else Fowler had said ('I heard a certain amount of gossip about Mrs. Manson'). But she had not known until now. How could she not have known? Manson secretive, all to himself, standoffish—even with a wife, especially with a wife, Manson being Manson. She knows now. Why just now, why did he come out with it like that? No illusion that he might be more jealous of me than any of the others. Why should he be? The lid on the kettle just so long, that's all. It had to blow off sometime... And how will she feel about it now?

Intellect, yes; understanding both sides; but I could admit to myself that I felt more sympathy for her. And what a mess, what a sordid tangle of emotion and motive, the kind of thing behind the divorce proceedings in camera, this was. I wanted no part of it.

Another primitive holdover. Where there is a fire, a man will stare into it, perhaps making pictures in the flames. Now suddenly I leaned closer. Resting half on the firelogs, almost in the heart of the flames, was a book. I obeyed my first impulse, reached for the poker and raked it out, and with it smoldering coals and ashes. A book. Manson was burning a book. Well, presumably he had paid for it and it was his fire.

I got down on hands and knees, handling the shapeless thing delicately, trying to decipher the title. The paper was gone, only a margin here and there left. The cover had been cloth, and part still survived, discolored. Even in that state it had a vaguely familiar look and the few gold-filled letters remaining identified it for me. It was the book Manson had loaned me, had insisted on loaning me: Seabrook's *Witchcraft*.

*　　*　　*

Eve did not appear for tea. For the first time, without her presence to distract me, I found myself speculating about Miss Manson. Like a ghost in the house, I thought. You seldom saw her except at meals, and for the most part she was silent. A queer old lady, certainly, and when you thought about it, much of this was her blame. ('I met the uncle once, a vague sort of man, you hardly knew if he was there.') Manson had got away from her physically, but he never would entirely in other ways. Yet had she such a hold over him now as Eve implied? Manson treated her casually enough, sometimes a trifle arrogantly, and her manner toward him was deferential. (Natural: she belonged to a generation whose women were expected to be deferential.)

She spoke not at all, and Manson was preoccupied, avoiding my glance and some secret concern in his own eyes. I made an excuse, glad to leave them, and went up to my room. Smoking by the window, I remembered the morning I had stood here and watched the boy climb the wall... Well, Fowler could be contemptuous, but there was something in it, you couldn't deny that. This was the sort of background that could not result in a normal child. The child—it all began and ended there. The child was a kind of storm center. Bad, very bad. And none of my business at all.

I smoked too many cigarettes, at last went across to the nursery, as I had promised, to tell the boy about his dog; and afterward, I bitterly regretted that little lie, to make him easy. I came back, lay down, and though I did not expect to, slept, waking in time to wash sketchily before going downstairs to dinner. I had thought the weekend would drag. I seemed to have been here forever, and it was still Friday.

CHAPTER TWENTY-TWO

She was very late appearing for dinner, so late that I thought she would not come, would send down an excuse. The convenient feminine headache, and I could not blame her. Manson fidgeted about the room, talking sporadically. The old woman knitted some nondescript gray thing in silence. When Eve came I was doubly startled by her appearance. She was dressed as if for an evening in London: something dark, smart, expensive, unsuitable for this place and time. A row of rhinestone buttons glittered, and the diamond on her hand, the diamonds in her ears. For the first time I could remember it was obvious that she had used cosmetics, to cover traces of tears? No, she had not wept. She was a painted woman of marble, expressionless, and little lines about her mouth and eyes.

'I'm sorry to be late.' No, she had not wept. Her voice was clear and hard. That gown, that voice. Did you say involved, Harkness? You should have run while there was time. She has taken it this way. She means to defy him directly now, the natural human reaction: *If that is what you believe, and what use to deny it, believe it and let me show you how right you could be!* I wouldn't have expected anything different from her, or any woman, but as it was, well, I was the only man available. It looked like being a difficult evening.

'Thank you so much,' with a brilliant smile, as I seated her at the table. 'Let's change around, shall we? My right, Mr. Harkness, not that it makes much difference with one guest, but just for a change. And really, it's rather silly to go on calling you Mr. Harkness, isn't it?'

'Very,' said Manson. 'Very. Under the circumstances.'

She divided a smile between us. 'Of course. But you don't like to be called Johnny, do you? I'll remember. I'm afraid we've been neglecting you today, but you understand.'

'Yes, certainly.' Be damned if I'd play up to her. 'I hope the boy is all right now?'

'Oh, yes, thank you. He ...' The interruption came from an unexpected quarter.

'I was so frightened,' said Miss Manson. 'So good to hear you say that, Eve. The doctor says he is quite safe now? Such a blessing, yes. One cannot be too careful. Perhaps, since that is so, Richard, we might...'

Manson frowned at her. 'It doesn't matter,' he said sharply.

'But we agreed it might be so helpful. You know, my dear, we have experienced some difficulty in the sittings. So interesting, and some very strange things have occurred, but we thought if you would not object, it would be so helpful if you would agree to let James sit with us.' Plaintive, placid tone. She might have been commenting on the weather. 'He is so directly concerned, you see, and the spirits...'

And now Eve needed none of the rouge on her cheeks, the bright angry flush making it stand out starkly.

'You're suggesting... You don't imagine I would agree to such a thing? A child, to be frightened that way! Wasn't the first time enough for you? I...'

'It was Aunt Belle's idea,' said Manson. 'It doesn't matter at all.'

'Oh, was it? Yes. But, dear Eve, surely you see.'

'I won't have it, I won't have him involved in such nonsense. You heard what Dr. Dyck said, Richard. It's criminal. How you can think of such a thing. A child.'

'Oh, yes. It doesn't matter,' repeated Manson. 'Don't keep on at it, Aunt, if Eve feels that way.'

'But you were so eager to try it, Richard. James understands it, my dear, we have explained it to him, you know. I can't help feeling...'

'Criminal!' Eve said. 'I think you must both be mad to think of it. If I have to lock his door you'll not...'

'Really, my dear,' Manson broke in gently, 'is it necessary to make such a scene before a guest? I've said I agree with you. I considered it but it's not important. I shan't press it. Control yourself, Eve, please.'

She had half risen and now sat down again, her mouth tight. 'So long as you take that as definite, Richard.'

'But I do, I will. I've said so. It doesn't matter at all.'

'Oh, dear,' said the old woman. 'I had such hopes of it. I thought you really meant to try, Richard. My dear...'

'I said let's not go on about it, Aunt.' There spoke the master of the house, definite, firm. But in good humor. With something like dismay I realized that at least there would be no scene from Manson. He was pleased at Eve's reaction. He would be kept in good humor all evening, watching the two of us. Watching her prove he was right about her, to salvage his pride further.

The old woman subsided after a glance at him (yes, who ruled there after all?) but there was still anger in Eve's eyes as she turned to me. 'Do forgive me, but I know you agree with me about these absurd superstitions.' Surface, stilted language from a bad play. I would not sit here through an interminable meal with her flirting with me out of anger at Manson. In defensive desperation I began to talk, about London, about my job, the recent influx of Americans, anything to keep the conversation away from her in her present mood.

Manson listened, smiling, watching her. She listened, smiling, never looking at Manson. And when the inevitable pause came, the old woman said, 'We are going to try again this evening, Richard, aren't we? You said...'

Manson shrugged. 'Why? We don't seem to accomplish much. I've rather a headache. I hadn't thought of it.' It was absently said.

Her mouth drooped. A child deprived of a promised treat. 'Oh, but Richard! We must not give up. We must go on trying. So important for the boy's sake!' She glanced at Eve and me appealingly. 'We should be happy for you to join us. It is better with a large number, you know. More psychic forces. The last time I felt the power very strongly. I'm sure we shall begin to achieve results quite soon.'

'It doesn't matter,' said Manson. And then suddenly, 'All right, we will, Aunt. Of course. You two will excuse us, I know. Shocking bad manners, but there, Johnny, you're an old friend. You'll understand. You can keep each other amused, can't you?'

He would sit in the dark with her dry wrinkled hand in his and dwell pleasurably on us alone, on what we were saying and doing

237

in the sitting room, perhaps upstairs in her bedroom. Revulsion, other unnameable emotions swept over me. (Very well, admit it: left alone, and Eve behaving this way. Who knew? No, not in Manson's house. You could not know.) I opened my mouth to say, yes, I would join them, anything preferable to that. But the maid forestalled me.

'Excuse me, sir, Evans wants to speak to you.'

'Evans? At this hour? What on earth about?'

'It's the dog, sir. It's gone. He can't find it nowhere, and the gates are shut.'

'Well, they weren't shut all day,' said Manson. 'It's got out and strayed away somewhere.'

'Oh, Richard, he doesn't,' said Eve. Natural now, in concern, surprise. 'Are you sure, Elsie?'

'Yes, ma'am, the dog wasn't there when Evans went to give it its dinner.'

'It's out chasing a bitch,' said Manson, his eyes bright on Eve.

'Tell Evans to look again. He doesn't stray as a rule. If he's not back in the morning, we must look. Oh, dear. Jimmy will be so upset. And we were going to let him up tomorrow.' She put a hand to her head. Now this, said the gesture.

'After a bitch,' repeated Manson. 'All right, Elsie, tell Evans to have another look

238

about. We'll see to it in the morning.'

'Yes, sir.'

'I can't imagine what's happened to him.' She half rose. 'Perhaps if I called...'

'Sit down, finish your dinner. The dog's all right. What does it matter?' She obeyed, but the little interruption seemed to have changed the whole atmosphere. She made no further overtures to me. The meal was finished almost in silence.

'Will you want coffee in the sitting room, ma'am?'

'Yes, please, Elsie.'

'Not for me,' said Manson instantly. 'Shall we get started, Aunt? It sometimes takes the whole evening, you know, waiting. One has to concentrate.'

'Oh, yes, not for us, Eve. You will excuse us?'

'So rude,' said Manson, smiling at me. 'But if you don't care to join the fun ... I hope you won't find it boring, without your host. Be kind to him, my dear, won't you? And, Johnny, if you should want something to take to bed with you, please don't hesitate. Bookcase in my study. Help yourself.' He was still smiling as he went out.

There was a little silence then, but oddly not tense: only a time when neither spoke. She looked about the denuded table. 'You'd like coffee? Of course. Shall we go into the other room?'

I followed her there. The maid came with a tray, heavy Georgian silver pot, Spode china. Speak of a prewar existence... Eve sat down and filled two cups.

'Sugar? You don't take it, of course. I don't know why we use these things. Such lovely work, but impossibly heavy and awful to wash, you know. Not to speak of polishing. Those modern electric chrome ones are much more practical, actually.'

'I should imagine.'

'Of course, they're valuable. You can't throw things away, just because they're rather a nuisance.'

'No,' I said. 'No.'

She raised her cup. Her hand was shaking and a little coffee spilled into the saucer. She set it down again and covered her face with one hand.

'What am I going to do? My God, what am I going to do?'

CHAPTER TWENTY-THREE

Melodrama always makes me uncomfortable. I made a little play lighting a cigarette, stirring my coffee. But she dropped her hand and looked at me, and it was the Eve I had known and liked in London. 'I think I owe you another apology. I'm sorry. I haven't

240

meant to behave like a child.'

'It's all right. I understand.' The clumsy overworked phrase. 'I ought to confess, I was an unwilling eavesdropper this afternoon.'

'Oh ... but you knew before what he thought. You implied that. How did you know, when I never did? Did he say it to you?'

'No,' I said. 'Someone else. I think probably—others.' Fowler ('I heard some gossip') yes; other men, the wrong ones or the right ones; because of that need to salve his ego, and it would be the same if she was guilty or innocent. For there Manson was beyond the truth. And true or false, believed. For he was the husband, and who was not eager to believe that of a beautiful woman? There would be those who could confirm it, and would, in private. My mind shied away from that like a skittish horse. I did not want to think of that here, now.

'I want to know who. What did he say? When? I never dreamed.'

'Better not,' I said uncomfortably. 'Better leave it there. Does the rest of it matter?'

'No. I don't want to know now. But, in London, that long ago? I see.'

I said abruptly, 'Drink your coffee before it's cold.'

'Melodrama, I know. I'm sorry. I wonder why I can talk to you. I don't mind. Because we are strangers and not strangers. Last night . . .'

Only last night. Not twenty-four hours. She looked away and down. 'I don't want you to think . . .' she began painfully.

'I'm not thinking anything. It's none of my business at all. I don't know what I'm doing in it. But as long as I'm here I won't sit on the sidelines and keep quiet. I said some of what I thought last night. Perhaps you're seeing a little clearer now.'

The coffee was hot. I scalded my tongue, all the anger rising in me again, madness, nothing personal to it, all because of this lost lovely woman (oh, you should have run, Harkness, while there was time).

'There's nothing for you, no reason . . . when he's like this. You see what it's done to him. I don't believe he is quite sane.'

'London,' she said. 'Then! And I never—he has always been jealous, of course.'

'Insecure, immature. People like that always are.'

'Never wanted to go out with me, have people in. Like a dog with a bone. All to himself. But I never thought . . .'

'Well, now you know,' I said angrily. 'What are you going to do about it? It's an impossible situation as it is, you see that. I haven't any right to offer advice, but I think you'd be a fool to stay with him any longer. As it is . . .'

She looked at me curiously. 'What concern

is it of yours?'

'None. I've said that. None at all. I'm sorry for both of you,' I lied, 'and that's all. I don't like waste, and you're wasting time, effort, patience, your whole life with him. And you know how bad it is for the child.'

'You're saying I should divorce him. Why?'

I did not misunderstand her. The instinct is not as old as man but as old as civilization. Take care: woman the huntress, man the trapped! I said, 'I don't give a damn, Eve. It's none of my business what you've done or what Manson thinks or what either of you does about it. I've no rights over you.' And I want none. Or rather, one, but not the legal one. Oh, no. 'However,' I added rather maliciously, 'I'm far enough involved that I might have a certain right to give an opinion, don't you think?'

She looked at me steadily for a moment without speaking and then gave me the ghost of a smile. 'Oh, yes. You could say that.' She would be a difficult woman to quarrel with. Almost every other woman I had ever known would have retorted to that, and we would in an instant have been snapping at each other, little mean words, calculated. But strangers cannot quarrel. Strangers.

'I beg your pardon, that was childish.'

She was lighting a cigarette. She got up and went to the fire, tossing the match into the flames, stood half turned away from me. 'It's

243

all right. We were both rather out of control last night, and I suppose that's why we can talk like this now. After all, we don't know each other very well.'

'No. I never apologized.'

She shrugged. 'No one's fault, or mine as much as yours. Each of us is two people, aren't we? The nice modern civilized one, and the other. Or do you call it the spiritual side and the animal? Rather orthodox and puritan, I've always thought, that idea. They're not that far apart. But I've sometimes thought it would be a lot easier if we could just dispense with one or the other.'

'Which? I don't know,' I said, 'that I'd like to dispense with the animal. Think of all you'd miss. It's not just the one thing, you know.'

'No. Be a lot less complicated. And that's all it was,' she added hurriedly, 'you know that. I'm ashamed of it now. I don't want to think about it.'

'Then don't,' I said shortly. Of course, if not for that we could not talk this way. Ashamed? Well, very likely she had been accustomed to more finesse, more leisure and discretion. Probably with the others, with Templeton. I had said, jealousy immature, but a little was only natural, the dog with the bone. I had not even the right to be jealous, and God help us, I was more jealous of Templeton the dead man than of Manson. Of

244

course. Involved was the word.

I said, 'It's an impossible situation for both of you, that's all I see.'

'Do you think I don't see that, too?' she asked in a low voice. 'The way he is, all this time, never coming into the open with it, never giving me a chance.' But he could not. Not Manson. It is bound up with the other fact, that he dares not admit or think about. And with his resentment of you, who were the means of his learning that incompetency. 'I don't know what to do,' she said, and the edge of panic was in her tone again.

'You can't go on with him.'

She turned and looked down at me, and I knew how she would look when she was old. Beautiful always, that was in the bones, not the flesh, but—old. She said quietly, 'Do you think for one moment he would let me have Jimmy?'

It brought me up short. The boy. The one thing, for both of them. The thing each would fight for. And she could not risk it, for Manson might have evidence. 'That I hadn't thought of. I see.'

She threw her cigarette into the fire. 'I hate this place,' she said. 'I hate the country. I always have. I hate the everlasting sound of the sea down there, and this house: all the rooms too big, always drafty, creaking floors, and the stairs too steep. All that, just little things. But what it is, it's an old unhappy house and I hate it. I hate having to drive a mile to buy cigarettes or toothpaste, and mostly finding Mrs. Beech is out of the kind you want, and no other place to go unless you drive twelve miles into Truro. I hate there not being anything, shops, theaters, people—not that I've got to be forever going somewhere. In London I might not go out of my own garden for days and be perfectly happy, but it's just the feeling that they're there. I enjoyed London again, that little while. I never thanked you for it. It was fun. Until just—the last. Spoiled it . . .

'I hate the fog and being shut up in this house with nothing, nothing, nothing to do. You can't read all the time. You can't make a life teaching one little boy sums and reading three hours a day. And the old woman giving the servants different orders from mine, and having always to remember not to fuss at her because this was her house to manage so long. And both of them talking that nonsense to him but not quarreling in front of him, not letting him know. I hate almost everything about this place and about Cornwall. I've never been happy here and I never will be. But I'm tied here. I can never leave, because it's where he is and he would never let me take my son away.'

I had nothing to say to that, for she was right. Manson would be vindictive and jealous. Evidence or no, he would lie, beggar himself, to keep the boy. And not to have the boy, not primarily, but to deprive her.

'I don't hate him. Perhaps if I did it would be easier, I don't know. I am only sorry for him, and a little afraid of him. The things he says and does.' She looked at me. She said, just discovering it, 'I know you better than I know him. After twelve years.'

I ignored that because I was afraid to go into it.

'Are you still saying what you said to me last night, that you're not blaming him? After what he said to you?' For, I thought, though she may be venal, it is from him the hatred comes. She might be innocent as day and Manson still what he is; it is of his own creation.

'I don't know. It's nothing to do with you. I won't go on talking about it. It's my own problem.'

She turned suddenly. I had risen, and we met face to face, unexpectedly.

'Let me alone,' she said. 'I don't know where I am or what I'll do. Twelve years. I thought I could bear it. You get used to anything. I wish you would go. Please go away.'

'You didn't want me to stay. I knew that.' And suddenly, now, our voices had dropped to intimacy, so close.

'No, of course I didn't. Reminding me. I wish you'd go.'

'All right,' I said absently. 'I'll go. Monday.'

It was a foreordained thing. In just a moment now I would reach for her and it would be like last night, and both of us knowing it, postponing the moment out of fear, out of the intensity of our desire.

'I don't know how you got into this, really a stranger, my fault, I remember.'

'Yes, it was.' But not as she meant. Plenty of chances to get out, but you stayed in, because of her. I reached out and took her by the shoulders, and she settled against me with a little moan. But then she wrenched away.

'No, not anymore. Not again. Stop it, John!' She backed away, curious blindness in her eyes on me. 'I won't, I can't. Not now, here. Ever. I think all of this is my fault. From the beginning.'

And I was ashamed, and said honestly, 'I'm sorry.'

'I can't talk about it anymore,' she said, and turned and ran from me, and I thought she was crying.

CHAPTER TWENTY-FOUR

Sunday morning, and had I been here forever? Facing myself in the glass as I shaved, I wondered why I had stayed, after what she said. If I needed to be rude to break away from Manson, what would it matter? I had no intention of pursuing the relationship. Either of the relationships, I amended wryly. Yet I had stayed. Bored, embarrassed, angry, I had stayed, neglecting my own job. Irresponsible. Why?

Because of that strange feeling: another kind of job to be done.

For now it was not Eve, but something other, something nebulous, uneasy at the bottom of my mind. Something to do with Manson. I did not know what it was. I thought about yesterday.

The dog had still been missing yesterday morning, and Manson was impatient with the child. 'How should I know where the dog is? It'll come back or it won't, that's all, and small loss.' Difficult to find anything to say for Manson, saying that to a child, and the dog all the child had. Yes, she had said that. 'All he's ever had was Roddy.'

'But, Father, he might be hurted somewhere.'

'If it had been run over on the road someone would have found it by now. It's just strayed.'

'Roddy wouldn't go away from me,' said the boy miserably. 'He wouldn't.'

'Well, it has.'

'Father, d'you think the witch could have taken him? You said...'

'Oh, very likely,' said Manson, looking amused.

Manson, yesterday, assiduous to the guest. Insisting on taking me out for a country walk, chattering at my elbow all four or five miles of it. A walk I might have enjoyed alone. The landscape was grand, strong and bold, like Evan's old smugglers. Chattering about half a dozen topics and never once mentioning his one erstwhile topic, until I deliberately asked him, when he frowned and shrugged.

'Oh, that. Actually, I'm ready to give up trying. I suppose it's a talent I haven't got. We don't seem to be achieving anything. My aunt's very keen, of course, and I thought for a while ... but I'm afraid it's a waste of time. Definitely. Now you can see some of the mines, up there on the hill. We won't go up. It's a stiff climb this side, but if we did you'd see they're not awfully deep, as we think of mines.' Manson perfectly friendly, only with secret amusement in his sidelong glances. Knowing I knew and was deliberately not challenging him; and of course, by not bringing it into the open I only increased Manson's certainty. I had the feeling that if I had come out with it (and just how should one broach the subject, according to polite usage?—excuse me, sir, but you're quite wrong, you know, I am not one of your wife's lovers) Manson would remain as surface-cheerful, undisturbed (no need to apologize, old man, I know how these things happen).

Yesterday, Manson: and nothing of Eve. She had not appeared all morning, excused herself from tea and dinner (the expected excuse, a headache, so sorry). Today I would escape Manson at least a little while, to more boredom at church. Convenient excuse. And prolong the escape by walking in and back.

And this morning we were both grateful for the old woman, to make a third at the table. Manson was absent, and from the study came the gravely triumphant counterpoint of Bach, insistent, dominant. We ate in silence. Eve was pale and would not meet my eyes, and the other woman gave me only timidly hostile glances over the cold toast and lukewarm tea. I thought they were both relieved at my announcement that I would attend church, and I left early, myself relieved that it was a clear enough morning to make my fiction of wanting a walk plausible.

I took my time walking in. It was still early when I came into the village. I recognized Dyck's car before the inn, and Dyck's stocky shortish figure approaching it. Seeing me, Dyck stopped and waited. We exchanged greetings.

'Church?' said Dyck. Just faint contempt. 'I wouldn't have said you were one of the faithful.'

'Not as a rule. An excuse to get out of the house, I'm afraid.' But I did not want to talk

251

to Dyck. I was not, in fact, in a mood to talk to anyone, and went on with a nod, feeling his eyes on my back. Dyck speculating: something in Manson's hints after all, when I was still here, feeling as he knew I did about my host? Damn Dyck, let him think what he pleased.

I sat through a somewhat rambling sermon on the subject of sacrifice. Mr. Silver dwelling on Abraham and Isaac at gruesome length. At the church door the rector shook my hand warmly.

'My dear Mr. Harkness. Always a pleasure to welcome the stranger in our midst, and when he is so faithful in attendance. Not everyone, especially away from home. I find people very lax these days. Yes, indeed. Good morning, Colonel, good morning! Won't you give me the pleasure of entertaining you to luncheon? No, no, no trouble at all, I assure you. And you know we promised ourselves another talk.'

I was not overanxious to return. Suffering mild guilt at having used Mr. Silver's service as escape, I accepted, to do penance. We lunched well, accompanied by the rector's Cornish werewolves, which I found considerably less gruesome than his sermon. I should have called to let Eve know I'd be out for lunch; perversely I did not. They would only be relieved to be rid of me.

'Which reminds me, that other legend we

were speaking of—the curse, you know—if you believe it, I have heard several references to it recently. At the inn the other day ... but of course, you were with me, we commented on it at the time. The little boy being so nearly drowned. I trust he is recovered now?'

'He's lost his dog,' I said. 'Manson seems to think it wandered off.' Seems to think? 'It's a red-and-white spaniel—not a young dog. I shouldn't think it would stray. Yes, a pity, his only playmate, it was.'

'Dear me, how dreadful. One grows so attached to them, doesn't one? I am fond of spaniels myself. I will surely keep an eye out. It may only have strayed.'

When I left the little rectory, it was long after two. Still half unconsciously postponing my return, I took another, longer way back, going up the hills across the road by the rector's vague directions. I was of two minds about Cornwall. It was bleak country, nothing pretty-pretty about it, strong-profiled. And I was not shod for rough walking, but once started I kept on. A faint track led me up almost to the brow of a line of little hills marching along above the coast road, and there vanished. In the distance I could see Poltressor House. Manson and I had come somewhere near here yesterday, but lower. Yes. There were the little dark marks in the hillside that Manson had pointed out as abandoned tin mines.

In idle curiosity I took the trouble of climbing higher to inspect those. A grand view of the water and the cliffs from here, the headland jutting out beyond me with the house at its far end. I could see the white line of surf for a little way and even part of the stone steps at the shore below the house. It was a clear afternoon. Later the thin sea mist would blow in.

I came up to the mine lowest on the hillside. Its lip was overgrown with coarse shore grass, and it did not look big enough to be called a mine. I bent over the edge and was disappointed to find it so relatively shallow. Of course, these were old excavations, some pre-Roman, and the tin gone long ago. Thirty feet deep at the most. Over the centuries, perhaps, it had been filled in by wind and silt.

I bent closer. Something was down there at the bottom of the shaft. It looked ... I went round to the other side, and from there the sun gave more direct light on a shapeless furry thing lying down there in the old dust and mud of the mine, on dirty red-and-white splotches of coat.

It was the dog, the boy's dog, and it looked very dead.

*   *   *

I sat back slowly on my heels, steadying myself with a hand on a rock by the edge.

254

What dog but a blind and deaf one fell into a hole in the ground this size? And the fall, to drifted-silt bottom, would not kill. More likely the dog had been put there. I looked around. My hand fitted the rounded top of the rock so snugly, and no other rocks were nearby at all. I picked it up. Blood and a few white hairs on the jagged underside.

Someone had killed the dog, brutally, deliberately, and put it down the mine out of sight. Who and why?

I got up and went on quickly, and once again anger rose in my mind. But the dog! It was wanton cruelty. The friendly, quiet little spaniel the boy had loved. It made no sense. Or did it? I walked now not noticing the landscape, and it was some while later I found I had come on another path. It led me down out of hills toward the road, and past a thin tangle of undergrowth. Little cover on the bare Cornish hills as a rule, but a reason for it here, I saw. There was a pond, by courtesy: brown, stagnant—looking water, perhaps salty this near the sea, and not large. This must be Pigeon's Pond.

And here were Manson and the boy, at the water's edge. At the sound of my coming, Manson whipped round startled. It was a steep climb here from the road. His face was white and little drops of sweat glistened on his forehead. He stood motionless for a moment, then lifted a hand in greeting.

'Well,' I said inanely, 'out for a walk?'

'That's right,' returned Manson. 'A walk, yes.'

The boy was poking about the edge of the pond with a stick. He looked round at us, smiled at me. 'We're looking for Roddy. He hasn't come home yet, and Father thought he might be up here, but he isn't. This is the pond I fell in, you know, but Roddy wouldn't get hurted here, he knows how to swim.'

Manson was watching me, watching the boy. He reached slowly into his pocket, brought out cigarettes, offered the packet. 'Been to church,' he said. It was not a question. 'Eve said...' But he was not interested, instantly. He fumbled again and brought out a lighter but never offered to hold it for me.

'Yes, that's right.'

'But I don't know where he could be,' said the boy. 'I wish we'd find him. I wish he'd come home. I miss him awful.'

'Waste of time,' said Manson. Yes, it was. I looked at him, started to speak, stopped.

'Did you see him anywhere, sir?'

'No,' I said. 'No, I'm sorry, Jimmy. I haven't.'

Impossible, of course, to tell the boy, have the boy all concerned, run back and see the dog like that, skull smashed in. A thing you could not do to a child. I could tell Manson afterward. Tell Manson. Did Manson need telling?

I found Manson was looking at me, and the cold hostility in his eyes was startling. 'And what prompted you to come back this way, Johnny? Wanted a walk . . . oh, yes. It's a fine day, but we'll have rain before night, you can smell it in the air.'

In the strong salt wind my cigarette burned unevenly, tasted only of sulfur from the match. I threw it down and stepped on it. I said, 'I came by some of those old mines we saw yesterday. Interesting. I had a look down one of them.'

'Oh, yes?' Manson was watching the boy again. 'Don't go too near the edge, James. Oh, yes? I told you they're not very deep, the oldest ones.'

'No. You can see the bottom of the shaft quite clearly. I was surprised.' But this play with words, like a bad detective novel. Manson! Surely even Manson . . .

'James!' called Manson abruptly. 'Come along, we'll go home now. Tea by the time we get there.' Glancing at his watch, 'Had enough walking, Johnny? Come along, that rain will blow up fast now.'

'Oh, but, Father, we've only just come. We haven't . . .'

'Come along, no argument.' Manson started swiftly down the hill. Like many small men, he was a tireless walker. Unwillingly the boy came after.

'But we never really looked at all. If he was up here somewhere, he'd come if I called.' He began to call the dog as he walked, his shrill boy's voice piercing in the clear air.

And Manson glanced over his shoulder, quick, uneasy. He snapped, 'Stop that! A waste of time, that's all. The dog's gone and that's that. Be quiet. And hurry, we'll be late for tea.' It was just on half past three by my watch.

'Yes, sir,' said the boy. He stumbled along between us, head down, probably biting his lip to restrain tears. What did you say to a child? Not that. The anger for brutality was stronger than curiosity. I put a clumsy hand on the boy's shoulder.

'Dogs don't live as long as people, Jimmy. And sometimes they run away, or get lost. You have to—to get over losing a dog.' At least I knew enough not to say the unforgivable thing. You'll have another dog one day.

'Roddy wouldn't run away from me, sir. We're friends.'

'Actually,' said Manson, 'I'm inclined to think someone hit the dog in the road and hid it somewhere. Avoid paying the damages, you know. People go to extraordinary lengths.'

Well, yes, if you're suggesting some passing motorist carried a dead dog half a mile up a steep hill to drop it down a mine shaft, all to get out of five pounds' conjecturable damages. I glanced at Manson curiously, but Manson was looking ahead, walking fast. Nothing further was said until we came in sight of the house, and then Manson spoke only to urge more haste on the boy.

We came into the house and Eve was in the doorway of the sitting room. 'Mother, we didn't find him, Mother. I called. Father says he might be runned over.'

'Oh, darling, I'm so sorry,' she said helplessly. And afterward I would think of that moment with a kind of horror, her kneeling there embracing the child, rising, trying to smile down at him. 'Come along, we'll find some cake for your tea and I'll have it with you, and we can read *The Wind in the Willows*.'

'I don't want any cake,' he whispered.

'All about Mole and Badger, and Mr. Toad,' she said, a brave attempt at cheerfulness. 'Come on, darling.' Looking brief excuse at us, leading the boy off upstairs. Manson's urge for haste seemed to have vanished now. He stood staring into space, lighting another cigarette precisely, snapping the lighter shut with a little vicious click.

I said deliberately, 'It's a pity about the dog. What do you think could have happened to it?'

Manson never looked at me or answered.

He went down the hall rapidly, quietly, slammed the study door after him. In a moment, from behind the door, sounded the first compelling, delicate measure of Ravel's *Bolero*.

CHAPTER TWENTY-FIVE

Despite the walk and the fact that I'd not had tea, I had little appetite for dinner. No one seemed more cheerful. There was small attempt at talk, as if I were in truth not a guest here to be entertained. In the spaces of silence the rain was loud against the windows, and when the rain dwindled for a moment the surf was audible on the rocks at the foot of the cliff. Manson ate little, and when our glances crossed there was veiled bitterness in his eyes on me. The welcome worn thin. When will you go?

The old woman slipped away almost unnoticed before coffee was served, and Eve excused herself soon after. Would she have stayed, to make polite surface talk, if she knew Manson would go off as well? I wondered when Manson, with only a muttered word, had shut himself up in the study again. He must have played *Bolero* over a dozen times, and there it went again. Not the most soothing music available for a man already tense.

My welcome worn, yes. She had said, I wish you would go, and Manson might as well have said it. And I had not in the first place wanted to stay. So why not go? Nothing was holding me here. Go back to town, forget these people caught in a trap of their own making. Nothing to do with me. Well, I was going in any case day after tomorrow. And something did hold me, now, making that small unease at the back of my mind.

The dog. Manson and the dog. Who else, and for what reason? Even Manson, what reason? You could make a case, oh, yes, of a sort. The dog had led the boy into the pond, and he nearly drowned. So Manson killed the dog. Retaliation, vindictiveness, temper? Hardly that, so long after the event. Who else but Manson? The leash had been taken, the dog deliberately led up there and killed. Killed brutally, savagely. And either way, whatever the reason, no reason a sane man would do that. Blaming the dog? It was, it might be, the kind of logic a man not quite sane would use.

You never knew what a man, not quite sane, might do. Manson, snapping at the boy that way. (All you have left me to think about, the one thing.) Manson, burning a book in the sitting-room fire. That book. Manson, so enthusiastic about his amateur séances and then suddenly uninterested. And

Dyck: 'He is not in a normal state.' Often found such abrupt shifts of mood, of temper, in a neurotic. Manson, nervous little Manson, God knew what devils torturing him inwardly.

Well, and what exactly could anyone do about it? Tell Eve; frighten Eve. Call Dyck; but you could not force a man to consult a doctor.

I went upstairs at last, the *Bolero* still building to crescendo in the downstairs passage. I had found a stack of old *Spheres* to take with me, but in the bedroom I did not open one immediately. As bad as Manson, fidgeting about: smoking too much. The rain had stopped. I heard the door across from mine open and the child's voice tearful, the comforting, comfortable voice of Nanny in reply. The door shut.

I undressed, got into bed with the ashtray and the magazines, and read myself to sleep with the light on.

*   *   *

I woke in a great fright, heart thumping, body cold with sweat. I had seen Manson running after the dog, and shouted and run after, and suddenly found I was the dog running from Manson. I had run, panting, panicky, over miles of rough ground with Manson close behind wanting to catch me and

262

kill me, and at last came to the edge of a tall sheer cliff with the sea seething on rocks below. There was no place to turn. I was trapped. And then Manson seized me and flung me over and I was falling, and woke.

For a moment I lay, orienting myself to reality. I was trembling. I sat up, blinking in the light, looked at my watch. It was three in the morning. I lit a cigarette. Only one of the nightmares I still occasionally had. Fowler and his fear of boats. These things hung on. My own dread of heights, of falling, went back to the time Alex and I were climbing in the Appalachians, and I slipped and fell on a long scree, broke my ankle, and the rest of me well bruised.

I finished the cigarette and switched out the light, but lay awake, restless, until the first faint gray of dawn crept in the window. Sleeping then, I overslept, and woke past eight. I shaved and dressed with two opposing forces talking in my mind. Go now, they want you to go and you do not want to stay, and, Don't go: there is something, some imperative reason you must stay here.

I came downstairs and met the maid Elsie in the front passage. 'Good morning, sir. There's a letter.'

'A . . . ?' Surprised, I took it. Certainly, it bore my name, and in a familiar hand. Then I remembered that I had written Fowler on Friday, and it was a silly thing to have done. I did not then know how long I would be here. You can say what you like about England, but the British post office is something. It was just as well Manson had not seen the post first. I could imagine the look in his eyes. Planning on settling down with us, are you, changing your address? I ripped the envelope open hastily.

Fowler's large impatient scrawl. 'What are you doing in Cornwall again? I thought I warned you. Templeton's crash was second week of January year after the war. Why?' And a curly single C for signature.

But, I thought numbly, but ... Templeton. Taken it for granted it had been Templeton. 'He'll be eight in November.' March, then. And Templeton killed the January before. So, it was someone else, and absurdly I was as angry at her as if I had caught her out in a deliberate lie. She had told me nothing at all. I had no right to expect that she should, either lie or truth, and what did it matter? But she had been in love with Templeton.

I thrust the letter into my pocket and went into the dining room. Manson was alone at the table. He looked up and said 'Good morning,' shortly. No pretense now. He had urged me to stay, then, because it was pleasurable punishment to catch us together—imagining, dwelling on it. Now it was not. Now something had happened to change him. He was hoping for an announcement of departure. When I said nothing he asked with small attempt to conceal irritation, 'Well, what are you planning to do with yourself today, Johnny? Not very suitable for a country walk.' More rain threatened momentarily.

'No. I'll drive into the village for one thing; I need cigarettes.' Manson looked a little, only a little, relieved at that.

*   *   *

It was raining lightly by the time I got into Pentressor. I left the car outside The Drowned Man, crossed to the little row of shops, bought cigarettes. I went into the other one, the one housing the telephone exchange. The mountainous woman was behind the counter knitting.

'I'd like to make a trunk call,' I said. 'London.'

She looked at me indifferently. 'Right there.' Old-fashioned telephone on the wall, no enclosure. 'Marge! Gennelmun wants Trunks.' This evidently to someone in the rear premises where the board would be. A cheerful 'OK, Mum!' came back. I took down the receiver, remembered that I did not know the number offhand, reached for my address book in an inner pocket (times it was useful to be methodical) and found the page.

The usual delay, the mysterious clicks, the bright voice of the London operator, and at last Fowler's secretary.

'Mr. Harkness? Well.'

'It's rather important.' It was not of course: only curiosity. 'I'll wait if necessary.'

'Just a moment, I'll see.' And finally Fowler. 'That you, John? Are you still in Cornwall?'

'That's right. I . . .'

'What's all this about Templeton? What are you up to?'

'Nothing,' I said, 'Nothing. I'm, er, calling from the local exchange. I just . . .'

'Oh,' said Fowler. 'I see. Well?'

'I just wanted to ask if you'd had Manson's manuscript safely.'

'It arrived in the morning's post. I was, um, surprised,' said Fowler.

'Yes, so was I.' Belatedly I thought this had been a mistake. We could not talk freely on the telephone, with no way of knowing who was listening. Country: another disadvantage. I said, 'You haven't had a chance to read it then?'

'As a matter of fact, I was so curious that I'd just begun it. How long have you been down there?'

'Since Friday. Just over the weekend. I'm coming back to town tomorrow, I expect.'

'Not sure?'

'Not exactly,' I said. I was, of course. I was

266

leaving tomorrow morning. I would be back in London by late afternoon.

'How are the Mansons?' asked Fowler abruptly.

I hesitated, undecided what to reply to that. When I answered conventionally, 'Oh, just fine, thanks,' it was too late to sound convincing. I heard Fowler's familiar grunt.

Surprisingly, 'And the youngster?'

Again I paused. 'All right. I—that is, Manson just wanted to be sure you had the manuscript. I suppose you haven't got far into it.'

'No. It looks interesting. Interesting.'

'That's good,' I said. 'Charles...'

'Yes?'

'Nothing. I ... we can discuss it when I see you.'

'What's wrong?' asked Fowler in a lowered voice.

'I don't know. Nothing. I'll see you soon. Good-bye.' I heard Fowler speak my name as I replaced the receiver.

I came out to the road and crossed to the inn. Legitimate hours now. Just why had I called Fowler at all? Curious. What kind of thing had Manson written this time? Another best seller perhaps? Or, as second novels often were, disappointingly mediocre. And that did not matter either.

I was inside and had given the order to the landlord before I realized two things: that it was much earlier than my usual drinking time and that Dyck was the only other occupant of the inn. We nodded at each other. The doctor strolled over to join me, carrying his glass.

'Two sinners together,' he commented, indicating the clock over the bar. 'But I've an excuse; up all night. I'm just on my way home.'

'And stopped for breakfast?' I smiled. 'I hope it wasn't wasted effort.'

'I wouldn't say so. An eight-pound boy. And how,' asked Dyck abruptly, 'is young Jimmy?'

All this concern. Psychic forces, I thought vaguely. Child crying in the night for his dog. I looked at Dyck, reached a sudden decision. 'Come and sit down. There's something I want to tell you.'

CHAPTER TWENTY-SIX

She was, of course, avoiding me. I had no chance to speak to her privately until that evening. And the knowledge of Manson's suspicion, lying almost tangible between us, turned us as self-conscious in public or private as if it were justified. Once again, that day, I felt the wires between us. I had thought once, in this the child was the center. So for them he was. But for myself, I was here and entangled because of Eve, only because of Eve. So many chances to disassociate myself, and I had taken none of them. And was it rationalization to tell myself it was not only because this was a beautiful woman to draw any man's interest, but because of a truer interest in the woman herself? Probably. She had said, and it was true, we were strangers really.

I could not, when we rose from the lunch table, make any open overtures with Manson's eyes on me. And with Manson removed into the study, she had gone. I wandered the house as much as I dared, looking. She was in her own room or with the boy perhaps. The rain had kept up. At least it made a valid excuse for me. No one would set out on a long drive in such weather when it was avoidable. And the reasonless unease grew and grew in my mind, while Manson played *Bolero* over and presently set Beethoven's steps of doom marching through the house. Manson brooding all to himself in there. On what?

What is going to happen here, I wondered? For as I'd said to her, it could not go on. Figures in a tapestry, frozen in a scene of tragedy, stayed in their course. With human beings, there is constant change and flow. She said, I don't know what to do. And what I had to tell her might be the motivation needed. I thought of it. It passed across my mind in a series of pictures: the proceedings, the sordid hearings in camera, the decision. I saw her in London with the child, without the child, and it was nothing at all. It would never happen, because there was something else not yet known. And it was the rain beating on the windows that made me so uneasy.

Never should have got involved. Go away, right away from it now, back to a sane existence. Tomorrow.

But I caught her after dinner, for Manson, with a dark vacant look at us, went back to the study before she could excuse herself, and common courtesy forced her to stay, not looking at me, offering more coffee, discovering the pot was lukewarm, rising to get some fresh.

'It doesn't matter, leave it. I must talk to you, I've something to tell you.'

She sat down again unwillingly, her expression tensing. In three days she looked thinner, paler, and I did not like her dress. it was the wrong color for her, turning her skin sallow. or was it the light? 'I'd really rather . . .'

'It's not that. Please, Eve, just listen. Dyck said you ought to know and I think so, too. I don't want to frighten you.' How to say it? Say it and get it over, let her know the worst. 'Damn,' I said. 'Maybe it's a mare's nest, but you'd better know. I found the dog. Up in one of those old mines. It ...'

'But Roddy? How on earth ...'

'He's dead,' I said baldly. 'Someone killed him with a rock. Smashed his head in and put him down the mine. And I'm afraid it was Manson.'

She looked at me, not saying anything, and then said, 'Oh, no. No.'

'I think so.' I told her about it in more detail. She listened, once put a hand up to her face.

'I'm sorry. We had him since he was a puppy. Mr. Treherne gave him to us. He raises them, you know. I'm sorry. I ... go on, please.'

'The leash was gone. And now it's back. I looked. On its nail in the tool room.' I waited, watching her.

After a little silence she said, 'Yes. No one else here. I see. He's never cared especially for animals. But to do that. No reason at all.'

'No sane reason, Eve, no. That's why. You see what we thought about it.'

She nodded abstractedly. 'Because of Jimmy. You mean, that's why he did it.'

'When people aren't thinking quite normally, they're apt to reason like that. He'd think, the boy nearly drowned because of the dog, and it might happen again, so get rid of the dog. You see.'

'Yes. As bad as that. I didn't think it was as bad as that. It's never been good for him, here. Too isolated. He's always been nervous, imaginative, anyway.' She bent to the match I held. Her hand was steady on the cigarette. 'All right,' she said. 'You needn't look so uneasy, John. I'm not going to have hysterics. Will you tell me what the doctor said?'

I told her some of it. What I remembered most vividly was myself saying angrily, 'Anyone who could do a thing like that would do murder,' and Dyck blowing smoke down his nose and saying, 'Well, you know, I think there'd be people capable of murder who couldn't bring themselves to kill a dog.'

'He said nerves, probably a treatment of a medical sort would help, but an examination...'

'I see.'

'He mentioned something about that to me before, I may as well tell you. When he was here the other day. He said he didn't like to see Manson so nervous, not normal.'

'No, but he's always been like that, too, hasn't he?' She was smoking rapidly, sitting up alert. 'I'll tell you something odd. I feel so much better about it now. It's something understandable. It explains so much. He's really just ill. Like a nervous breakdown. It isn't Richard himself, really, only that he's ill. It's frightened me, the way he's been the last year. More. But if he's just ill, and something can be done to help him...'

I lit a cigarette, got up to stand before the
272

hearth, to think before speaking. 'It may be a bit more than that, you don't know. If you can persuade him to see Dyck. I know you don't like him, but he's quite competent.'

'He doesn't like me, that's all. Yes, I see. Of course, that's all it is really.'

'All. Eve, if . . .'

'He doesn't really think all that,' she said. 'It's just that he's ill. A nervous breakdown. It's been coming on. I can look back and see now, of course. All he needs is care and looking after, and he'll get all right. Everything will be all right again. It's just that this has made him behave the way he does.'

'You don't know. Let's hope so.'

'Of course,' she said. 'Of course. He hasn't been really himself for a long time, I should have known. I should have seen he was ill. He never used to be so irritable, so changeable. Always nervous, but . . . and then that other thing, the way he's been about that idiotic curse. He laughed about it when he first told me. Oh, just after Jimmy was born and we came here. It's only the last couple of years he got serious about it, believing in it. Yes, it was after Jimmy fell on the stairs and had concussion, after that he first began to agree with his aunt about it, and make a fuss. That was just over two years ago. Miss Manson always went on . . . but he only laughed before. All the other things, it's come on

273

gradually, used to frighten me sometimes, but I see now. He's really ill and needs help.'

Going to take it this way. Women. I was angry at her, suddenly furiously angry at her softness, her readiness to overlook, take the blame. Manson, neurotic pampered little Manson, not worth it. People had no business letting themselves get into such a state. Nerves. My God, that's a convenient excuse for selfishness, self-indulgence. No, we were not quite strangers, she and I, for I wanted to quarrel with her. Suddenly I wanted to hurt her, and I said, 'Well, when it comes to the Curse of the Mansons, you could have cured him of that many times if you wanted to, couldn't you? If you'd cared to let him know the boy isn't a Manson at all.'

She looked up at me slowly as if she had not quite understood.

'Just out of curiosity,' I prodded further, savagely, 'who was his father? I don't suppose you'd tell me. None of my business anyway. You . . .'

'You thought,' she said with a little gasp, 'you thought, that?' And I saw belatedly that she had not believed all she said, that she had been talking to bury the fear in her mind. My anger died as suddenly as it had risen. There had been, strangely, no anger in her voice at all, only pain and surprise. She stood up to face me.

'Why, damn you,' she said, 'damn you!

274

Thinking ... was that why you stayed, then? Thinking I might...'

'I'm sorry. I shouldn't have said it, I'm sorry.' And still I did not understand.

'You haven't any right to ask,' she said, 'but I'll tell you. He is Richard's, of course. Of course. He couldn't be anyone else's. No other man. I never intended to say all that I said to anyone, but I thought you understood. Do you think, if I was like her, any woman like that, I would tear myself to pieces over it, the way you said? It wouldn't matter then, to me. Easy. No responsibility. No remorse. There've been times I've thought I'm a fool, but you don't get rid of a sense of responsibility overnight.'

'Eve, I'm sorry. My God, I...'

'I mind your thinking it almost more than him. If you knew the times. It hasn't been easy. But every time she was there at my shoulder, saying, "Go ahead, you are mine, part of me, you always were," and I was strong enough to get away. I wonder if I would have, from you. It was almost better even than with Kenneth. He was so amused, and angry, because I couldn't. And when he was dead I wished I had. But he was no good ... I like to think I would have, I'd have saved myself again. It's not a question of sin. Not that at all. I don't know if there is such a thing. It's the irresponsibility,' she said. 'The awful, damnable weakness. And breaking a

275

promise.'

I caught her, though she tried to evade me, pulled her close into my arms. I said against her cheek, 'Eve, Eve, I'm sorry, I'm sorry. I should have known. Forgive me!'

I had known from the beginning. I had been briefly convinced of her venality against my will. I realized that now.

'But it wasn't a promise to serve a life sentence, my darling. You can't go on like this, Eve.' And all the caution, all the experience in me was setting off alarm signals. No, don't say it, you can't know, don't be a fool! 'Eve, listen, leave him. You can't go on here. Leave him and divorce him. I want you. I want you to marry me, Eve.'

Too late not to say it, and I was a fool to say it. No, sane for the first time in years. She was mine, and I knew it, and I wanted her. And this time there was no fierceness of passion in our embrace, only a warm closeness, and only for a moment. She drew away from me. She stepped back, and she was smiling very slightly, a little sadly.

'You know I can't do that. I'm not free. And you don't really want it, I know. You could never be sure about me. Maybe I can never be quite sure about myself. But, no. I've a job to do here. My job. One I contracted to do. It says for better, for worse, you know.'

'Eve.'

'Maybe I'm sorry. Maybe I'll be sorrier. But there it is. You've been very kind, John, thank you. Not about that'—a little laugh—'everything else. But this is all rather a mess. You've hated being involved, haven't you? You're leaving tomorrow. Better make it for good.'

'Good-bye and good luck and that's that?' Are you sorry or relieved, Harkness? A man can be such a fool.

'That's right.' And just as she had the very first time we talked alone, she seemed not to know how to end it, to feel suddenly awkward. She looked away, looked down, put one hand to her cheek. She said, 'We'd better leave it at that. And say real good-bye now, because tomorrow . . . So, thank you again for everything.' She stepped back, went to the door, and then she turned and added, 'Especially London,' and went out quickly before I could say anything more.

CHAPTER TWENTY-SEVEN

I slept little and restlessly that night, my last night at Manson's house. Confused dreams chased around my mind, and each time I came to the precipice and felt myself falling, I woke in a sweat of fear with my heart pounding. I woke for good before dawn, and lay waiting for the light, and thought, if it is another wet day, an excuse. But I would not use it, I could not stay another day here. And she wanted me to go.

When the dawn came it was clear. Restless, I lay until I heard sounds of rising in the house, then got up and dressed. There was again something circling at the back of my mind, trying to tell me, trying to let me know. What? Something you have forgotten, it said. Something you must remember.

I came downstairs too early, before anyone else. I wandered the empty sitting room smoking, not conscious of hunger, only emptiness. Presently I heard a step in the passage and turned quickly. Manson or Eve? It was the old woman, the little gray woman. She checked when she saw me and then came in slowly.

'Good morning,' I said. 'Fine after the storm, isn't it?'

'You're leaving today,' she returned to that. 'Right away, aren't you?'

'Yes, that's right.'

'Good riddance,' she said. 'Good riddance.' She came up to me closer, facing me accusingly. 'You are an evil force here. I felt it when you first came. Evil for him, for Richard, turning him from the right way, so he is once again a mocker and a scorner. And for Eve, I have seen that, too, in your eyes when you watch her. You are one of the devil's. A mocker, too, and a fornicator and all evil things. It will be better when you are gone.'

I stepped back involuntarily, feeling foolish, embarrassed. But she turned and sat down as composed as if she had made some ordinary remark.

'I daresay you will be happier away, too. I have called upon the beneficial spirits to contest with the evil ones you bring with you. Perhaps you have felt that. And when you are gone I can talk to Richard again, make him understand. He escaped me once, and walked in the wrong way, the way of the world. Then he came back. But now he is gone again, and just as I thought he was safe. Your fault,' she nodded, 'yours. But I shall make him understand as I did before.'

'Aunt,' he said from the doorway.

'Oh, Richard. Good morning, my dear.'

He came into the room with his eyes on me. Impossible to know if he had heard all his aunt said. He ignored it. He looked as if he had not slept at all, or gone to bed. The same suit he had worn yesterday, the same shirt and tie, and though he was so fair, it could be seen he had not shaved. 'Well, Johnny,' he said with a sidelong smile, 'a nice day for your drive up to town. You *are* leaving today?' And his eyes added, at last.

'Yes. Yes, certainly.' I thought I heard from somewhere the sound of Eve's voice, low-pitched. But before anyone spoke again, Manson lighting a fresh cigarette from the stub of the one he had smoked, she came in. Say for good, Harkness, and run away and never come back, but no guarantee you will not be hunting after her ten years from now, this woman. Mysteriously fresher, younger, lovelier this morning. But she would not meet my eyes.

At the table Manson was cheerful, of course. Getting rid of me at last. 'Now don't forget to drop me a line when you find time. Always good to hear from you.' Fidgeting with the cutlery, eating nothing, chain-smoking over three cups of tea. Chattering. 'And do stir old Fowler up over that manuscript. I'm really anxious to know what he thinks of it. Quite a joke if he turned it down, after *Troth*. D'you think he'd dare? If he didn't like it personally, I mean. After all, *Troth* made quite a lot of money for him.' And, 'Eve, my dear, I wanted to speak to you about it. I've been thinking of plastering up the rear gate. The boy's just at the adventurous age and those steps are dangerous, dangerous. You can't be too careful, you know. What do you think?'

'If you'd like. I don't think it's necessary, but if you like.' Quiet, easy with him.

I had a second cup of tea I did not want, delaying. When it was no longer possible in decency to go on sitting there, I went upstairs

280

and packed my bag. This was definitely the last time I would be leaving Manson's house. Had I left anything? I opened all the bureau drawers, knowing they were empty, delaying again, that little voice in my mind saying, take care, there is something else, do not go yet. I brought the bag down to the front hall. I saw that Manson was hastening my departure. He had had Evans bring the car around from the garage, and the door was open.

'Well, Johnny.' Manson's tone was almost gleeful.

We said all the right things, the polite words, and none of us meaning any of it. Manson: For God's sake go, and I never want to see you again. And myself: I don't want to go, to leave you, but there is something else, too, some reason, and I wish I knew what it was. And Eve: Go, and let us have it finished, let me get on with my job. Old Miss Manson had vanished, but I knew how she felt, too.

Interludes. You stumbled across these strange stories, no beginning and no end, and passed on wondering: not your story.

'I hope you'll have a good drive up.'

'Oh, yes,' I said to her. 'It looks like staying fine.'

'May be raining in London, of course,' said Manson. 'I believe our storm's over. Now this would be a good day for a country tramp, wouldn't it, Johnny? I think that's just what

281

I'll do, when you've gone.'

'Yes. Well...' Not possible to delay any longer, but she delayed me, perhaps thinking it would be easier with me present, perhaps wanting moral support.

'As a matter of fact, I wish you'd stay in, Richard. Dr. Dyck is coming out to see you this morning. I'm expecting him any minute.'

Manson turned to look at her. For a moment he was silent, regarding her with a little fixed smile. Then he said gently, 'To see me?'

'That's right,' she said easily. She put a hand on his arm. 'I haven't liked the way you've been looking, you know. And you said you weren't sleeping well. I thought it wouldn't do any harm for the doctor to see you.'

'To see me,' repeated Manson. He stepped back from her touch. 'But you might have said something. Just tell me like that. Not a child, am I?'

'No, of course I didn't mean it that way, Richard.'

And now I was ready to go. I wanted to go. Why had she started this before me? I said loudly, too heartily, 'Well, Dyck can probably fix you up with a tonic or something, do you a lot of good. He's a good man, isn't he? And I must be on my way if...'

'Tonic,' said Manson, and laughed. 'Is that

your idea, Johnny? Oh, yes, of course, I see. Not acting quite right lately, want you to have a look at him. Nerves. Consultation. All nice and neat and easy. Tuck him away somewhere, private sanatorium, forget about him. Your idea, Johnny? I see.'

'Richard—'

'Or yours, Eve. More likely. Yes.' He turned on her. 'Come on a bit from your mother's method, haven't you? No need to kill him. Just get him declared incompetent. Oh, very good. But you'll never touch the money, you know. I've arranged for that. You needn't think you're so clever.'

She went dead-white, but she reached to him again, soothing, calm. 'My dear, you're taking it all wrong. We want to help you, Richard, we aren't thinking . . .' And the little pronoun nullified all her sympathy, her calm. He flung off her hand with a violent gesture.

'We, we! The two of you. You can't deny it! I should have known, I was a fool to let you stay.' He turned on me then. 'Interfering, always interfering! I talked too much to you. It was clever, the way you made me persuade you to stay. You didn't want to, oh, no, it was my idea! I should have seen that then. Interfering. I wonder, I wonder now if it was such a coincidence, your turning up here, first place. I wonder if it was you. Yes. It could have been. You were in England then, weren't you? Could have been any of three million men. Was it you, Johnny? I never thought you knew my wife then, but she knows so many.' His tone was conversational now, and he smiled slowly at me. 'Was it you, Johnny, gave her the child?'

'Richard,' she said. 'Richard.' Blank of all emotion but the one, sheer surprise.

'I never thought of you,' said Manson, and he sounded surprised, too. 'I wonder ... it never tricked me, of course. Never. Always knew he was a little bastard. Little bastard. But Templeton died too soon, and I couldn't be sure about any of the others. All the others.'

None of us spoke for what seemed a very long time then, while Manson stared at me absorbed. There was nothing to say. Time slowed and dragged and stopped altogether. None of us moved. We might all have been frozen there.

Then slowly Manson's face changed. His little color faded and the small smile began to grow on his mouth. His eyes changed. With a sudden sharp intake of breath he said, 'Go to hell. You go to hell,' and turned and ran from us up the stairs, sharp clatter on the landing.

After another moment, I found my voice. It did not sound quite right. I said, 'Better sit down,' and reached to her because I thought she would faint, she was so white.

'No. I'm all right. But all these years,' she said numbly. 'Always. No. I can't.'

I scarcely heard her. All the little alarm signals were ringing frantically in my mind now.

'He's mad,' she whispered. 'Must be mad. Say that. I don't believe...'

And the little voice in my mind was whispering, the Manson Curse.

She was staring after Manson. And there was the sound of a car outside, a step on the flagstone, and Dyck came up to the open door. He spoke, but I never knew what he said. I was absorbed with those alarm signals setting up a clamor all through me. She spoke to Dyck, and I did hear Dyck say sharply, 'What is it, Mrs. Manson, are you faint? Let me ...' but not her reply.

It was like a jigsaw puzzle. You had so many pieces, and somehow you had it fixed in your mind they belonged to two different pictures, and you fitted a few together on that basis. Then suddenly you got hold of a big piece, the center piece, and saw it was all one picture, not two. And Manson had made you a present of that center piece, unthinking, unrealizing, and as soon as he understood what he had done, as soon as he knew you would be putting the whole picture together...

I turned and plunged for the stairs. I did not get beyond the first landing, because I met an obstruction coming down. The Nanny, stout in starched white apron, much

285

on her dignity, forcing me to give way and intent on her own grievance.

'Excuse me sir, excuse me, Miss Eve. I don't want to step out of place I'm sure, but you know, Miss Eve, the trouble we have getting him to take his milk, and if Mr. Manson is going to come just as I've settled him down to it and snatch him off to play somewhere, I'm sure I don't want to seem unreasonable, Miss Eve, but the doctor himself, and here he is, too, good morning, sir, he said milk, and what's the use of getting an extra ration if...'

I turned back down the few stairs I had climbed, and because I did not know the house, where the rear door was, I plunged between Dyck and the Nanny and out the front and around the side of the house. Dyck said something after me in a startled voice. Of all incongruous things there was a taxi just turning in to the gates, a town taxi. I caught a glimpse of it, noting it without paying much attention. All my attention was on something else. I came round the rear of the house and saw Manson.

CHAPTER TWENTY-EIGHT

Manson had the boy, carrying him in one arm high against his shoulder. He was struggling with the other hand to turn the key in the rear gate. He glanced round and saw me.

I shouted, 'Manson! Stop, wait!' The gate swung back and Manson stepped through. He reached back to shut the gate and delay me even a moment, but it had swung too far and he dared not take the time. He started down the steep steps. I ran. I was almost to the gate when Manson, at the first turn, looked back and saw me that close. For a flash he hesitated. He looked ahead, and saw that the steps would slow him, cut down his lead. He turned and ran back the six or eight he had descended, to the little landing outside the gate, and just as I came up he started down the old path that clung and curved its difficult way down the cliff.

'Manson! Wait! Stop!' I paused on the landing, my breath short.

Manson looked over his left shoulder and saw me stopped there. He smiled. He called back, 'Come and get me, Johnny!' and went on around the first turn, picking his way carelessly.

I stepped out on the path. I dared not look down. Eighteen inches to my left, a three-hundred-foot drop, and on my right was the bare face of the cliff, no handhold. I came around the first turn and saw Manson ahead.

'Manson, listen to me. Listen. He's yours, Manson. It's not a lie. Come back. Listen to me.'

Manson threw an epithet over his shoulder. The boy was facing backward over Manson's shoulder. He looked excited and afraid.

'Don't talk to me,' said Manson. 'Don't lie to me, don't try it. You won't stop me this time—you or anyone else. Seven years. Always someone interfering.'

I heard sounds, voices, behind and above me, but I could not look. It was a hell of a path, rough and steep and too narrow, much too narrow. It sloped sharply away, and ahead, beyond Manson. I could see it narrowing, a place where it had almost worn away. I heard myself say helplessly, 'For God's sake, Manson.'

With the boy to overbalance him Manson could not turn. He had to go delicately down this steep slope. Small stones fallen from above, accumulated rubble of years, roughened the path further. Manson was talking, to himself perhaps, or perhaps he did not know he was talking, and his voice thin with anger came back to where I followed, sweating, over the stones and rubble.

'Interfering, always interfering. And it was wrong. He was frightened but he would not die, he would not die. Seven years I waited. To have it just right, and you'd think it would be easy, so damned easy. But always interfering. Little bastard. Never knew whose, and what the hell does it matter? I wonder if she ever knew herself. So many.'

'Manson,' I said. 'Listen. Wait.'

I'd never been good on heights, since that time or before. They said you could walk a strip a foot wide along the level, think nothing of it, but put it up twenty feet and it looked like a tightrope, made you giddy. Something to do with the inner ear, same thing that turns you seasick. The thing to do was not to look down. Look straight ahead, and hurry, and get to Manson. After that—think about that then.

The boy said, 'Father, you're holding me too tight. Let me down. I want to get down.' Manson paid no attention to him at all.

'I thought of it so many ways, but always someone interfering. Water and fire. Water best, of course. Symbolic. Always something wrong. Had to, have to. They won't stop me this time, the last. My own fault, then. I talked too much, thought so clever—but I was, I was! Damn you, stop following me! You can't stop me. I swear I'll get it done this time. Last thing I do, I swear.'

I stopped a moment and leaned on the cliff—don't look down—and wiped the sweat from my forehead. Manson came to the place where the track was worn away. Only a ledge for three, four feet. Perhaps a boulder fallen from above, perhaps only time. 'Manson, you can't make that. Stop!'

But he had. He balanced delicately on this

side and leaped it, and I thought they would both go over. The boy suddenly struggling, Manson staggering. Then he righted himself, stopped, and shifted the boy higher against him.

'Manson, listen to me.' Why are you talking, Harkness? He is beyond hearing or convincing.

'Think it would be so bloody easy.' Manson furious still at bewildering circumstance. 'Seven years, planning it. Any little thing, you'd think, but it took seven years. Stop following me, damn you. Go back.'

I could not get across that place. Had to get across. Don't look down. Don't shut your eyes. Manson around another turn now, out of sight. Here it was. Must cross.

I was taller than Manson, my legs longer. I got to the edge and stepped across the gap. Almost too long a step, and nothing to grasp. I fell forward to hands and knees, but I was over, and got up and went on. I heard the boy say, 'Put me down, Father. I don't like this. I want to go back. Please, Father.' I came around the turn and Manson was halted ten feet away. Manson reaching his free hand to slap the boy, deliberately, hard.

'Little bastard. Stop saying it. Father, Father, Father. Obscene lie. Tired of it, playing up to it, pretending. Stop saying it, do you hear? Stop it.'

The boy was staring at him, wide-eyed, lip suddenly quivering. 'Yes, sir.' A whisper I could only see, not hear.

'Manson, I'm here, listen to me. It's not a lie, he's yours. You can't do this. Stop and listen to me.' Reflex action, talking. No use here.

'Go away,' said Manson, not turning. 'Go back. Nattering at me. Lies. I'm tired of people nattering. And all of it lies, all of it always. This time too late. Nobody can interfere. By God, I will if it's myself, too. Thou shalt not suffer a bastard to live.'

He did look back then and saw how close I was, and his mouth tightened and spread in something like a snarl and he slapped the boy and started on.

Everything had gone away from me but the track and Manson. There were sounds and voices, but in another part of the world, nothing to do with me. Manson was out of sight again and I tried to hurry. Catch up, yes, and then? One blow aimed, landed or missed, on this narrow footing, and one or all of us would go over. Nevertheless, hurry. Catch him.

I came around that curve and saw that Manson had stopped again, and quite suddenly the answer slipped into my mind. Absurdly easy. How had I been confused? A child would see it. Only the cliff frightened me, taking away reason. The track went down to the shore, blessed level ground, and I had only to follow. Twice the size of Manson. Once there, easy. Get the boy away, subdue Manson. That was a good useful polite word for it. Little Manson. Then I saw why Manson had stopped.

There was a place there, just ahead, no one could get by. ('No one's used the old path in donkey's years.' Not since the smuggling days, perhaps.) A fall of rock, something, had taken away a section of the path in entirety, not even a ledge left, and the gap was too broad to leap. Six feet—too broad at least for little Manson burdened with the child. And just beyond the gap, another sharp turn where the cliff bulged out.

Manson swore to himself in a whisper. He turned in the path and faced me, ten feet away. His face glistened white with sweat, his nostrils flared.

'Stay where you are. Stay there. Don't come any closer or, by God, I'll put him over right now, right here.' I stopped where I was.

'Damn,' said Manson. It was an oddly fretful exclamation, small circumstance confusing his plan. He looked ahead, behind, out over the drop. He said to himself, irritated, frustrated, 'But it can't be this way, all the wrong way. Interfering. Always something interfering. Damn. This isn't the way. Water, that's the best, the right way. Decided that. This is all wrong.'

'Listen to me.' My voice was, I thought impersonally, listening to it, remarkably normal. 'I'm not coming any closer, you can see I'm not, I'm just talking. Listen, Manson. You've believed a lie. He is yours. You can't do it, when he is yours. Other people than me know it. They're watching, listening to us now. They'd hang you, Manson, you know that. I want you to put the boy down now, and let him come here to me. Then I'll see they don't hurt you, don't do anything to you. Do you understand?'

Manson laughed, genuinely amused. 'But you're talking as if I were mad,' he said. 'I'm not mad. I'm not a child. That's funny. Damned funny. Nobody's going to hang me. I see now. The only way. Go with him myself and make sure it's a job. Thou shalt not suffer a bastard. But not this way. I don't want it this way.' He looked over the cliff again and involuntarily, for all my self-control, I looked, too.

Vertigo seized me and I swayed inward against the cliff face, keeping my eyes open with effort. We had descended, but not too far. Still a drop of well over two hundred feet, and the sea seething white on black rocks below. Manson drew in his breath with a little hiss of pleasure.

'I see, I see. It's all right, after all. The tide is coming. I should have remembered that. High tide in an hour, give or take a little.

293

That's good. That will do.' He looked up at me and smiled. He put the boy down carefully in front of him, keeping a grip on his shoulders and a tight grip; I saw his knuckles white.

'High tide,' he said. 'It rises nearly twenty feet here, you know. Covers all those rocks down there. Plenty of water, quite enough. That will do. We'll just wait for it.'

One blow, landed or missed: safer to wait? Wait for the tide, a fall to water a little safer, just a little. Or not at all, for an indifferent swimmer? The boy, too. Think about that. No time, in fact, no real necessity to think about anything else.

The boy tried to pull away. 'You're hurting. Let me go. I want to go back to Mother. Please.'

'Be quiet,' said Manson softly, still smiling. All problems solved now, no more temper. 'Only a little while, now. Be quiet.'

Yes, what else? The oldest trick. Sometimes it worked. Sometimes. I began to smile myself, my mouth stiff on it. I said, 'Don't be too sure, Manson. Not so clever after all.' And I let my eyes go over Manson's shoulder. I nodded to a man not there and took a step forward.

Manson never moved, his eyes turned a little. Still in that soft voice, 'James. Look and tell me, is there anyone behind me?'

The boy was frightened now, not

understanding but aware of danger as an animal is aware, and inevitably associating it with the unknown, not the known. He leaned against Manson, into the grasps of Manson's hands. He whispered, 'No sir. Nobody.' And Manson let out his breath and laughed.

'The oldest trick. Someone always interfering, but I'll make it this time. Go myself and be sure. Only got to wait for the tide, not long. Stay where you are, don't come any closer, or we won't wait. I don't want it that way, but we'll go now if you try to stop me.'

It was not, of course, possible that Dyck should be there now behind Manson, coming slowly around the bulge in the cliff. Dyck was somewhere behind and above, on level ground. This was simply not so. Dyck coatless, shirt all grimed down the front, a serious intent look in his eyes, coming around the turn of the track below, beyond that gap where there was no track. Dyck, therefore, of no use at all, out of reach.

I must have started, changed expression. Manson laughed again. 'You tried that. I said, stay where you are.'

Dyck was moving slowly to avoid any sound. Now he stopped, bent down, steadying himself with a hand on the cliff, and pulled off his shoes, setting them down delicately behind him, side by side, neat. He looked absurd. I wanted badly to laugh at him. A stoutish, shortish, middle-aged man in shirtsleeves creeping along like a burglar in broad daylight. He might as well stop where he was—for all practical purposes he was a thousand miles away. But he came on, and stopped four or five feet from the gap, measuring it with his eye.

It happened with curious leisure, like a slow-motion film. I saw the instant before it began what it would be, and saw my part. The boy. The others might go over, would go over, and perhaps all of us anyway, but I had to make a try for it. For the boy, the one important thing.

Dyck took a run and leap and cleared the gap, and at the same instant I plunged forward and took the boy around the waist. I went down with my arms around him, covering him, shielding him, and lay flat. Manson and a great weight came with a crash on top of me, and I lay, spread-eagled, there above the boy, clinging desperately with my whole body to the ground. The weight struggled and wrestled on my back, lifted, and my left leg slipped into emptiness and I squirmed as far right as possible, trying to drag the boy with me. No one spoke at all, even to curse, through the whole moment. It was enacted in dreamlike silence. Then suddenly nothing was happening. I was only lying there feeling bruised and tired, the weight gone. I raised my head slowly and pulled myself to my hands and knees.

The boy lay white and still, flat. I turned my head and moved a little and saw Dyck. Manson was gone. Dyck was sitting, incongruous, in the middle of the path, his ring of ginger hair rumpled, his shirt torn open down the front to expose a white soft chest with red hairs in a little patch. He looked tired. He said, 'He never made a sound. Not a sound.'

I said carefully, apologetically, 'I don't think I can get back. I'm no use at heights.'

Dyck looked at me. 'You'll get back,' he said. 'You'll have to carry the boy, I think the bastard's broken my arm.' He looked at his left arm hanging at his side. He said, 'Darned nuisance,' and crawled forward and put his other hand on the child. After a moment: 'He'll do. Unconscious from shock. Come on.'

I was never sure how I went back, only that I did. I saw, after a long while, the square stone landing ahead, and then I was standing on it, and going through the gate. Someone took the boy away from me. Someone else put a hand on my arm. I looked around and saw it was Fowler. I said, 'What are you doing here?' and then I leaned on the wall and was violently sick.

CHAPTER TWENTY-NINE

There is a thing called collusion, and it was really remarkable how little of it there was here, considering everything. We'd had no time or chance to collect privately and decide on a story, but all of us seemed to know in some occult way what to say, as if we had planned it beforehand at leisure. The police were very polite, very helpful.

Dyck had been taken to the cottage hospital. I had not talked to Fowler at all, or anyone. But I answered the questions smoothly, and a sergeant wrote down what I said and the local inspector (a snob, and that was helpful, too) thanked me and said that agreed substantially with what he had, a pity, dreadful thing, and went away. The mundaneness of things intruded on me, reminding me as I washed that I had no clean shirt to change into. I had no idea how much time had passed. I came downstairs again, resisting an impulse to cling to the banister, and Fowler took me into Manson's study and gave me whiskey.

All I said to Fowler was, 'The servants?'

Fowler nodded. 'All right. It probably seemed eternity to you, but it was all over by the time anyone else realized something was going on. Evans and the two maids got there just as you started back up. Didn't see anything.'

Dyck came in then, a slightly more respectable Dyck, clean, clothed, with his arm in a sling. He nodded at us and took the chair behind Manson's desk, the chair both of us had tacitly avoided. He said, 'They didn't want to let me come back, but I wanted a look at the boy. He'll be all right, I think. No idea how much he understood, how much he'll remember. But he's alive, and well enough. Only bruised.' He smiled tiredly at me. 'Your doing. I hadn't a chance to tell you what to do.'

'You did most of it,' I said. 'I'd like to know where you came from. I didn't believe it. I thought you were a vision.'

'First time I've ever been called that. I came over the cliff on a rope, below you. I'd have been quicker, but it took the two of us to hold Mrs. Manson for a bit, when she realized what was happening. I didn't know about that gap or maybe I wouldn't have risked it. I used to do quite a lot of mountain climbing. Afraid I'm out of condition now.'

'My God,' I said, and poured more whiskey. 'What did we all tell the police?'

'Accident, wasn't it? Tragic accident. All going down to the shore to watch the tide come in. Didn't know about the gap. Manson slipped, almost took the boy with him, we tried to hold him, almost all went over. That

299

explains all the dirt, I should think. They're down there now,' said Dyck, accepting the glass, 'after the body, but I think they'll have to wait for the tide and by then it'll be taken out to sea. May never get it.'

Fowler broke some minutes' silence. 'They'll see the rope.'

'No, they won't. I pulled it up before they came. And,' said Dyck regretfully, 'I've lost a pair of shoes. I shouldn't think they'll find them, and if they do there's nothing to connect them—we were this side of the gap when we went over.'

'I thought we were all going over.'

'Oh, so did I,' said Dyck.

'He was mad,' said Fowler. 'I thought so when I read that manuscript he sent me. It's—I believe it had better be destroyed, but it's part of the estate, of course. I'll have to consult Mrs. Manson. Publishable? Good God, no. Incoherent obscene nonsense. When you called me yesterday morning...' Yes, several eternities ago, that was, '... you sounded strange. I'd just started the thing, as I told you. It's got a woman and a child in it. Not hard to place them. And that's why I asked about the youngster. You sounded so very odd.'

'I thought you were being psychic.'

'It's revealing,' said Fowler with a grimace. 'I've got it locked up in my safe at the moment. A good deal of it is merely ranting about whores and bastards. It was quite obvious to me that the man who'd written it was as near mad as makes no difference. And you had sounded so strange. I thought it over, and finally I got the evening train down to Truro. Couldn't find a cab to bring me on at that hour so I stayed there last night. I thought someone ought to know. Madmen often seem quite sane.'

'Until you touch on their one delusion, yes,' I agreed.

Fowler said, 'I wonder if it was all that much of a delusion.'

Dyck eyed both of us thoughtfully, curiously. I got up and retrieved the whiskey bottle.

'I'm damned tired of hearing you say that, Charles—and you implying the same thing,' I added angrily to Dyck. 'You don't know. Talk about delusion! You don't know what she's been through with him.'

'Do you?'

I passed a hand across my face. I was very tired. 'Yes, I do know—some of it. And I can guess the rest. Well, she's free of him now. You know what started it, don't you? Just two little facts. That she was Eve Henrys, daughter of a promiscuous mother. And that he, for a variety of reasons probably, was not exactly sexually competent.'

'Oh, Freud again,' said Fowler.

'Yes, all right, but you can see it, Charles.

You can trace how it began. He was a strange, nervous little fellow—imaginative. You said to me, about that time when he came to you, no man would talk that way about his wife unless he was sure. But he had to convince himself, you see. He had to justify himself, that it was her fault. I rather think you weren't the only one to have confidences from Manson. I think he'd be under compulsion to accuse her, to anyone and everyone. But he wasn't so crazy as not to care about his own safety until just at the last, and he was careful. He must have decided to kill the child as soon as he knew there was a child, but he was so careful, so clever about it. Just as he said, you'd think it would be so easy, but it wasn't. It had to be an accident, to look natural, and that would be difficult to arrange, you see.'

Dyck drank and said, 'I'm wondering now, looking back, just how accidental it was when the boy fell down the stairs.'

'I think that *was* an accident. He hadn't gotten so far as attempting actual violence, never did until today, as I see it. Until his one great scheme failed. You've got to understand how his mind worked to see it. He would recoil from violence in the ordinary way, he wasn't that straightforward. We'll never know what he intended to do, up to a couple of years ago, but after that I can tell you. Eve said to me—'

I was absorbed in thinking it out, and neither of them commented on the little familiarity.

'—It wasn't until then that he began to be serious about the curse. I wonder how much superstition he really had kept from being brought up by that woman; I don't think much. He never believed in the curse, of course. But enough, maybe, to make the imaginativeness of it fascinating to him. And he got hold of that book of Seabrook's somewhere, and his imagination seized on the theory.'

'Which is?'

'I mentioned it to you, Charles, remember? Explaining witchcraft as autosuggestion, self-hypnosis by fear. If you believe a curse can kill, sometimes it can. But Manson wasn't interested in explaining it. He saw, or thought he saw, how it could be used. When you come to think of it, it was attempted murder by witchcraft.'

Dyck made a derisive sound.

'Oh, it wouldn't work, of course,' I said. 'I'm not saying it would or wouldn't, on an adult. You can suggest a person into being clumsy, or seeing things that aren't there. Just look at all those old accounts, hundreds of people swearing they saw it rain blood, and so on—nothing but autosuggestion. Or even into being ill. There is such a thing as hypnotism. And maybe it's possible to suggest a person here and there into thinking he's so ill that he dies. But I don't think you can do it with a child. A child lacks the concentration, if you want to put it that way. He forgets things sporadically. And then, too, I suppose you could tie it up with Freud's life-wish and death-wish.

'Anyway, if it ever would work, it didn't. And he had never really expected it to. I believe it must have been his first serious attempt on the child's life, if you can call it serious. He certainly made a strong effort on it, two years and more, pretending to believe it himself, taking every chance to fill the boy's mind with fear and belief. It must have pleased his aunt; in fact, she said something to me—that he'd got away, rejected everything she'd taught him, and then suddenly seemed to accept it again. I wonder if he didn't actually in the end. There'd be a holdover of belief from childhood, you know.'

'But it's absurd,' said Fowler blankly. 'He believed the boy would just die of fear?'

'He gave it a thorough try, yes. That séance. He was delighted at that chance, an opportunity to frighten the boy further. He told him to come down and watch, of course. Then, when he saw it couldn't happen, just the other day, when he burned the book, he must have decided that it was necessary to make some more active plan. It pleased his imagination, you see. And he saw how it could be done.

'My God, when I think that it was right there in front of me. The boy nearly drowned in the pond, sort of silly thing a child does, going in after the dog. It showed him how he might do it, I think I know what was in his mind. He got rid of the dog so the boy was worried about it. That was the excuse for the boy being near the pond again, to look for the dog. And I think, you know,' I said slowly, 'that killing the dog, like that, made him begin to think in terms of more violence. A lot of pent-up violence in him, of course. Maybe that was just enough to release it. He was going to put the boy in the pond. He would have said the boy wandered away from him and by the time he got there it was too late. The boy was looking for the dog. Only I came along.' I remembered that moment. 'Someone interfering again.'

Fowler got out his pipe. 'You interfered more than that, John,' he said dryly. 'I'm inclined to think you set off the whole thing, hastened it along, I mean. You gave him his first real outlet for jealousy since he brought his wife down here, to keep her away from temptation.'

'I don't know, I don't know about that. I think it was time. He'd brooded just long enough. All those years, my God. And she never knew, not any of it. You see? He kept it all inside, torturing himself—the lid on the kettle—and there came a time when it had to blow off. I just happened to be here.'

Fowler looked at his pipe and said nothing. Dyck said, 'I'm glad he went over. The best way. No mess.'

'I wonder,' I said. 'Have you ... Mrs. Manson? How is she?' I had not seen her.

'Women are rather surprising. No hysteria.' Dyck smiled tiredly. 'She's thinking more of the boy.'

'Yes, I'd have expected that.'

'I think they'll both be all right.' Suddenly Dyck yawned. 'I'm going home to bed. I've had a full morning.'

'Haven't we all. Well, you've saved one life anyway, if not as a doctor.'

Dyck cut the yawn off in the middle, looking a little startled. He hoisted himself up out of the chair, a gray-faced, balding, exhausted man. His voice had lost its accustomed vigor and resonance. 'Yes,' he said absently. 'A life I owed, a life I owed.' He nodded at us and went out.

'And what did that mean?' said Fowler.

'I wonder. His wife committed suicide, the rector said. I wonder if she did. It doesn't matter.'

Fowler looked about the room at all that was left of Manson: the shelves of records, the books, the heavy old furniture, the silver cigarette case and lighter on the desk, a

306

fountain pen, letter basket with no letters in it.

'Manson. You wouldn't believe it in a book. I'd say, sorry, it's implausible, unconvincing. People don't behave that way.'

I laughed. 'For me, to pursue the metaphor, it started out like a ghost story. And ended like a detective novel. But at least, Charles, it had a happy ending.'

'Did it?' said Fowler. 'Well, he's gone, yes. If that's what you mean. We'll never know the whole story. Fact or fantasy.'

'All the fantasy was Manson's,' I said shortly.

'I'll always wonder about that, too.'

★   ★   ★

Strange how an orthodox childhood holds on, influencing the more tolerant and rational adult. I told myself I was thinking with repugnance of the usual funeral oration. It was even possible the rector would imply Manson had died in saving the child. Eve, all of us, having to sit through it impassive. But in any case Mr. Silver was safe. He was also distressed.

'Oh dear, oh dear, what a dreadful story, dreadful. I regret to say I do not know Mrs. Manson well. Perhaps I have been lax. I should have called, sought them out. Who knows but that spiritual consolation... But she has always impressed me as a lady.' And consequently, in Mr. Silver's lexicon, patently innocent. 'Dear, dear, what a dreadful thing, dreadful. Of course, you may rely on me, Mr. Harkness. Naturally such a story must not get about, no, no. The funeral, of course, I understand. Only an ordeal, under the circumstances. Dear me, how incompetent, how venal, this makes me feel, to think that while I blithely pursued my ordinary life—and I should have made a greater effort with Manson, tried... Oh, dear, dear, a horrid affair. I hardly like to intrude in such an unprecedented event, but I wish you would tell Mrs. Manson, anything I can do, if she would like to call.'

'That's very kind of you, but I think she'd rather be left alone. I haven't seen her myself.' I had by then removed to The Drowned Man with Fowler. 'There's nothing much anyone can do now. It was the service I was thinking of.'

'Of course, of course, I quite understand. Very short and simple.'

It was that, and with no long oration, for they never recovered Manson from the sea. The tides were strong along this coast, and swept out in force. So Manson was tumbled out with them into the wilderness of water somewhere in the channels, companion of drowned ships and other dead men, and all the land given him was a square in the churchyard corner bearing a plain stone with his name and the date.

I sat between Fowler and Dyck, the day after the inquest, with most of the village which welcomed an opportunity for an hour's holiday, and listened to Mr. Silver, rather more quavery than usual, regret a sad accident robbing a man of life in his very prime, and admired Eve's calm white profile across the aisle. She was not in black: something dark blue, with touches of white, and a sober hat. She went forward to speak to the rector afterward. I came out with the others and stood smoking in the road in front of the church. The village dispersed to its business. The local gentry, well represented out of decency, seemed indisposed to linger, and went off in its cars and on foot, with a few curious glances at the two strangers.

Dyck said, 'She's taking it well. I'm surprised. I'd have expected more display.'

'You once told me I didn't know her well. Mind if I say the same thing to you?'

'I daresay, yes. You're going back to London?'

'Immediately. Only common courtesy to say something to her, isn't it?' I was annoyed at imagined implication. Dyck and Fowler exchanged glances.

'Oh, certainly.' Dyck suddenly tossed away his cigarette and said, 'Well, nice to have known you. If you're ever down this way again, drop in and see me, won't you?' offered a firm hand and walked off rapidly.

And Fowler said, 'I'll meet you back at the inn,' and followed him. I turned and saw her coming out of the church. She came up to me and paused.

'I think I have you to thank that it wasn't such an ordeal after all.' She smiled faintly.

'That's all right.' I was unintentionally brusque. I was suffering sudden embarrassment, worse, fright. Involved, you said. That, all right. One little moment of impulse, sympathy. You have implied to this woman that you would marry her when she was free. If she was free. Well, she is. And a stranger. A lovely, unknown stranger.

I said, 'Can't I drive you back to the house?'

'No, thank you. Mr. Silver's gone to fetch his car. He insists on coming back with me.' Another faint smile. 'He belongs to the generation when women were given to swooning and sobbing, you know, and he's terrified I will, but determined to do his duty. Such a nice old man.'

'Yes. Yes, he is.'

There was a little pause. 'You're leaving for town?'

'Yes. If there's nothing I can do.'

'You've done enough, haven't you? I'm sorry, I'm not going to be embarrassing. There's nothing I could say anyway, properly. Only thank you. Very much. Sounds so silly. I'm sorry.'

'It's all right.' Another pause, and was she expecting me to say something else? It was not an occasion when you could even cover silence with a comment on the weather, any other inane phrase.

'Well,' she said at last, and was suddenly brisk. 'Here's Mr. Silver. Good-bye, John, thank you.'

A gloved hand briefly in mine and she was going. I stood and watched her go, all of it unsaid between us, the expected things, the right things: let me know if you're going to be in London; mayn't I write to you; I hope everything will be all right; do let me know if there's anything I can do. She got into the rector's ancient shuddery Austin and never looked around at me, and then they were gone.

I went back to the inn. Fowler was standing at the bar talking to the publican. He looked at me expectantly, curiously, but I only said, 'One for the road? It's after twelve, we should be on our way. Stop for lunch in Truro?'

'Fine. Beer for me.' And the publican produced whiskey silently for me.

Back on the carousel again. Only one old fisherman and the young one this time, but at the same table. 'Well, it do show how God move in myster'ous ways, all right. Might be

311

that old curse lost some power in it after this time.'

'Never had none at all. Bloody nonsense. You heard what old parson said. Tragic accident, he says, and that's all it ever were when it happen like that.' The young one drained his glass and pushed back from the table with heavy finality, went off leaving the old one shaking his head stubbornly.

'Well?' I said.

Fowler finished his beer. 'I'll fetch the bags.'

And I never, I thought, waiting for him under the swaying inn sign, I never want to set foot in Cornwall again.

CHAPTER THIRTY

It was May when Manson died. I came back to London and settled down to my own job for a change, and to coping with Mrs. Bunch and her notions of cleaning and cookery.

I heard nothing of or from Eve at all. When I saw Fowler we mentioned Manson, but did not again discuss her. Once, some time in June, I did ask Fowler what had been done with Manson's manuscript.

'I destroyed it. I spoke to Mrs. Manson about it and she told me to do as I liked. It wasn't a thing to preserve, except possibly as being of interest to a psychiatrist.'

'I don't expect so. Is she still in Cornwall? I wonder.'

'I've no idea, but I shouldn't think so. The house was left to the aunt. Don't you know?'

'No. Really,' I said. 'Well, I don't imagine she'd regret that.'

I heard nothing at all for three months, and alternated among curiosity, surprise, relief, and irritation. (She might at least have dropped a note saying where she was. Of course, under the circumstances... But still...)

*   *   *

Barclay had been switched to a job at home after his sick leave. A good deal to my surprise, I was offered the editorship in his place, permanently, which put me in the devil of a spot. I didn't much want to stay abroad, but it's not too good an idea to turn down a promotion, and as far as that went, I'd have jumped at it at home.

Well, in the end I wrote Thompson what I felt quite frankly, and he was damned good about it. How did I feel about coming home and taking on a syndicated column on a permanent basis? he asked. How did I feel? Just about as if a million dollars had dropped into my lap. I felt fine.

I thought about a new car, and somewhere

to live other than the shabby apartment I'd kept for six years out of inertia. I could afford better from now on. But in spite of all the congratulations and my excitement about it, for the first time since Betty died I realized that half the fun of succeeding in personal ambitions is having somebody close to tell. You know? To share the pleasure and anticipation.

It's odd, the reputation newspapermen get. We're just individuals, like other people. I expect Vicky was right about me. I'm conventional.

I had a month still in England.

Of course, I'd thought about Eve and wanted to see her, and I'd also thought very sensibly that it was better to let it go as it was. The thing was finished. I didn't try to get in touch. For one thing I wasn't by any means sure she'd want to see me.

Thought about her, I say. She was what had kept me in the affair from the beginning. The first time since Betty I'd felt that way about anyone. Well, I knew about her then (didn't I?) and there were times in those three months I wanted her desperately, and times I told myself that if I was going to do anything about it, I'd better start. And then I thought, which God knows was true enough, that she'd have small reason to want to see me ever again, reminding her. And I thought, too, trying to argue myself out of emotion, that we were really little more than strangers, who had veered close to each other very briefly through outside circumstances. No real reason I should want, or hope, or expect, or consider anything more.

And then at the end of that week, when my days in England were numbered, I came into the flat late one night and on the telephone table beside the door was a note in Mrs. Bunch's large childish scrawl. 'A mrs manson calls at benson hotell ate oclock wants you shd ring.'

I looked at my watch. It was after eleven, but I took up the phone and called. There was a little delay, a sleepy night clerk, and then her voice.

I said, 'I shouldn't have called so late. I just got in.'

'That's all right, I just thought I'd call and ask—how you are... Oh, settling things up. We just came to town yesterday. No, actually we've been in Bournemouth for a couple of months. I—we thought a change of scene. Recuperate, you know... He's fine, thank you.'

'Can't I give you dinner one night?' I asked.

She hesitated and then said, 'It's not at all necessary. I'd like to see you, of course.' Formal, one saw friends when one was in town. 'If you're free tomorrow afternoon, I was going to take Jimmy to the park if it's

315

fine. You could meet us and give us tea if it wouldn't bore you.'

'Hardly. Of course.' And the arrangements made, she said a firm good-bye and was gone.

★　　　★　　　★

I met them in the park that afternoon. I had wondered what to expect, if she would be changed, but except that she looked calmer and happier and even, perhaps, lovelier than I remembered, she was the same: in a light summer frock, and hatless. And the boy a bit plumper, a bit taller too even in three months. He said a sober 'Hello, sir.' He had a little wooden sailing ship with him. I said, to cover the first awkward minute, 'That's a nice boat.'

'Isn't she? Her name is *Wanderer* and she sails like anything.'

'We thought after tea we'd find a pond where she can sail.'

'Fine, we will.' And so it was not until after we had tea, sitting sedately opposite, talking about Bournemouth and the fine summer this year, civilized people making harmless conversation before a child, that we could talk about anything real. We came back to the park and found a sailing pond with a few other children around it, and, for a wonder, an empty bench.

I said, 'He's all right, isn't he?' The boy

had chattered at tea, just like any almost-eight-year-old.

She nodded, watching him at the water's edge absorbed with his boat. 'He's all right. I don't know why. I talked to him, of course. They say you ought to tell children the truth, all stern and realistic, or they get frightful shocks when they grow up. Well, I don't know. I don't think they understand some things until they do grow up. He didn't understand. He was just terribly frightened, and he's over that now. We just tried to help him forget.'

'Of course. He certainly seems quite normal.'

She smiled at me. 'Of course, he isn't normal. He's very much more handsome and intelligent than anybody else's, can't you see that? Maybe when he's older, if he asks, when he's quite grown up, I might tell him. But it doesn't really matter, do you think?'

'No, not now. You don't mind talking about it?'

'Not now. Why, would you like some of the loose ends tied up?'

'We don't have to talk about Manson,' I said.

'All right, but I wouldn't mind, you know. I haven't let myself go all broody about it. No point in that, is there? And I haven't had time.'

Yes, even more beautiful than I

remembered, the smooth-polished dark-brown curls, the deep-fringed eyes, the generous red mouth. And the indefinable elegance, sleek, neat, City. What got you involved. What kept you involved, damn it, for there is unfinished business here and you both know it.

'Perhaps you'd be interested,' she was saying now, still watching the boy. 'You remember he said I'd never touch the money. He left everything to his aunt: the house, everything. The lawyers said something could be done, some statute about it, I don't know. They're still wrangling about it in ... would it be Chancery Court?'

'I don't know, I think so.'

'I wouldn't have cared for myself. But Jimmy, he's entitled to something. Education and so on. There should be enough for that anyway, when I've paid the lawyers. We came right away, you know. I couldn't stay any longer, I couldn't. And I thought it was best for Jimmy. We went to Bournemouth, the first place I thought of, I don't know why. And it was full of tourists and holiday people. Very good for all of us ... Oh, Nanny Edwards. I don't know what I'd have done without her. She's funny and old-fashioned—old-fashioned even when she was *my* Nanny—and she's past seventy now, but she's awfully good with him, you know, and always so kind. That's the main thing. I told her I wasn't sure I'd be able to pay her any longer—I haven't much of my own, you know—but she's got a little pension and she absolutely refused to leave. She said, what would she do in hired lodgings somewhere with no children to fuss about. And whatever the lawyers decide, I shall probably have to take a job—heaven knows what, I can't even type, but I'll find something, or do some training. So I'm lucky to have her to be with Jimmy.'

'Yes, I see.'

'It's funny,' she said, 'how things turn out. Just as you think you've got it all planned, you can see years ahead, know just what's going to happen and what's not going to happen. And then someone shakes the dice somewhere and—and it comes out three instead of seven, so to speak.'

'Yes.'

So what about it, Harkness? Here it is. You asked her to marry you, and she said she would not leave him. But she never told you no, if she was free. You were not exactly in a normal state. You did not exactly mean it, did you? Impulse. No, damn it, you meant it as deep as you could mean it. And now how do you feel about it? What is she expecting? Strangers, really. Don't look at her. Think about it. You look at her and it only tells you that you still want her, so damnably, that she is what you've waited for, the ultimate, the

319

best. But you really don't know, you just feel, you don't really know her. Kept your freedom all this while, since the bad luck with Betty. Give it up now? Freedom—the immature word for it. Women like Vicky. You have seen Vicky, taken her out, these last three months, but it's never been what it was—she seemed suddenly so obvious, so boring.

What it comes back to is your uncomfortable Presbyterian conscience. You offered a bargain under certain conditions, and those are now fulfilled, and in honor you must honor the bargain. Want to? Of course you want to, like hell: but that is only emotional thinking. How about five years from now? You couldn't know. A chance you took.

So I said it baldly, no preliminaries. Get it over. 'Eve, you know what I want to say. I said it once before. I'm saying it again. I want you to marry me.'

She let out her breath in a little unconscious sigh and turned to me. Yes. She'd been waiting for it, expecting, hoping for it. You see? Woman the huntress, man the trapped. But she did not speak, looking at me, and then she smiled, but the smile did not touch her eyes.

'So your conscience is salved,' she said, 'you've said it. Funny honorable man you are. Were you afraid I'd say yes? You don't really want it.'

'But I do, I do, you mustn't think . . .' And I did. I took her hand, but she drew away, shaking her head.

'I don't think so.' Looking away from me now. 'You were . . . we both were quite a bit upset that night, weren't we? You were sorry for me, and I . . . And the other time was just bodies, after all. I wonder why we always say "just" about that. No, thank you very much, John, I won't embarrass you by accepting your very kind offer.'

'Kind? But, Eve, it's not like that.'

'But it is,' she said. I had thought once, infinite woman. Yes, wise. 'It's all right. You felt obligated, I know. I think that's why you met me today, just because you felt obligated to renew the offer. I'm not going to hold you to it. Look'—and she turned to me again and her smile was genuine—'I'm not angry, no, how could I be? But this is embarrassing for both of us. Anticlimax. I think I'd like you to say good-bye and go away now, and if some time later on you want to see me again, just as people who know each other, no strings attached, we can do that . . . I'm looking for a flat, but I'll leave an address at the hotel.'

'That's the way you want it?' I said after a moment.

'That's the way I want it. We're all even now, aren't we?' Her smile friendly, steady. 'And if you don't call, that's all right, too. I

321

understand. You never wanted to get involved in the first place, did you? That's right, you go now and we'll stop embarrassing each other.'

She held out her hand. I got up.

'It's not the way I want it. I'll go if you want me to but I'll be back.'

'Not for that. You've done your duty and we can forget it. Thank you again—for everything.'

'Well,' I said. I took her hand. It drew away from mine after conventional time. I stood awkwardly, looking down at her. 'Well. I will call, you know.'

She said nothing, and then, 'Thanks, and good-bye, John.'

'Good-bye,' I said. Absurd, stilted talk. I looked at the boy, kneeling by the water with his boat. I said again, 'Good-bye,' and walked away. Aimlessly, not knowing my direction. I didn't look back. I came to the crossing of paths in the park, by a large rhododendron bush, and turned left.

Are you relieved or sorry, Harkness? Freedom, you said. Freedom to be alone, to be the perennial uncle. And philanderer? Strong word for it, in your case, but still . . . Freedom. A succession of flats large or small, a succession of Mrs. Bunches, a succession of Vickys.

I stopped to let a family straggle past me, indeterminate number of children like steps, all with striped sticks of candy, all shouting. 'Ernie, mind the gentleman. There, 'e's gorn and dropped it.' A loud wail. ''Ere, love, Mum'll wipe it orf for yer.'

Just as well, of course. Of course. A man my age mightn't settle down in marriage. Used to a different routine, doing as I pleased. The boy, too. Might resent it. And for myself, I might resent her affection for the boy. No, that was absurd, impossible. They said that happened. Handsome, nice youngster. A good boy, he was. Might be said I'd the right to feel some proprietary interest.

Aren't you relieved, Harkness? Quite a responsibility. You're not used to that. No, and a man without responsibility is a useless man. A man without responsibilities is a lonely man.

I came past another pond where children sailed wooden boats and parents watched them. I turned up another path aimlessly and passed a man selling ginger beer from a little cart.

I began to walk more and more slowly. Tell yourself, Harkness. Only because she is a beautiful woman. Freud's Id saying, I want. Nothing more; nothing softer, nothing more meaningful.

But it isn't so. Emotional thinking... And what in God's name would life be without emotional thinking once in a while? A cold sterile thing with not as much meaning as—that. And you know it isn't so. She did not mean any of that. She is alone, and lonely, and frightened a little about the future. But you know her and you know her pride and her obsession about responsibility. She was giving you an out, just in case. That she should never be an obligation, something acquired on impulse and regretted. She did not mean it.

And you took what she offered all too gladly, all too quickly, and she let you go. She told you to go while she could smile and never let you see the bitterness she felt—and what else? Please God, what else?

I turned and began to walk back. I passed the man with the cart and turned back down the path.

A man can be such a fool. Shake the dice and it comes up seven instead of three, and there you are on a different road altogether, for a while. The raise I was to have would come in handy. There would be a house somewhere, a house with a garden, and a red-and-white spaniel for the boy. A large enough house for other children, yes. The new car did not matter.

But ten to one, Harkness, you have lost her, because you ran away. She said, 'No obligation,' and you shook her hand and left her, so she will never believe you again and you have lost her.

I was walking fast now. I came by the

second pond where children were sailing boats. I got all entangled with the straggling family of children. 'Gloria, mind the gentleman! For 'eaving's sake, Doreen, watch 'er, do!'

She was gone, of course, she would be gone. Nothing to wait for, nothing to stay for. She would have called the boy and gone away, back to the hotel, somewhere, perhaps not to the hotel and I'd never find her again, never see her to tell her—

I came around the rhododendron bush at the path's curve. She was sitting there, just where I had left her, alone on the bench, motionless, looking straight ahead, and the child still playing by the water's edge. I began to run.

Photoset, printed and bound in Great Britain by
REDWOOD PRESS LIMITED, Melksham, Wiltshire